G. 7 2

TURNING THE TIDES

Allen

About the Author

Allen was born in 1933 in Lancashire. He left school at sixteen and went to work on an arable farm and a dairy farm, one year on each. He then served two years of National Service with the Royal Army Medical Corps.

He studied Agriculture at degree level at the University College of North Wales and spent two years working on a 150 acre farm on Pabbay, an island in the Inner Hebrides, fifteen years market gardening in Anglesey and two years with a pitch in Covent Garden and Bayswater Road selling his own paintings, drawings and sculpture.

He has held various exhibitions of his work in North Wales and London over the years.

For twenty years he was a special needs teacher in Islington, London.

Two marriages, one divorce and two children later, he is still painting, growing things organically and writing in No. 6 Stanley Street, Beaumaris, Anglesey LL58 8ET.

Ring 01248 810 661 for a visit.

Contents

Prologue

I am eighty-two. The year is 2065.

I have been asked to 'write' these memoirs as a sort of history of Anglesey during my lifetime and, since I have nothing better to do except relive my memories while enjoying the company of my second lovely (they were both lovely in their different ways) wife, Elen, I have agreed to do so: provided somebody else will do the editing, correcting and putting into reasonable English.

I will sit and reminisce and talk into one of those things that listens and writes it into its computer mind and will print it if you want it to. Somebody else, however, must correct the grammar. The older I get the more I find myself thinking in Welsh, that being my first language. While I have spent much of my life using English as a working tool, now as I get older I prefer speaking and reading Welsh, enjoying the turn of phrase, the picturesque language, the down-to-earth allusions, the homely often agricultural references, the innumerable anecdotes that enliven the older writers.

So if I sometimes use a Welsh turn of phrase not in tune with common usage, or if the computer uses the wrong words or punctuation, somebody else will have to put it right.

They have asked me to make it a personal account, which will go in the records beside the papers in the County archives.

Well, there's a thing!

If it is to be a personal account then it must contain personal details! And this to go in the public records along with planning applications, receipts, formal letters, and all the stuff archives must hold?

I have never delved into archives myself, dry stuff for the most part I presume. Well, anybody reading what I have to tell about will not find it dry!

A joke, really, to put my life into the archives!

Well, I don't mind if they don't, so here goes…

You will have to excuse an old man if he rambles a bit sometimes, philosophises sometimes, takes things in an order not always chronological...

How to Swim

I was eighteen when I made the first fin turbine to produce electricity from the small river that ran through the grounds of my parents' estate.

I say 'estate' although by that time it had been whittled down to a largish farm of two hundred and fifty acres and a big old ruined mansion with derelict grounds.

My parents, Llewelyn and Marged Cliffourd, (Cliffourd – all that was left of our Norman origins, their first names being a sure sign of the strong Welsh side of the family), were doing their best to farm those 250 acres and, in fact, had produced a very good standard of living by running a pedigree Welsh Black herd of cattle for beef and, each year, buying castrated male lambs from the mountain farmers around Eryri to fatten on our lowland grass and crops.

But, in 1997, when I was fourteen and attending the nearby secondary school in Menai Bridge, mad cow disease had put the fear of a fate worse than simple death into the people of Europe and America and the bottom had fallen out of the market for British beef.

Completely.

Instead of a good income from the sale of pedigree breeding stock and a premium paid for the quality beef they sold, my parents, along with very many British farmers, faced an immediate drastic cut in income with no clear way forward and a terrible reduction in the capital value of their animals. With no likelihood of matters improving for years to come.

Of course, anyone stood a far greater chance of death or serious injury from an accident on the roads than dying of mad cow disease, but this was a statistic that, it seemed, only we fourteen-year-old pupils in our P.S.H.E. citizenship classes were aware of. For the rest of the beef-eating world, everyone was likely to go stark raving, dribbling, slavering mad with one bite of a beefburger, let alone a slice of roast.

At that time I hadn't even made the first of the windmills producing electricity to heat the greenhouses for the organic gardens, let alone even begun to think about the fin turbines that were eventually, to revolutionise electricity generation throughout the world and make me a millionaire twice over.

By 1999, some years after the onset of mad cow disease, British farming was in very dire straights, many British farmers, including my parents, were near bankruptcy and a few had been forced out of business.

By drastic culling of the national herd: by slaughtering and burning supposedly infected cattle at great cost to the nation, with only a nominal recompense to the farmer for every beast slaughtered, British beef was declared free of the disease by European health experts and exports were again possible. But great damage had been done to customer confidence in beef, not only in the home market but also in Europe, with France unilaterally continuing the ban on any imports from Britain.

The only way any British farmer could be sure of selling any beef by then was if it was one hundred percent guaranteed organic and here there was greater demand than supply, but even that demand was limited due to the cost of production. And, by then, the price paid for ordinary beef was uneconomically low and calves were of no value at all, farmers could not sell them and had to pay to have them slaughtered since it was no longer worth keeping them alive.

So. I remember when I was about sixteen, in 1999; old enough to understand the implications of all this and, being an only child, likely to inherit the family estate, I was included in the heart-searching and endless discussion that went on about how we were to keep our heads above water.

Heart-searching because we were great friends of a farming family, cousins on my mother's side, who had sold their farm in Sussex and moved lock (but not stock, because of the risk of 'mad cows') and barrel and bought a large farm with wonderful, but old, buildings and a small acreage of vines in France. They, after only a year in business, having purchased local animals, could already see their way to not losing money and were having a lovely time, with a better climate, into the bargain. The National Farmers' Union had told my father, upon enquiry, that to date about six English farmers had upped and gone and many more were thinking seriously of doing the same.

My mother was enthusiastic. She had seen my father growing more and more morose and despondent as the last few years had gone by and seeing, instead of a reasonable return from his farm, a steady decline in income coupled with the threat of having to give up his pedigree herd. He had become very quiet indeed, given to going for long walks by himself around the farm and on into the desolation of the old Plas gardens that ran in a riot of overgrown rhododendrons and fallen exotic pines along the valley of the small river – the Afon Wen – as it rushed and tumbled its way from where it entered our land at the top of the farm, pushing through the flat, upper fields, down past the ruined Plas, stopping for a while to gain courage and strength in the man-made lake, long filled with mud and weeds and fallen trees, before tumbling, first over a now breached and jagged retaining stone embankment, and then running on through arching caverns of monstrous ferns and a whole area of umbrella forest of gunnera grown wild and black and exciting in which I and my ten- and eleven-year-old gang had roamed and fought cowboys and Indians and space invaders only a few years before. Then on and on down it went, over moss-covered rocks, past old and twisted oaks into a wild hazel and willow and hydrangea bog area before seeping into a small cove with a rotten, collapsed boat house and so out into the Menai Strait and the open sea.

All, once, a thriving bustling Plas. With domestic servants living in the top, third floor, vast kitchen and sculleries, a dairy and laundry, stables and gardeners and the accompanying large walled kitchen garden, with greenhouses, hot beds and double deep digging, potting sheds and ornamental lawns and landscaped gardens that swept down through the woods to the sea.

All, now a ruin of a house, the roof gone, dripping and moss-covered walls, sycamore and ash saplings grown to trees pushing their way through the jumble of smashed slates, rotten rafters and soggy, broken beams where once apple pies and all sorts of wonderful pastries were made, pheasants and duck, lamb and beef roasted, and cooks and maids scuttling to and fro. All signs of the upper floors gone, except for the black ends of beams still jutting from the walls and gaping empty fireplaces below chimneys leaning or fallen into the abyss beneath.

My father's inheritance; mine to come.

It had been like this – a ruin – since the end of the 1914–18 war in which nearly all male members of the family and very many of the gardeners and stable boys, grooms, butler and housemen were killed.

My great great-grandmother, Anghared, moved out of the Plas into the farm where we live now taking the then sixteen-year-old Tomas, my great-grandfather, with her. She employed an agent to manage the estate which, in those days, included five other farms beside the home farm.

Death duties and another world war had reduced the property to its present size, nobody wanted the ruined Plas buildings or the neglected gardens in a deserted, now wild and tangled wooded river valley and my father, after studying agriculture at Cirencester had married my mother, a fellow student, and had continued running the home farm after his father's early death of lung cancer in 1983, the year I was born.

But now my mother wanted to join our cousins in France. She wanted to buy our own place near them with the warmer climate, the romance of having a French-style kitchen, her own wines to cook with, herbs aplenty and, above all, the far better chance of financial security that farming in France offered; where it seemed, the French Government recognised the value of its agriculture and supported it accordingly. The British Government seemed bent on turning farms into amenity playgrounds for city folk with the right to roam anywhere and they were encouraging, and giving grants for, the conversion of farm buildings into holiday cottages.

We spent a month in the summer of 1999 in France. Partly staying with the cousins, mostly looking at farms for sale in the whole of the region and some of the time visiting gardens and the chateaux because my mother was a very keen plantswoman, her father being a professional landscape gardener and plant collector with his nursery and show garden on the Llyn Peninsular in North Wales.

Dad got more and more quiet as Mum became more and more enthusiastic and the cousins joined in with their exuberant excitement at having made the move and wanting another English-speaking family within calling distance.

Not quite true, the latter qualification, since we were a Welsh-speaking family by preference, background and education.

All junior schools in North Wales teach through the medium of the Welsh language so all junior school children grow up Welsh speaking and very many families, like ours, think and speak in Welsh, although nowadays are just as much at home with English: truly bilingual. Able, as a population, to switch from one language to the other but using in everyday conversation, in shops and in the home, on Welsh Television and in Welsh language books, Cymraig – Welsh – and very proud of the language and the culture too.

Dad was a true Welshman, of the uchelwyr (gentry). His ancestors, although Norman way back, became assimilated into the Ynys Mon (Anglesey) gentry and a later ancestor fought with Owain Glyndwr, paying a heavy fine for the privilege of staying alive and on his own land after the death of Glyndwr. Dad didn't want to sell those ancestral acres, give up the pedigree herd which his grandfather had started – and his French wasn't up to much either. Nor was mine.

So we came home and spent the winter of '99 brainstorming the problem, giving ourselves until New Year's Day, the first day of the new millennium, to simply talk, explore, take advice and look around. Only after free-wheeling in and around a host of ideas – practical, idealistic, fantastic or real – only then would we, must we, commit ourselves to either moving to France or selling up and Dad retiring on the proceeds, or staying here and making a go of it. Somehow. It seemed auspicious and logical: a new century, a new way of life. Perhaps.

The day after we came back from France, Dad had taken Mum and me for a walk round the whole estate, prefacing the walk by saying, 'We've been around places in France thinking positively about them, now lets go round this place in an equally open, optimistic, creative frame of mind.'

So we walked in the sunshine of a lovely late summer's day from the small river 'Afon Wen', 'White' or 'Whitewater', where it poured over a stony outcrop of rock. We walked along its banks a bit through a wet, marshy area, then he took us through the good, well-drained fields where the pedigree Welsh Black cattle were grazing. A healthy pile of silage in its round, black polythene bags was stacked near the buildings; very heavy bags these only to be lifted by the front-end loader of a tractor, but one barn was full of old fashioned hay in bales of a size and weight that a man could handle. Dad liked to give his cattle a warm dry feed as well as the cold but nutritious silage.

No sign of sheep at this time of year. These had been sold to a local butcher who knew the quality of what he was getting. They had gone in batches since early spring as they became plump enough.

(I am conscious as I write this as to how such a sentence, such an attitude to animals, such a carnivorous bald statement must strike animal lovers and vegetarians and sensitive people alike. And yet it is only recently, in terms of centuries, that mankind [how in the world do I reconcile recognition of the equality of the sexes with the use of the word 'mankind'? Write 'and womankind' I suppose! Or 'humanity'?] So, it is only recently that humanity has been able to afford the choice between meat eating or not. This dichotomy formed an early part of our discussions, as you will hear.)

Provided we continued to be meat producers, (outrageous exploiters of poor, dumb, sweet animals!), then Dad would be buying in another crop of lambs from the mountain farms in the autumn ready, as I have written, to plump them up nicely for the table. So two fields of young kale were sprouting green and growing for them to enjoy next March and April.

Another field of swedes was halfway to maturity for the cattle to feed on over the winter. Cattle that, in the present state of the market, were virtually useless, would cost time, which is money, and feed, which is also money, and who would sell for less than it cost to feed and look after them and whose calves farmers could not even give away. A sure, and rapid, route to bankruptcy.

We walked on, past the ruin of the Plas, through the walled kitchen garden, pushing aside brambles and overgrown blackcurrant bushes, looking momentarily at ivy-grown, broken-down, dangerous greenhouses, vine houses, hot houses, potting sheds; down again, keeping to the river, past the lake and water-fall, only just able to make our way along old paths hidden by the leaf mould of years, climbing or fighting our way round fallen trees, brambles, nettles, elder bushes, ash saplings and sprawling, ever-encroaching rhododendron into the more natural riverside woodland. Wild sessile native oak for the most part, moss-grown and damp and beautiful. Then down into the boggy area, resplendent now with hydrangea flower heads, mostly of varying shades of blue that would later, with autumn's cool weather, turn darker and richer, to purples and plum colours and wine reds, but straggling and struggling in undergrowth grown rank and smothering from years of neglect. And out onto the little gravel beach with its ruined boat house, wet muddy bits of boat ribs still stuck underwater in the tumble of sagging roof and walls, the little jetty not much more than a jumble of stones but still discernible as the tide receded.

We sat on the rocks, in the sunshine, Mum and I taking off our socks and boots, paddling our feet in the water; Dad sitting pensive, looking across the Menai Straits at the distant mountains, blue and hazy in the distance.

They had always been there for Dad, growing up as he had here, at school in Beaumaris, then farming, working in the fields with a clear view across the water. I had attended the same school, seen the same mountains as I walked down the hill to sit in the same classrooms. Mum also grew up with those mountains in the background, never far from the sea, from a slightly different viewpoint, down on the Llyn peninsular.

Sometimes they loomed high and dark and threatening, seeming close and enclosing our world; sometimes they vanished in rain with only a hint of their presence as clouds scurried over the lower, nearer hills. Sometimes gleaming white and cold and far away, snow covered and remote or, like today, very far away indeed, hardly mountains at all: gentle hills, warm, blue and hazy, lazy in the heat of high summer.

'So...' said my Dad pulling notebook and pencil from his pocket. 'We've walked round what we've got. Shall we sell up and move to France? Or try to stay? Or we could retire from farming and live a life of ease in a bungalow somewhere by the sea.'

Mum dipped her hand in the water and threw sparkling drops at him. 'Can't see you retiring, you old goat, you'd be bored to an early death and you'd drive me crazy in a bungalow, under my feet all the time. Let's go and live in France and drink wine every day!'

'Less of the "old", Marged,' grinned Dad. 'Goat, perhaps.' And he moved to get to his feet, an evil, anticipatory grin on his face, reaching out to grab at her, fingers groping.

They were good, my parents, still in love and showing it. Not afraid to hug and kiss in my presence. I was the one, in adolescence, uncomfortable to be seeing even the mildest of sexual behaviour in my, as I thought of them, elderly parents. But reassured by it all the same since many of my friends' parents were divorced or separated or living uncomfortable lives 'making the best of things'. In two cases among them one was aware within their households of the tensions and frustrations, and so were their children, we often talked about it, we youngsters, among ourselves. Asking each other, 'What would be "the best of things" if we were grown up and in that situation? Split, or stay?'

I moved a bit away, to give them a chance... and heard Mum say...

'Get away with you, Llewelyn, you are a *very* old goat. Good only for retirement. I'll keep you in the garden shed down in this old bungalow of yours. Go on, stay where you are; what's the notebook for?' Her voice changed from banter to pointed interest.

'Right, you – later!' He continued to grin as he called to me.

'Come back here, Davydd. Now, let's write down any ideas we have about how we can stay here on the farm. I don't really want to leave this place – will if we have to, but I'd rather stay if I can.'

I came and sat nearby.

'I want to stay. Talking in French isn't easy and I want to study engineering here in university. I'd never manage that in French!'

'You could come back here to college if you wanted to,' said Mum. 'All right then, I'll do bed and breakfasts and we can get some of those lovely government grants and convert the buildings to holiday accommodation. I'll learn "haute cuisine" and open a restaurant in the cowshed. That way we'll get the wines and the cooking with herbs as a perk from the business.'

I could see Dad starting to make a list in his notebook.

'Bloody families with kids all over the place,' I groaned. 'They'll invade the farm and leave gates open, Mum will get overworked and overtired doing all this cooking and where does Dad fit in with all this?'

I could feel myself getting more anxious than angry. Not wanting our present way of life to be drastically altered, not wanting our peace disturbed, resenting the intrusion of change and, behind it also, the looming advance of my adulthood; half welcoming and half fearing, as one does in adolescence, the beginnings of the need to be responsible for one's actions: the taking up of a career, earning a living. Money, sex.

'Let's not discuss the pros and cons of anything now,' said Dad. 'Let's just write down any ideas of what we could do, get a good list, even if some of the suggestions are crazy. We can have some fun talking about all of them, build some castles in the air, find out about things, and then, as we have said, aim to be making decisions around about Christmas time ready to really make some changes in the year 2000. We certainly have got to decide something by then. The bank manager is after me!'

So we sat there, down at the water's edge, in the sunshine, throwing ideas at Dad which he wrote down, adding his own contributions, nobody saying 'no' to anything and some of the ideas sounding impossible at the time. But many of them in some form or another have become reality now, in my old age.

Bed and breakfast.

Self-contained holiday accommodation.

Restaurant.

19

These had been my mother's immediate reaction suggestions, putting herself in the front line to save Dad's farming and ancestral home. I had kept very quiet, I remember, intentionally.

In no way did I want Mum to be enslaved in a kitchen although I knew that with her organisational abilities if any of those three alternatives were adopted then she would quickly find good staff and not have to do all the cooking. But one of my best friends in school was the son of a restaurateur/hotel owner in a country mansion not far away and I knew the long hours they worked. Financially they seemed okay though. But it was not what I would have called a fun life. Or interesting. And since I was likely to end up keeping the project going when my parents retired then I had better make my preferences known. But not yet...

'I want, if I can, to keep the pedigree herd,' said Dad writing,

'Pedigree Welsh Blacks – organic? Organically produced lamb.'

'If you're going organic, why not veg and fruit of all sorts, pick your own?' I had asked.

'Already being done on the island,' said my father. 'And it's hard work, needs more intensive labour than conventional production and you don't get all that much more of a price for your produce.'

Nevertheless, he wrote 'Organic fruit and veg. Query – pick your own.'

'If you are going to grow fruit and veg then I want to grow flowers for sale,' said my mother emphatically. 'And, perhaps, plants and flowering shrubs; propagate and grow our own, not buy them in. Still all organic. I know more about plants than cooking.'

Down went 'Organic Garden Centre'

I kept quiet about that idea, I didn't want to inherit a garden centre manager's job either! So I suggested something that came to my mind – extending the concept of a garden centre with its play area.

'Let's turn the whole of the river valley with this cove's access to the sea into an outward-bound managerial training centre. And use the self-contained accommodation that we convert the buildings into to put the trainees in, and Mum can feed them in her restaurant.'

I liked this idea. I could see myself leading groups up the mountains, taking kayaking training teams around the Menai Straits and building bridges out of tree trunks across the river.

Dad grinned and wrote. 'Managerial Training, chief physical instructor Mr David Llewelyn Cliffourd. A.M., P.M., Inst., B.Sc.(Hons).'

Unfair that, since he knew how much I enjoyed outdoor activities. And I wish to record here that I spent many happy hours, and some dangerous ones, as part of the Bangor University mountain rescue team as well subsequently doing a lot of sailing on the Menai Straits. But, in the end, it was somebody else who started the Managerial Training Business that became international in its appeal, in another of Anglesey's many ex-landed gentry mansions.

Bed and Breakfast.

Self catering in converted buildings.

Restaurant.

Organic beef.

Organic lamb.

Pick your own organic fruit, veg, and flowers.

Managerial training.

That was our list, with the last one not being serious, me still being in school. By the new year they had found out all about 'going organic', intending to keep the pedigree Welsh Black cattle because they were Dad's pride and joy – to do away with them would make a nonsense of all the work done over the years by my father and grandfather. But he would go on a course to learn how to cut up meat, have his animals killed in the nearest abattoir and returned to him, and sell his meat direct to customers – and continue selling pedigree breeding stock as and when he could.

At that time the only things that kept any money coming in for Anglesey farmers were the fattened lambs. But, since everybody had realised the same thing, everyone was after all the young lambs they could get from the hill farms for fattening. Prices were high, and demand exceeded supply. Dad was thinking about starting his own small flock.

None of us wanted to change the nature of our farm buildings, which were well built Victorian cowsheds and barns, by applying for grants and changing them in to tourist accommodation. Mum said she would prefer plant growing to running a restaurant, so we opted for pick-your-own vegetables as a joint effort between Mum and Dad but Mum was also to open a small garden centre using stock purchased wholesale from her father as a start, with the whole enterprise going organic as soon as possible.

Going organic in those days was difficult, costly and took two years of using no pesticides, herbicides or fertilisers except as allowed by the Organic Inspectorate. You had to pay a lump-sum fee to register and be subjected to random inspections to see that you were not pulling fast ones hurling chemical fertilisers left right and centre. And until you had your certificate at the end of the two years it was illegal even to mention the word organic when selling anything. Thus you had to produce food by costlier methods for two years but were only allowed to sell at 'normal' prices.

So we were likely to be worse off for the next two years!

However, Mum got a present that Christmas from her father which changed the direction of everything we proposed doing, enlarged the scope of everything we had talked about doing and started me off, first of all towards my being a millionaire twice over but also, more importantly or perhaps I should say subsequently – since the latter could not have happened without the former – on my course towards being deeply involved in the declaration and continuing state of Anglesey – Sir Fôn – as an autonomous, self-governed, organic entity.

Organic meaning organic. No pollution. Energy from natural sources. Healthier.

The present was a book, *The Lost Gardens of Heligan*, which details the rescue of an overgrown, neglected Victorian garden with its stream, ponds, walled garden, fallen-down greenhouses, rampant rhododendrons, hydrangeas, tree ferns and all. It tells how the whole of the 'gardens' were 'discovered' and rescued over a period of about five years. Funded by local industry for the most part. Developments followed by a television company and now a thriving tourist and gardeners' paradise.

Well, our overgrown 'gardens' were created during the same Victorian and Edwardian era, using many of the same plants brought back from all parts of the world by the famous plant collectors of those days, they were laid out in a similar manner and our climate is nearly as temperate as that of Cornwall and Devon.

Having read the book, and before the new year was in, Mum had determined to do the same for our Plas gardens and was off, with Dad, even in January, to see the 'Lost Gardens of Heligan' and other similar old estate gardens open to the public down in that part of the south west.

They stayed in an hotel down there for the best part of a week, talked to as many of the owners and managers of the 'Grand Gardens of Cornwall and Devon' as they could and came back full of enthusiasm, determination and advice as to how to set about getting planning permission.

The week that they spent away was the most wonderful one in my life so far! I received, thankfully and joyfully and comprehensively, an intoxicating introduction to sex. And, while not becoming an addict, I certainly consider all aspects of this delightful part of human life to be important – virtually essential – a pleasure to be cultivated, much as music, good food and wine and intelligent company are to be sought after and cherished as much as one can while pursuing the basic essentials of reproduction, the need for food and a roof over one's head.

In at the Deep End

Take that last bit I told you about where my mother and father had gone off to visit gardens in Cornwall and Devon and I spent every moment I could in bed with Maggie Evans.

What are the important things in life for you?

We all need to have the basic human needs met. We all need food, shelter and warmth.

To be satisfied human beings I think we need love and a job, our good health and the company of others.

If this is to be a personal account of my life then I must include all those aspects of living that go to make a man's life in its entirety and I will give equal pride of place to food (and drink!), the houses I have lived in, the friends I have made, my sex life and my wives, as well as the ups and downs of my working life which is what they were really after, I think, when they asked me to get all this written down.

I don't need to say much about health since I have enjoyed very good health all my life, although there is one aspect of my body's performance that saddens me these days.

Impotence.

It is very sad, as you get old to find that your mind and sexual urges remain alive but your penis, while he sometimes gets halfway there, or even gets an erection for a very short while but doesn't hold it long enough to be effective, is not the man he used to be.

All the mind's sexual activities remain! And I have now got in Elen a wonderful woman of sixty-five, and I hope she won't mind me telling you! She was very happily married to a kind and gentle man I had known and worked with for many years – a farmer who embraced the organic concept in its early stages and who died tragically from a heart attack while saving two children cut off by the tide in Red Wharf Bay.

Elen knows more about gardening than I do and is a most understanding, and still co-operative and initiative lover, likes to dress well, flirts with me and all and sundry, bringing fun and joy into all our lives. We have done, and still do, a lot of gardening together, both of us being relatively fit and active. We are both interested in cooking, eating and drinking well.

But I'll tell you more about her when we come to that part of my life.

Maggie Owen was something else again!

I have said how teenagers in general, and myself in particular, think that their parents, probably aged between forty and fifty by then, are too old for sex and the said teenagers don't like to talk about sex or even think about sex in relation to their parents.

I used to go out of the room, or at least away from their close vicinity when they started any 'fooling about' as I did down on the shore that day we were discussing our future and my Dad started acting up.

Until then the only personal physical contact I had had with a girl had been with Jenny Crick. We were both gymnasts in the school team and, together with the team, had travelled around by coach to other schools in other parts of the country and even, once, down to London to compete in the schools' gymnastic competitions. We did quite well among our Welsh school competitors but only came twelfth, over all, down in London. Jenny and I sat together on those coach trips for the whole of one winter's gymnastic season. Cuddling and kissing in the back seat on return journeys, going swimming together and going back to one or the other's houses, or the houses of others in our group. And towards the end of that winter we used to creep into my Dad's hay barn, making a hide-away among the bales at the top of the stack under the beams and slates of the old barn roof. We got as far as taking off our outer clothing, in spite of the cold, touching and kissing, using hands and mouths, tongues and fingertips, exploring and learning about each others' bodies and achieving orgasms for us both, without penetration or any risk of babies.

That friendship faded away during the summer and I was playing rugby for the first fifteen the next winter. I still see her occasionally; twice divorced, and living in a bungalow near Beaumaris, crippled these days with arthritis, walking around shopping, with two sticks that she waves in my direction when she sees me.

I met Maggie when Tom Pritchard and I returned to his house after a rugby game on our home ground where we were hopelessly beaten by a school from Cardiff. We were showered and clean but shattered and shaken. Exhausted.

Tom had played a brilliant game as scrum half, repeatedly squashed flat by their fast-moving wing forwards and I, as prop, like the rest of our pack, had been run off my feet, pushed off the ball and out-manoeuvred by a very skilled but lighter set of opponents. We had run out of breath on the field and still felt the effects as we tottered into Mrs Pritchard's kitchen demanding sandwiches and coke.

Helping Mrs Pritchard prepare the evening meal and invited to share it herself was Maggie. Average height, strange fluffy fair hair like a halo around her laughing cheery face. Big green eyes wide set, sparkling with humour and tease, tiny twitching nose and generous smiling lips. Older than us boys. But I was old enough and not too exhausted to register her strong, athletic figure and firm shape beneath the jumper and skirt above black tights and trainers.

We lads grabbed our sandwiches and drink and went into the sitting room to collapse into soft armchairs, put on a disc and start to recuperate. Maggie joined us in a few minutes with a sherry – a very large sherry even to my untrained eye – and she listened to our comments about the game with understanding but little sympathy.

It turned out that she was a PE teacher from North London taking time off, 'for personal reasons', which I later learned about from her while lying, just as exhausted as I was after the rugby game, beside her in bed in her cottage down on the shore in Red Wharf Bay.

She had married a young property dealer from Islington just over a year before, and been severely bullied and beaten up by him before six months of their marriage had elapsed. He had proved to be a very insecure and jealous man although doing very well in his profession and he refused to let her out on her own in the evening even though he often had to work late. She had rebelled against this and gone out to a pub with a group of teachers from her school and he had followed her there, hauled her out from the bar, and beaten her up when they got home. She had left the next day, gone to stay with another female teacher colleague in her flat, and had had to put up with one or two difficult encounters with her husband. With divorce proceedings started and an injunction against his trying to see her she had nearly had a breakdown and her doctor had recommended a period away from work and the area. This would end at Easter when she would return to London and teaching. She had rented a tiny cottage by the sea in Red Wharf Bay to get over the shock and strain of the whole escapade.

She'd been there since September and, it now being early December, was feeling very much more herself and ready to cope with life again. She had met Mrs Pritchard while shopping in Beaumaris, got talking, found that Tom's mum had been teaching before she married, and was invited to the evening meal.

Tom was – still is – short of stature, strong, wiry and fast, ideal for a scrum half. I am fairly tall and well built and, at seventeen and a bit, could pass for an adult in a pub anywhere, Maggie started teasing us, me more than Tom, about our failure to beat Cardiff that afternoon.

We had an uproarious meal with Tom's dad and mum drinking wine, Tom and I allowed beer and Tom's two younger sisters officially on coke but nicking some parental wine with their tacit agreement and Maggie offered to drive me home afterwards.

I pleaded homework as an excuse not to stay for coffee after the meal so Maggie and I left there fairly early and I accepted her offer to show me the cottage and have coffee there instead.

On the way over, a matter of about twenty minutes, she rapidly established that I had not got a permanent girlfriend at the moment but that I had one for a while and that we had gone so far and no further with our sex play.

She was a very frank and forthcoming person, Maggie. She soon made it clear that she fully intended going back to teaching in London, that she was not in the habit of running around cradle snatching, yet physically I attracted her and did I think I could cope with this?

By this time her left hand, when it was not changing gear, had come to rest on my knee and I had the hardest erection I had had in my young life! Who was I to say no?

I muttered something about being older than my years and before we arrived at the cottage her hand had crept up my thigh and taken hold through my trousers of that hardened member, squeezing it gently.

I began to realise why that husband of hers didn't want to let her out of his sight and, when it came time for her to leave my life, I didn't want her to go either.

I owe her a tremendous debt of gratitude. She showed me, early enough on in my life, what fun and pleasure sex was. She came totally equipped from her marriage with contraception skills, spermicidal gels and a coil fitted so we were free to enjoy.

She put a match to the sitting room log fire, put the kettle on, told me where the toilet was, told me she was going to switch on her electric blanket and then came back to make the coffee.

We shared the sofa, sitting close, drinking coffee while the fire burned up, talking a bit, about mountain walking and sailing, both of which she enjoyed doing and she agreed to join me sailing the next day 'whatever the weather'. Then, coffee drunk and a fire blazing, we kissed and touched and kissed again and, slowly, bit by bit, removed each other's clothing.

A most wonderful experience, touching, exploring, being touched and explored, gently at first, finger tips along your back, nails gently dragging up thighs, hands cupping breasts and balls, fingers round a penis, erect, hard, squeezing gently, moving up and down. Fingers exploring moist places, entering and moving into a flood of juices, finding the clitoris and, very softly, soothingly, incessantly, caressing.

Maggie laughed, told me I was good enough to eat, that her bum was burning from being too near the fire and come on, up to bed. I had an hour, she said, before she would take me home 'to your own bed, lover.'

And in bed, after many other, to me, new experiences, she used her mouth to give me such exquisite pleasure that I could hardly contain myself and we both achieved ecstatic orgasm together.

We went sailing next day – Sunday – in half a gale and back to early hefty tea and bed.

We spent every moment together that we could without making it too obvious to my parents. When, after Christmas, they went off on their garden hunt down to Cornwall I virtually lived in the cottage for the week, missing the first few days of term, loyally covered by Tom writing a note, on behalf of my parents, saying I was going with them to Cornwall, transferring all telephone calls from them to Maggie's phone and Tom fed the dogs at home for me.

In many ways I grew up a lot thanks to Maggie and from then on I always felt myself older and more experienced than many of my school friends. Anyway, after she had gone, I was often busy after school helping Dad in his workshop, first of all building, together, the wind turbine to heat Mum's greenhouses and, later, me working more on my own, developing the fin turbine to use the flow of water in the river to generate electricity because wind power isn't constant and solar panels are expensive. In those early days we had to keep expenses to a minimum so heating the greenhouses, if it could be done by home made wind generator – or water turbine – made good sense.

Maggie left at Easter, as she said she would, and she made me promise not to write or try to get in touch with her. That parting was very difficult. I was deeply in love and craved her body daily. She was warm hearted and wonderful. I never heard from her again and do not know what happened to her. True to my promise, I never tried to find her again.

The Early Farm Years

Back came my parents from Cornwall and things started moving. At this time, of course, I was still at school – seventeen and a half years old – my birthday is on 25 June, every year! I was there for my final year of A levels and the pace in school was hotting up. Everybody, well, nearly everybody, revising and panicking, most of us anxious to go to university, all of us worried about how to pay for it, many, including myself, having no choice other than to go into debt.

I gave myself that half week away from school after Christmas, spending as much time as I could with Maggie and she, understanding woman that she was, interspersed our love making with revision, as we lay naked in bed, in such subjects as she felt able to help me with. I am sure there is no better way of seriously revising!

Be that as it may, I did well enough in all my exams and was accepted by Bangor University – just across the Menai Straits – not quite simply down the road but down the road, over the bridge and back up the parallel road to Bangor. My parents gave me a reasonably roadworthy car to celebrate, taxed and with MOT, but I would have to pay for petrol out of my own money.

I intended living at home, so saving residence fees. Mum said I could continue getting food free from her but there would be jobs to be done in the gardens. Petrol would not be much more than bus fares so, compared to many fellow students I was well off.

So, what with sex, revision and exams, my time until June was fully taken up.

I was a bit involved with the 'gardens' though because Dad had started making a wind turbine to heat Mum's greenhouse and I often looked in on him, as he worked away on wet days at the weekends and in the evenings in his fairly well equipped farm workshop, giving a hand when some bit of the job needed four hands instead of two. Glad to get a break from my books.

Mum at this time couldn't do much about the gardens in any physical sense but she and Dad almost immediately after their return from Cornwall went down to the county planning offices to find out about permissions to open an organic garden centre, a pick-your-own fruit and veg unit and opening the Plas gardens to the public with all the reconstruction that would entail.

At that time the council was doing all it could to help and encourage tourism and small businesses. Farming, which had been a major contributor to the island economy, was in the doldrums and, like everywhere else, too many people were out of work so the council was glad to hear of any enterprise that would create employment. If it also increased the tourist attractions on the island, so much the better.

In principle they were all for what was proposed and various members of the different planning offices were going to come and walk around the property within the next few days.

They arrived in a group of five, in three different cars at ten in the morning on a blustery, damp Tuesday, 26 January with wellingtons and weather-protection clothing in the boots of their cars. Mum took them into our capacious farm kitchen, gave them tea (or coffee) and gingerbread – delicious, soft, warming gingerbread that I still make for my grandchildren and all other visitors, very popular – while Dad presented them each with a large sketch map of the place and a brief resumé of the proposals. Then they all went out to have a look.

They returned damp but, on the whole, encouraging. We were to submit details and plans with the filled in planning application forms and the whole thing would progress from there; with a lot of subsequent discussion and amendments no doubt but a lot of goodwill coming from the county offices. Toilets, refreshments and car parking would need full and careful consideration.

Handshakes all round and off they went.

I have had to deal with plenty of planning applications and planning officers, architects and engineers in my life since then but, thank goodness, I was on the periphery then. There already was a farm office for Dad with a Packard Bell computer armed with special programs relating to farm accounts etc. and I used it to write essays and things but, from then on, I had to book ahead to get a place at the keyboard!

Capital was going to be a problem in all this, clearing the Plas gardens and rebuilding would take a lot of money that we had not got. My parents did not want to get involved in raising capital from local industry as had been done down at Heligan gardens but they did decide to contact the Welsh TV company in Harlech. A film had been made and shown of the rescue of the derelict Heligan and there was tremendous interest in gardening with three different gardening TV programmes being shown at that time. A television programme, when we opened, would be a great publicity boost. Mum volunteered to write a proposal and contact the company.

We all helped to formulate that proposal though Mum wrote it and made contacts and in due course a team arrived under their presenter Marie Roberts. They fell over tree stumps and tripped up over brambles making a record of what it was like before we started; they slipped over in the mud of our reclamation work, they stumbled into holes and over strings as we replanted and they rejoiced with us as shrubs and flowers came into bloom and people began to visit the place. They became friends over the two years it took to get the place open and were present at the party Mum gave on the evening when the TV programme went out.

They returned to continue film making, recording further developments and improvements, bringing families and friends to see the place on days off and it developed, after a year or two, into a monthly slot in their gardening series showing different areas of the garden as it came into its best and different parts of the whole project as they came on line.

The organic vegetable area got constant media attention, as did our generation of electricity from natural sources. And this media attention was invaluable in furthering the popular acceptance of the concept of having the whole of Anglesey go organic; of our use, as a county, of our natural resources of wind, sun and tide power to generate electricity and our eventual banishment of pollutants like petrol, diesel, cigarettes and drugs from our shores.

So, capital being a problem for us in those days, we decided to advance slowly, paying our way as we went, using one side of the business to finance another.

And the first policy decision Dad made was not to have anything more to do with lamb fattening. The price for bought in lambs off the mountains was relatively high and, although they would be eating 'organic' grass, he could hardly call the finished meat truly organic although there was not much chemical pollution, if any, in the lambs when they came off the mountain.

Dad would hold his pedigree breeding herd as it was and hope to cover costs. The land earmarked for the lambs would convert to wholesale vegetable and fruit production and he proposed growing fifteen acres of willow!

That took us by surprise!

The money he had put by from the sale of last year's lambs ready for the purchase of this year's lot would be used to finance the fruit and veg area. No refreshments on sale during this first year, a start with car parking where, in the end, the car park for the whole enterprise would be and toilets would be home-made straw bale buildings, the human excreta dropping down into compost pits to a design already proved and in use at the Centre for Alternative Technology (CAT) near Machynlleth.

Even the planning boys couldn't object to this since the centre had already won the planning battle.

I must state, in all fairness to the planning officers, they were more than helpful in everything we proposed, doing their best to help us get everything going, enthusiastic about going organic and using natural resources and only hampered by rules and regulations not of their own making. In later years, as the strength and independence of Anglesey as a geographic and demographic unit freeing itself from the devolved Welsh Assembly in Cardiff and the central government of England grew, the officers and elected members of the Anglesey Assembly, as it came to be called, changed the rules when needed and everything became much simpler and more directly applicable to our needs.

My father's brother – my Uncle Dafydd – had died of cancer in 1989. He was an engineer in Manchester with his own business making specialised packing machinery. I was only six at the time and don't remember much about him except the impression of little squeaks of released air when we went round his workshop unit while his machines under development performed their various small tasks. He used compressed air and micro gadgets to automate their functions.

Dad was very upset when Uncle Dafydd died. Dafydd was the younger brother. There was a sister, my Aunt Morfydd, who had married and lived in Scotland, we didn't see much of her.

But when Uncle Dafydd became ill my father spent quite a lot of time in Manchester in support of the family up there – Dafydd's wife Paula and their two children.

It rapidly became apparent that a serious operation needed to be done quickly, as the cancer was rapidly advancing in the space that surrounds the lungs. The doctors cut through ribs, opened up the chest cavity, removed what they could and sewed him up again. And told him he had about six months to live.

This proved to be true and the whole family went through a very difficult time.

After his death his business was sold but not as a going concern, which is why Dad inherited a lot of useful workshop machinery and tools. Aunt Paula married again after a few years and the girls grew up and used to bring their husbands and children to stay with us during holidays.

One of the lasting effects of Uncle Dafydd's death was my father's conversion to organic foods. He also stopped smoking; Mum never had smoked. Uncle Dafydd had recovered from the surgery quite quickly and had gone down to the Bristol Centre for advice and moral support, taking Aunt Paula with him of course because she needed the advice and support as much as he did.

And later, much invaluable nursing help came from the Macmillan Nurses. After that Dad had a standing order at his bank donating money each month, not a lot to start with but increasing later, and I have continued that donation, increasing it considerably when I became very well off.

The Bristol Centre had advised eating and drinking only organic food and drink – so much of the stuff for sale being polluted with carcinogenic chemicals in one way or another. In those days organic produce was difficult to come by and relatively expensive but they followed it up, found suppliers and lived with it until he died.

Dad was more than convinced by the arguments for healthy eating, knowing, as a farmer, how much fertiliser, particularly nitrogen, was poured onto the fields, how fattening hormones were injected into beef cattle and chickens, and how many sprays were used on crops to kill weeds and insect pests and cure fungus diseases.

From then on, the vegetables in our garden at home grew on compost from the heap and manure from the cattle, and we bought only organic produce within reason; by which I mean we drank ordinary beer and wines and Mum made our own bread. My parents were not fanatic about it, they just 'went organic' as much as was reasonably convenient. And, I must say, everybody who came to eat in our house expressed pleasure at the tastiness of the food. I grew up to enjoy raw carrot – but not the tasteless shop stuff! Dad grew lots of carrots in the garden. So he knew quite a bit about organic vegetable production long before he started growing them as field crops.

Dad made a couple of trips down to the Organic Research Station at Ryton under Dunsmore, near Birmingham; and came back the first time with a load of books and pamphlets. Having read those and sat around talking about things he went down there again and paid for a consultation meeting with one of their experts to discuss his plans. He also wrote off to the Organic Growers Association, (again in Bristol!) got application forms and details of how to register as an Organic Grower and we received their quarterly magazine from then on. And, every now and then, he would go off to visit other organic farms and vegetable growers and pick-your-own places to see how they were doing things.

Following the same principle, he went down to the Centre for Alternative Technology (CAT) near Machynlleth, to see what they were doing, bought books, and paid for a consultation about composting human excreta and building a straw structure to house our toilets. They have a big straw building down there and when it came to the construction of our straw village in later years their help and advice, and that of other experts from other parts of the country, was invaluable.

There are five different but overlapping areas for consideration in running a pick-your-own (PYO) organic fruit and vegetable farm.

There's

i)   Deciding on how much and where to grow the stuff.

ii)   What to grow.

iii)   What to compost and how to organise it.

iv)   Car parking and toilets.

v)   Covered sales place.

After considerable discussion with Mum and the planning officer Dad decided he would have to make provision for car parking near his crops rather than near where the garden and plant sales place would be. Car and coach parking for visitors to the gardens and the garden centre would have to be hardcore of some sort and very permanent with a good roadway entrance and exit. For the pick-your-own people, in cars and no coaches, with picking done mainly in fine weather and certainly not in the middle of winter, a reasonably dry grass field would suffice with the approach road being single track over grass and the exit a different grass track. Those tracks might have to be improved with loose grit if it got too muddy – the approach track Dad was proposing to use was already a farm track, well used by tractors and with ruts that would need filling in with stones and gravel.

The toilets (one for each sex) and the sales shed, would be semi-permanent straw bale buildings. Dad fully intended to have water laid onto all the vegetable-growing area for irrigation and he would lay water pipes to the toilets – for hand washing only, excreta and urine was to drop down into the compost bin; each day a layer of sawdust would be added to the compost and the toilet bowl washed with an organic cleaning liquid. The whole compost bin being removed weekly, emptied onto a central, special heap only for stuff from the toilets, the bin washed and replaced.

Toilet paper tissues are a very useful addition to the heap since they supply fibre to the other residue. It all rots down in about ten weeks in the summer time and is best treated as a separate heap from the rest of the compost material. In this way the resulting compost can be spread around the comfrey plants and so does not go directly in contact with crops growing for human consumption.

Let me tell you about Russian Comfrey because we have grown and used a tremendous amount of it over the years and its use has spread throughout Anglesey and in gardens everywhere. Visitors to the place have seen and heard our enthusiasm and the enthusiasm at the Organic Research Station praising its many qualities.

You can get a much more detailed scientific account of its value and use from Dunsmore or our own shop at the Plas. I'll just tell you a bit about it now.

Dad had read about it among all that stuff he brought back after his first visit to Dunsmore and had ordered a hundred root cuttings. These arrived in early spring as bits of black root with a growing point just beginning to show and Dad planted them in our own vegetable garden, in a plot that had main-crop potatoes the year before. They were to be his stock plants planted in rows three feet apart, twelve inches between each plant.

Every bit of root, chopped down to about two inches long, will grow again. This can be a problem if you ever want to get rid of it but is a great asset if you wish to multiply. And Dad intended to multiply a thousandfold. They were to grow in the garden for that first year then be dug up, roots cut into sections and replanted in the field. After three years Dad had all the comfrey plants he needed – running into thousands – and was selling potted-up plants in the garden centre. The variety is a particular one, Bocking 14, developed by Laurence Hills at the Organic Research Station for its non-viable seed habit and its ample top growth rich in plant foods. One cuts it just as the first flowers are beginning to appear.

I have told you quite a bit about comfrey because it deserves to be better known about but for all the yearly details of varieties of vegetables and fruit grown in the pick-your-own areas you must get the records and reports that are on sale at the Plas Garden

Centre. Dad had them printed out each year and they have been in great demand from visitors, amateur and professional alike.

Comfrey is very rich in plant foods and its roots dig deep down. It does not spread by seed because virtually all its seeds are infertile, unlike the wild comfrey and related plants that can spread their seeds like wildfire.

It can be used in three ways – four really since the young leaves can be eaten raw or lightly boiled and taste like a rough spinach, very good for you. As a plant food you can cut it and lay it alongside a growing crop where it quickly rots down and acts as a top dressing as well as a mulch. You can cut and carry it to the compost heap where not only does it add food value to the compost but it also helps to speed up the composting process. You can stuff the leaves tight into a bin and the resulting liquid mush, very smelly, is a good liquid fertiliser and very strong – dilute it with sixteen times as much water!

Altogether a treasure trove of a plant. It does not suffer from any insect or fungus problems. Occasionally, in dry weather, it may develop a white powder mould on its leaves but this harms nothing and you can still use the leaves – but perhaps not to eat! Anyway, Dad was laying on irrigation and, wanting as much growth from these comfrey plants as he could get, he would not be letting them go dry.

You can get five cuts of well-grown leaves in a year in our climate. The tops left on the plants in winter turn to nothing in a frost like any other herbaceous plant.

Discounting, for a moment, the questions of how much and what to grow, there are two problems that face the organic grower: how to get enough raw material to make enough compost to feed all his crops, and how to cope with weeds, pests and diseases.

To some extent growing in compost promotes healthier plants which cuts down the invasive effects of pests and diseases. But far from entirely.

Dad already used to buy in a couple of large loads of straw direct from a midland farmer to use as winter bedding for the cattle. He intended to continue to do this and the resulting straw and manure mix would be used in the early spring around the comfrey plants – remember that back in the early days we only had a tiny bit of compost from the toilets. Much later, when all Anglesey's sewage system was changed to an organic system and all organic waste was composted, everybody got free delivery of this material for their farms and gardens.

Anyway, just as Dad, and Mum, had their original, practical, non-purist attitude to our organic eating, so he decided that the rules and regulations laid down by the Organic Growers Association were too stringent for anybody to reasonably adhere to in the early years of setting up an organic unit without spending a lot of money, and he therefore was quite happy to buy in non-organic straw which would be used, mixed with the manure, on the comfrey.

This changed later when all Anglesey went organic and wheat was grown by the farmers to supply organic flour for bread, the resulting straw by-product replacing any need to purchase from the mainland.

More Early Farm Years

One of the basic principles that my father worked to was that of minimal digging and I have continued that policy. He had seen down at the Research Station how cardboard, newspaper, old carpet or black plastic sheet could be used to smother weeds on paths. He had noticed that carpet, after it had been down for a few years, left nylon thread all over the place and that the plastic degenerated leaving bits of the stuff blowing around. So these two were out. Newspaper is all right but difficult to handle if any wind is blowing, so Dad decided to use cardboard exclusively.

He used to take a trailer behind his old Volvo estate and go round all the big stores in Bangor, speak to the managers and get permission to take all their waste cardboard box packaging from their rubbish area. By handing out a few bunches of home grown carrots he even got the warehouse men to put the cardboard aside, ready flattened, to take away. Once they knew what use it was to be put to they were intrigued and very helpful and once the veg etc. was ready for sale, Dad would take their orders and deliver as he collected!

If you don't do any digging, or ploughing which is the same thing on a larger scale, you not only save yourself a lot of work, you also don't bury the lovely layer of compost on the surface which young seeds can revel in. Neither do you bring to the surface any weed seeds. If you keep that surface free of weeds then, after a year or so, you do not have any weed problem at all – the occasional seed blown in and growing needs to be removed before it seeds in turn and is put on the compost heap – and one of the main bugbears of organic growing no longer bothers you and there is certainly no need for any chemical killing.

One is always caught between two fires over this business of weeds. Weeds, before they go to seed, are a useful addition to the compost heap, but it does take time to pull them up. On the whole, the fewer the better and organic material can be got by other means.

Anyway, in the week before he started on his cardboard collection rounds in late February, whenever the weather and ground were dry enough, Dad wrapped up warm, sat on his tractor and ploughed all the fields intended for growing vegetables and fruit.

That sounds like a contradiction in principles but all the fields were down to grass and he needed clear soil so it all got turned over, including that field of kale meant to have been for the young lambs. He ploughed it as shallow as was consistent with burying it deep enough to prevent the grass growing up through again, and, of course, it formed a layer of compost ready for the roots of crops to get down to later in the season.

A word about the tractors.

In those days he had two old Ferguson diesel tractors. Old, yes, but in immaculate working condition. I've got a photo somewhere of Dad as a young man driving a Fergie. Most people will have no idea what a Ferguson tractor is. It's a small, light, tractor with the conventional two large wheels at the back and two lighter ones at the front. The whole thing cleverly designed so that as it dug into the soil while ploughing, or pulling a weight, the added traction gave a good grip. The bigger tractors that became all the vogue later depended more on their own weight and strength.

The cost of a Fergie was much less than a large tractor and Dad liked their manoeuvrability. Their light weight, adaptability and low running cost proved invaluable and nowadays we have a factory on Anglesey making tractors of a very similar design, electrically powered and exported all over the world: one of our many good sources of income as an 'exporting nation'; very useful to our island economy; Managing Director – Dai Jones – who helped me design the original fin turbine in our student days.

I tell you about the Fergie because, once Dad had ploughed the fields and had laid in the main irrigation piping – which I'll tell you about in more detail when we talk about irrigation – then he mapped out, on the ground, metre-wide strips on all the ploughed areas. These were to be cultivated strips and access paths alternately.

On every path strip he began to put down overlapping cardboard and, as he put down the cardboard, so he put a layer of wood chippings on top – to hold the cardboard down against the wind and to form a good, dry, clean surface to walk on. Workers were subsequently forbidden to drop any soil from the growing beds onto these paths and he had weed-free paths for evermore!

They need topping up every five years or so with another layer of chippings but this is far less work than having grass paths that need cutting, or simply leaving soil paths that would have needed weeding and on which you could slip in wet weather.

The Fergie wheels were set so that they straddled the metre wide cultivated strips with the result that the ground for growing in was never compacted by any wheels. Workers and pickers were forbidden, in the nicest possible way, to set foot on the growing areas; they had to stretch across half a metre from either side. No hardship.

Having the beds set out like this meant that all was plain sailing from then on. During that first year Dad went over any unplanted ground about once a fortnight rotavating with a rotavator – a machine set on the back of the tractor driven by a power take off at the back of the tractor, with blades that churned round and round. He set the rotavating blades to a very shallow depth and so killed off any weed seeds that germinated.

This rotavator was in continual use after any crop was cleared, just mixing the topsoil very shallowly, including any compost that would be spread on it at that stage, and in a year or two Dad had a lovely, rich, top layer of soil.

One needs to dig root crops like carrots and parsnips up by hand of course, using a fork, the tops being left to be rotavated in as soon as the patch is cleared. Old cabbage, cauliflower and sprout stalks were pulled up by hand, the soil banged roughly off them, put through a chopper – mounted on the back of the ubiquitous Fergie and therefore dropping the chippings directly back on the soil – and rotavated in a few days later.

As root crops were rotated onto different growing strips each year so the depth of rich soil increased over the whole area.

While Dad was busy at this, clearance had started in the gardens surrounding the Plas and all rubbish, bushes and branches from those fallen trees and unwanted ash and sycamore saplings – anything that would go through a strong shredder – was all chopped up and used by Dad to put on top of his cardboard paths. He never needed to buy in any wood shavings, which would have cost, and any subsequent prunings were used in the same way. The growing of willow was an important part of this because it meant there was always a good supply of chopped, waste, thinner, branches as the willow was cut and trimmed yearly.

So, while Dad got on with his organic veg, I got on with my schoolwork. When Maggie had gone there was a void in my life that I filled with revision and helping Dad in the evenings with his making of a wind turbine.

This wind turbine was nothing new – there were plenty of them about at that time, of varying design and power – and we simply went to look at a few already in use, down at the CAT near Machynlleth and in other places on the island and the mainland, and copied them, using our own materials as much as possible and buying bits we couldn't make.

There already was quite a good greenhouse in our farm garden that was used to grow tomatoes mostly, Mum propagated some seeds for the garden, much as anybody did, but there was no heating in it.

Dad wanted it heated for growing seeds for early veg and he also had plans for polythene tunnels for early produce but they had to wait until the following year. Heating the greenhouse was a priority however.

He dug out a deep pit within the foundation walls of the greenhouse – about six feet deep, and luckily not hitting rock, and lined it with very thick polyester insulating blocks, lined them with black plastic sheet to make a watertight reservoir, laid a floor on top using second-hand timber and builders' quality thick plywood, all treated with organically acceptable wood preservative; and the wind turbine heated the reservoir of water, a method already in use for many years at CAT where they used it to heat their main sales and information building. Even when there were days and days of no wind the reservoir continued to stay warm enough to keep the frost out and he had a thermostat to cut off the turbine if the water got too hot. He wasn't designing a sauna he said, and didn't want to cook his produce at that stage.

We discounted any use of solar panels at that time, capital and installation costs being too high then although, as with so many things, Anglesey now has a factory making its own photovoltaic tubes – also exported!

The greenhouse wind turbine was up and running by Easter. Dad was very busy in the vegetable fields, sowing seeds, planting out young plants started in the greenhouse and getting bought-in soft fruit bushes into the ground. In subsequent years he planted orchards of apples, plums and pears.

Anglesey's climate is not suited, ideally, to growing this sort of fruit but a man on the mainland, who later became very famous for his work, had begun to collect old varieties, looking for tastier fruit than those then grown commercially, and for disease resistance, and Dad bought his young trees from him.

At Easter Dad took on his first employee and Les divided his time between the pick-your-own farm and starting to clear the overgrown Plas gardens. It wasn't long before Dad needed to employ part timers to harvest some of the crops because many customers, when it came to it didn't want, or hadn't the time, to pick their own so stuff had to be there ready for them, and he needed sales staff as well.

There were plenty of local ladies delighted to take on these jobs and by the end of June Dad and Les had built the straw toilets and the sales shed, after which Les was working full-time clearing the gardens.

The Early Garden Years

I worked with Les all that summer holidays in the gardens. He had already done some clearance of paths using a bow saw and thick gloves for the brambles but we then tackled the job in earnest.

By then I had left school, knew I had a place in university, had been given my not so old and not so much of a banger of a car, passed my driving test and was glad to have something physical to use up my energy; rugby over, cricket not appealing and mountain climbing not so much fun in hot weather with too many people on the hills anyway.

Plenty of swimming and sailing though after work and I took a fortnight off for the Straits Regatta.

Which led on to someone else!

Another, a little bit older than me, woman.

If all I have told you so far seems to be just sex or work I can only ask you, 'What else is important at that stage in a youngster's life?'

House and food were provided, the car was useful and needed a bit of attention now and then, my work in the gardens took up most daylight hours, swimming and sailing filling the rest!

Leaving only my friends to tell you about. Tom Pritchard and I were very good companions but our attentions had switched by then to girls and going about in a gang to pubs and dances. And it was in the sailing group, as a member of the Anglesey sailing club, based mostly in the Gazelle, that pub down by the Straits between Menai Bridge and Beaumaris, among many other girls and women, that Glynis Williams appeared.

Twenty-three years old, tall as myself, slim, strong, long legs and well formed breasts; hair cut short and business like, bleached blond in the sun and salt winds. A very competitive, competent sailor with her own boat and already a key member of staff in a local estate agent's office. Lately moved to the area from Cheshire, living in a flat in Menai Bridge.

Looking for a skilled, permanent, for this season at least, crew member for her two-man Scimitar sailing boat.

After a few trials I fitted the bill and after a few weeks of intense close company, working together in sailing her boat and doing very well, as our teamwork improved, in competitions against other crews, I was invited to her flat for coffee after the pub and so to bed.

I don't intend repeating again details of our love making, pure sex really, there never was any question of a permanent relationship. Just healthy, rampant, romping, fucking – plenty of it.

In the boat on hot days with no wind, keeping low on the floor of the cockpit so as not to be seen by any peeping Tom, Dick or Mary-Jane. Up in the mountains on warm summer evenings, in the mud by the side of the lake where we were clearing the gardens and a swim in the lake afterwards; many, many times in her flat at all times of the day and night. My parents knew what I was up to by then and Dad just grinned and said he hoped we were taking precautions.

That relationship fizzled out when I went to college. I couldn't make the time to be with her as much as she demanded and she moved on to an older man with more money. We won a lot of races though, in that year's Regatta, I remember.

We're still friends. I have remained friends with all my sleeping partners, except Maggie of course, and even there I am sure friendship remains although we have never seen each other since.

I really enjoyed those summer months, on the one hand (well, more than a good one-handful if the truth be told!) was Glynis and the sailing, and on the other, cleaning and reclaiming the gardens.

Once I had my driving licence Dad gave me his second Ferguson tractor to use. Les was a competent and qualified chainsaw operator with his own machine so we used ropes and chains, fitted a scoop behind the tractor on its power lift linkage, got ourselves a strong scrub strimmer and got to work.

Nearly every day that summer the weather was good enough to work in, if it poured we gave ourselves time off, and we worked five and a half days a week stopping at around six in the evening. Mostly wearing only shorts, heavy boots and socks, thick fencing gloves and a safety helmet. Mostly covered in mud and scratches. Glorious.

Then, for me, home for a meal, and out sailing, or drinking in the pub and back with Glynis, who was insatiable, and I often went straight from her flat to work in the mornings. Mum, in her turn, saying she hoped we were taking precautions. And laughing at me.

My parents seemed to be getting younger as I grew older!

Les and I set the width of the tractor wheels to be fairly close together without running the risk of tipping the thing over too easily. We agreed that safety should come before speed and that always we would err on the careful side, me not wanting to spoil my fun with Glynis and Les having a wife and two kids.

Dad had taken out an insurance policy for me just in case of accidents and Les was covered by the special industrial insurance anyway that Dad had taken out with the National Farmers Union as many farmers do for their employees when tractors and machinery are involved.

We used the width of the tractor as a measure of how wide to go when clearing paths and by going forwards with a front end scoop (much as you see on those large council JCBs) we took off the layers of rotted old leaves that had covered the original paths, exposing the sea sand, small pebbles and shingle with which they had been originally laid.

The shingle and stuff had come from the small beach down on the Straits where it conveniently accumulated, so once we had cleared the path to tractor width down to the sea, we carried more shingle etc., back up, to consolidate the paths.

All the leaf mould and accumulated debris off those paths went into a small trailer parked in convenient places by the side of where we were working and when the trailer was full we connected up to the tractor and took it to make a compost heap in the compost area Mum had designated outside the walls of the kitchen garden but near the potting sheds. The mixture of already mainly well rotted leaves and some sand and grit made a perfect, easy to use, compost for Mum and her helpers to grow shrubs in. Perfectly organic! And by the time we had done all the paths there was plenty of it. Enough for a year or two anyway and by then other compost heaps were rotted down and ready for use.

We had done the main paths and cleared the ornamental lake by the end of that summer holiday. That was a glorious mud bath! Les went back to sharing his time between the vegetable fields when required and clearing the undergrowth of brambles and rambling rhododendrons further down the river, pulling out unwanted hazel and wild willow among the hydrangeas. He pruned those hydrangeas well back and, with additional planting as necessary, they have been a magnificent sight every summer and autumn ever since.

While he was clearing overgrown rhododendrons, just below the ornamental lake that autumn, Les uncovered a small building that none of us had realised was there. As with the main house, the roof timbers had rotted and the slates fallen in, but when we spent a day or so rescuing good slates and clearing out sapling growth and moss-covered, rotted oak roof beams, he found the remains of a water-powered turbine. This had been driven by a water wheel set in a sluice that took water, via a small canal, from the river that tumbled down from the ornamental lake.

Long ago, when the wall retaining the end of the lake had given way in places, the river had found its own way onward, the sluice gate, giving the water access to the canal, had become blocked and subsequently rusty and broken and the whole canal had silted up and become overgrown.

Les cleared the little building out and went on with his undergrowth removal. But he told us about it. And I, beginning to think of myself as an engineer, went down to clean up what was left of the turbine and find out as much as I could about it.

The brass plate giving maker and type of turbine was there, bolted onto the rusty body of the machine, so I looked in the industrial directory and spoke to one of the directors.

It had been a family engineering firm in Manchester back in the early nineteen hundreds and he knew little of the details of their business history. The name remained, the firm had prospered in those early days, diversified, family members had died out, and turbines were no longer made there. 'Sorry he couldn't help any more than that.'

Which was lucky for me really because the sight of that little building and the small silted-up canal, plus the concept of making our own electricity from water that was free, set me on a course that has lead on, for my entire life, to an overwhelming interest in renewable sources of power. This has also made not only a lot of money for myself, but, by the development of that interest and those concepts of using natural resources, enabled Anglesey (Sir Fôn) to become a world leader in the development of such things, to develop its own internal economy, become a thriving international tourist attraction and to virtually make its own laws.

The Plas estate in those Victorian times had generated enough electricity from that turbine, powered by the water running in its own little river, to give light and heat to the main Plas house and also to the home farm and cottages nearby. Quite a lot of electricity. And here were my parents paying MANWEB, the electricity board for North Wales, a quarterly bill for stuff that they could make for themselves! Or so I thought in the rather simplistic terms of adolescence and ignorance.

Dad encouraged me though; he, also, wanted to use our local resources rather than take electricity from the main grid. Not so much because of the cost but because he did not like the concept of nuclear power with its attendant risk to humanity, locally and globally, from radiation and waste pollution. He realised the extra cost involved in buying and setting up a turbine, the water wheel required, and the running of cable from turbine house to where the electricity would be used. Once set up of course then running costs would be negligible.

Dad set me a challenge: find out all about the harnessing of energy from water power to produce electricity; make an economic case for it to see if the initial capital cost would be repaid by having no electricity bills over the next ten years and he would help me to construct the thing – turbine, sluice gate and clean the canal. We could not afford to buy everything new.

I spent much of the time when I should have been reading course books about basic engineering in finding out about electricity from water-powered turbines. And, of course, got caught up in all the other technologies involved in the generation of power, heat, and gas from all the other natural resources.

I remember attending a two day conference organised by the group 'Energy 21' held in Gloucester at the end of November that year, at a special reduced fee for students thank goodness. That conference stuck in my memory because there I heard about using hydrogen in liquid state as a way of storing energy!

One of the main difficulties that delayed the proposed building of the vast dam which was built across the Severn River in 2034 to get electric power from the captured tidal water, was the fact that electricity demand is very high during the day and evening and drops to relatively little during the night. The cost of building such a dam and its attendant turbines was very high indeed; to build such a thing and only be able to use the electricity produced for two thirds of the time seemed, in view of the extremely high capital investment, to be unconomic to the government of the day.

One of the main factors in making it a viable proposition was the storage of energy as hydrogen; as indeed it made possible the two barrages built across the Menai Straits which we did in 2026 you will remember, setting the example for the Severn and other barrages.

The thing that struck me as vital during that conference was the fact that the stored hydrogen was made by the electrolytic breakdown of water, a totally natural source in abundant supply, and that the later use of the hydrogen returned it to its original state as water, using the power of water held back by the dams to separate the hydrogen from the oxygen in water in the first place.

A wonderful cycle of events that effected the environment only by building a few dams, and no release of carbon dioxide to cause any more global warming!

Why wasn't everybody doing it?

By the end of the conference I knew that the reasons were many and complex. The hydrogen storage and use technology was still in the development stage and the capital costs of dam building were greater than the government were prepared to pay. Electricity was being produced at a much lower unit cost than could have been done by damming the Severn and other ways of generating electricity were being developed. One of which was using wind power just as Dad and I had done, on our own local small scale, to heat Mum's greenhouse.

But the concept of hydrogen storage which I had heard about at that conference was one that fascinated me, as was the idea of growing willow to burn for fuel to produce heat and electricity. Dad had been ahead of me there, and already had a hundred cuttings growing, ready to plant in the fields next year. He hadn't said anything about building a small electricity generating station though and I had thought he was going to sell his willow for basket and charcoal making.

Willow is magic stuff! It roots from cuttings very easily indeed. You only need to stick an eight-inch length of it into the ground and it will produce roots and grow. Since each of Dad's cuttings would grow four or five shoots which would each be about three or four feet long by the end of the first year, all he had to do was cut them off, leaving a few inches of each shoot still attached to its root to grow on next year, and these would send up a total, per original rooted plant, of another ten or more shoots. Every three- or four-foot-long shoot cut off could then be snipped into eight-inch lengths and planted. Just about every single one would root and grow in turn. So Dad, or anyone else, could quickly multiply their plants and grow acres of the stuff! As indeed has been done here on Anglesey and we now have many small power plants burning willow wood grown on local farms, supplying electricity and heat to nearby houses, small industries and farms; sometimes able to add their electricity to the grid system that extends across the whole of Anglesey, belonging to Anglesey Power plc which in turn sells electricity to the mainland. But I'll tell you much more about that and the concept of local ownership some other time.

It took me and my father all of that winter to make and set up our turbine down by the river. It was quite a neat one really, supplying enough power to heat Mum's greenhouses, to warm and light the restaurant and the information centre at the gardens, plus power for cooking there as well.

We took ourselves, at the house and farm, off the main power grid that next spring by piping some of the water down from the river where it came onto our land and building a Pelton wheel, just as the Victorians had done on many farms where there was sufficient head of water. Rivers and streams run full in the winter when power is needed and photovoltaic cells on the farmhouse roof heat our bath water and give us electric light in summer when less is required and streams may run dry.

Mum's planning permission to rescue the gardens and open to the public as a show garden and small garden centre had come through by about June that year but she had already started taking hundreds of cuttings from her father's nursery down on the Llyn and from anywhere else where she could find suitable young growth. She had set up a mist unit for the very young soft cuttings in her greenhouse in the garden at the farm and had made some cold frames for hardier young stock. So by July, as became the case every year, she had hundreds, later thousands, of cuttings that were growing on in small square black plastic pots. These would either need protection over the winter or potting on into larger pots to be placed outside in their place of sale in the garden centre area.

As soon as the planning permission was confirmed in July Mum took on her first employee, a girl who had studied horti-culture in Coleg Menai, the further education college here in Llangefni. Bronwen Lloyd Evans lived at that time with her parents in Beaumaris and so could walk to work. She still frequently walks up from her house in the town to 'keep an eye on things', bringing grandchildren and visitors with her.

Bron was about my age, became deeply involved with the whole garden project, always seemed to be head gardener and was officially employed as such a few years later. She certainly became one of the most enthusiastic of all our gardeners and was one of the first shareholders when it was turned into a limited company.

Her task when she joined us was to help clear and lay out the garden centre area and to start on the continuous job of potting up the young plants. These, to start off with, were potted into small square three-inch pots using a general compost that my parents had made from garden rubbish, weeds, household waste and some cow manure. Being keen organic gardeners they had made compost for many years and seemed to make more than they needed. Anyway, it was all used up that year and the home garden didn't see any of it.

These full three-inch pots were placed in plastic carry trays holding about thirty plants each and put in growing-on areas on ground that was first covered with cardboard and then a two-inch layer of the shredded branches and stuff coming up from where Les and I were clearing the undergrowth.

There were two basic management principles for the gardens my parents decreed in those early days and that have continued to be viable all these years:

That full plant pots should be carried from place to place as little as possible.

That weeds are not a problem but an asset if dealt with properly.

So, when thinking about weeds, they did not insist that their potting compost was free of weed seeds, so their compost heaps for use as potting material, as opposed to the material composted to be spread on the ground, did not need to be built up and turned over two or three times to combust and develop a good heat that would kill off the weeds and troublesome insects and diseases. The material going into the potting compost heap could come from anywhere, could contain soil and did not need to heat up very much. The whole heap was covered from rain, left for a year to rot down and then used.

Of course weeds would germinate and grow as well as the young cuttings.

In the case of the three-inch pots these were allowed to grow because, before ever the weeds got too big, the young plant was transferred to a larger pot and at this potting-up stage the upper layer of growing weeds was scooped away off the top of the root ball, dropped into the bottom of the pot into which the plant was going and covered by the potting compost required for the bigger pot where they would rot down and supply organic feed to the roots of the growing plant.

This bigger, usually final before sale, pot was not filled to the top with compost, but a layer of shredded wood chippings was put on instead. Very few weeds grew through this and they could be seen and pulled when noticed.

Dad and I made a very simple, double-bottomed tank for steaming any compost required for seed growing and potting of annual plants for sale; steam raised by burning our own woodland sycamore and ash invaders and, later, Dad's willow branches.

The designated garden-centre plant area next door to the walled garden was first cleared of brambles, nettles and old rusty metal. Over the years this had obviously been the estate dumping ground not only for garden rubbish but also for farm machinery that had broken or gone out of use. There was an old combine harvester sitting drunkenly on flat and rotten tyres, an old Fordson tractor with no tyres at all, many bits of agricultural implements from days gone by and about half a dozen garden rotavators of varying ages which had been scrapped as better ones came on the market.

We put some of those on one side, which were later cleaned up and put on display, and the rest we persuaded a scrap-iron merchant to take away. The whole area was then cleared and laid out to beds at ground level for the plants for sale. You know what this sort of thing looks like in conventional garden centres and there was nothing new about ours except our use of gravel from the bay at the bottom of the property, underlaid by cardboard to deter any plant growth on the paths, the gravel was regularly raked in dry weather to kill of weed seeds blown in from outside. And we used our own wood chippings, initially from our own woodlands and later from Dad's willow plantation, as bed, with cardboard underneath, on which to stand the plants in their pots.

No weed was ever allowed to show itself in that garden centre area! And no one was more insistent that this should be so than Bron.

Bron spent the whole of her first summer and most of the following winter helping to create this sales area and then potting up stuff to fill it.

All this was work with no money coming in but Dad's pick-your-own organic vegetable project was beginning to take off, local people were keen to buy his produce, and together with the other two organic growers on Anglesey, he was finding that there was greater demand than he could supply. This augured well for next year and some of the takings went to pay Bron and Les as well as feed our family.

The outbreak of foot and mouth disease in the early spring of 2001 affected us indirectly only in so far as Dad had to keep his herd of Welsh Black Cattle and that part of the farm in complete isolation. His animals did not get infected, no farms neighbouring his got infected although there were a number of cases on Anglesey and many animals had to be destroyed. But it did affect all of us as people because we knew many of those directly involved for whom it was catastrophic. The epidemic was eventually contained although Dad continued to take great care about hygiene for a number of years, keeping customers to pick-your-own areas well away from the cattle.

The garden was not scheduled to open until the summer of the following year – 25 July 2002 was the date provisionally set. By the time I went to college in September 2001 Dad's pick-your-own was up and running well, the garden centre plant area was cleared and beginning to fill up and Les was working all that winter clearing undergrowth and paths through the woods. He also, with help from me at the weekends, was to repair the retaining wall of the ornamental lake.

Mum wanted two plastic greenhouses, one to be used to give some modicum of shelter and warmth while potting up plants, and the other to shelter tender young plants over their first winter. These were in place by that Christmas leaving the gargantuan task of clearing the walled garden, rebuilding the old potting sheds, hot and cool greenhouses and replanting the walled garden.

The Chief Planning Officer had suggested, and the planning authority had agreed, that to do anything with the Plas building itself would be impossibly expensive at this stage although, long term, it was hoped we would make the walls safe and give access to the public so that they could see what used to have been, much as has been done for ancient monuments by English Heritage and its Welsh equivalent, Cadw. Although neither body, when approached, considered the Plas to be of sufficient historical importance and so would not release any funds.

In the meantime, and therefore for quite some years to come, the Plas house was to be securely fenced off. This was scheduled to be done in the summer of 2002 before we opened to the public and would be a wooden post and rail fence, made of oak cut from our own woods, backed by large mesh-wire netting and topped by two strands of barbed wire, impossible to be got through by children or climbed over by anybody. Leaving a clear view of the ruin and with notices giving a ground plan and history. All part of the tourist attraction.

In late autumn, two men started work in the walled garden. They were a couple who lived together in a house in the nearby village of Llansadwrn. One, the older, was quite well off, a writer of books, and his younger partner was a keen gardener. They had made a beautiful garden for themselves on the banks of a stream running past their converted farmhouse and now wanted something with a challenge to it that would get them out in the open air when the writer was not writing.

Jim Blake and Glyn Roberts were elected honorary members of the Plas Garden Trust before they died. They worked, for the fun of it, all that winter, clearing the ground within the garden walls of nettles, brambles, old tin cans, dead blackcurrant bushes, dock roots and ancient, dying lichen-covered apple and pear trees. They picked up bins full of broken glass and carted away and burned rotten lengths of wooden greenhouses. They kept the Victorian cast-iron, big-angle, brackets that supported the roof timbers, they found and kept all sorts of old rusted garden tools that mainly lay on the floors in the potting and tool sheds which eventually were de-rusted, oiled and used for display within the rebuilt buildings.

None of the buildings were repaired by the time the gardens were open. Work started on one, the old potting shed, at the end of that first summer after we had opened, when it was seen that there would be enough visitors to pay the wages of a carpenter-cum-builder to re-roof and re-glaze the place. And one greenhouse or potting shed was restored to its original glory each year until all was as it had been.

By that time my water turbine down by the river was in place and working and the greenhouses had their cast iron hot water pipes full of filtered river water, heated by home grown electricity. We cleaned up the old cast iron boiler that used to heat the greenhouses but it was in too bad a state of rust and damage ever to use again so it was left as a show piece in its own special boiler house halfway underground.

Underneath the brambles and nettles, within the walled garden, were paths laid with gravel from the beach and edged with what had been dwarf box hedges. In some places these had been smothered and had died, in others they had grown unchecked and were scraggly two and three foot high bushes. Mum caused these to be cut back to about a foot high and transplanted temporarily into pots in the standing area. She took cuttings from all the top growth and, when the paths were cleared and the ground repeatedly tractored over by Dad with his shallow rotavating to kill off weeds, the old box hedges were replanted with the original plants and their offspring rooted cuttings, now grown to sizeable stock; the paths were covered with a new layer of gravel off the beach and Mum and Bron sowed seeds and planted plants in the spring ready for opening to the public in that July of 2002.

The planting plan for this walled garden was to reproduce, for the public to see, what had been grown in Victorian times and how they had done it in those days. But a compromise was agreed on. Visitors wanted ideas and demonstrations to show what they could do in their own gardens so the best of modern varieties were grown under an organic, no-dig, garden routine, putting all compost on top of the soil instead of digging it in. All growing beds were reachable from the paths, all paths between rows were permanent, as was done in the PYO (pick-your-own) fields, and weeds were either hand hoed in dry weather or hand pulled in wet and put on the compost heap.

No chemicals whatsoever. Unwanted insect pests controlled and deterred by mixing plants. Growing things like tagetes (marigolds) and garlic among vegetables and fruit. Surely everybody knows about these sorts of things by now – the information leaflets have been available in all the organic garden centres for fifty years or more!

Water available from standpipes all over the garden. Watering done by hand-held hosepipe, to retain the Victorian historic flavour, by gardeners dressed in historically correct gardening clothes.

Plenty of large galvanised watering cans in constant use, these to apply the diluted comfrey juice that was, and is, used as a liquid feed for all plants in the walled garden. A special, smallish area set aside in the potting-up area to produce comfrey leaves that were, and are, stuffed tight into lidded bins and the resultant liquid diluted one part comfrey juice to sixteen parts water.

The combination of compost and comfrey juice produced crops that amazed, and amazes, all visitors, and produce was, and is, eaten in the garden restaurant.

Turbines

Girls, during this time, were a disappointment.

There were some very beautiful students about. Intelligent, much more intelligent than myself for the most part, witty and fun to be with. They, mostly, seemed delighted to be invited to dances or pubs, to go sailing, walking or mountaineering, quite capable of initiating invitations themselves to any of these activities, but amateur at any sexual activity in bed or out of it. Disappointing after Glynis and Maggie. They didn't want to explore my more esoteric suggestions, in fact, they nearly all didn't really want any sexual relationship. A bit of kissing and sometimes a cuddle and such and then... 'No, no. No more. That's enough. Don't.' And hands pushed me away instead of touching and exploring. 'I came to college to learn, not to have babies.' And this in spite of explicit sex and sex education on the telly and in schools. Disappointing.

But it didn't seem to trouble me much, nothing like the frustration I felt in later years when my first marriage ground to a halt as Jayne and I matured into 'middle age', developed separate but equally valid interests and drifted away from each other, spending the last eight years of that marriage as strangers in the marriage bed, held together by not wanting to hurt our teenage children, both equally frustrated in other directions.

By the end of my first year in college, Dad and I had made the smallish generator using wind to power the four-bladed propeller that drove the turbine, making enough electricity to heat the greenhouse in the farm garden which we had had for years and which Mum used in the first few seasons of opening the Plas gardens to propagate cuttings and start seeds off.

The problem with wind is that sometimes it does not blow. And this can happen in the middle of very cold frosty days and nights when all is still and beautiful and sparkling crystals but the little seedlings, tiny cuttings, geraniums and fuchsias in the greenhouse freeze to death. This can be prevented, as we did, by having a heat reservoir in the form of a water storage tank under the greenhouse floor which gets warmed when the wind blows and steadily releases heat during calm weather, enough at least to keep the frost away if you line the greenhouse with polythene bubble insulation.

Wind power, in those days before the perfection of electricity storage in modern batteries or hydrogen gas containers, was not constant enough, by itself, to give a steady supply of either heat or electric power.

'Energy' is the comprehensive word for heat, electric power or light. And these days energy can be stored as hydrogen gas and converted, when you will, into any of the other manifestations of energy like heat, light or power.

But then, back in the winter of 2001–2002, in the middle of my first year in college, there were no ways of storing large amounts of 'energy' except perhaps as water behind a dam that could be steadily released to turn turbines driven by water released through 'gates' in the dam. And this 'storage of energy' was only possible, in large quantities, in lakes of fresh water, or behind a dam to hold back salt tidal water. Both having a period during the night when electricity demand is low so their potential electricity production is hardly utilised and so being a financial investment not in use for one part of its potential economically productive life. Or so the banks argued when talking about investment loans of millions of pounds. Anyway, we weren't, then, thinking in large quantities.

So from February 2002 onwards, in between attending lectures and taking late-adolescent females to dances and pubs and not getting very far, I worked first of all at the theory of energy production from water turbines driven by the stream down by the lake at the Plas and having persuaded Dad, although he didn't take much persuasion being as interested as I was in energy from renewable resources, that it would pay us to make our own electricity, he and I built a turbine from scrap machinery he bought from a dealer in Birmingham.

This was to a standard design, used and proved by the Victorians and good enough to heat and light, as I have said, the greenhouses and restaurant at the gardens, and supply cooking power to the kitchen there.

For our house and farm workshop etc. we turned our attention to the river 'Wen' – the Avon Wen – where it entered our fields at the top of the farm. We built a small dam and piped the water through a four-inch plastic pipe buried a couple of feet underground down to the farm buildings where it came out at quite a speed to hit the cups of a Pelton wheel – another Victorian invention still to be seen at work in some places. We made our own Pelton wheel, cutting sheet steel and welding things together, using bearings etc. from the Birmingham scrap dealer. Then we piped the water back into the river and said not a word to the Water Board because we had heard, years before, that they had tried to impose a charge on the woollen mills of North Wales simply for the use of water to drive the mill machinery. Such a high charge that one mill had closed and the others had had to contest it and had had a worrying few years until the matter was dropped. We didn't want any of that, thank you very much and, since the water was returned to the river, of the same quantity, we didn't see any reason for pay for it.

We also installed enough photovoltaic cells on the farmhouse roof to give enough heat for baths and a bit of electric light in the summer.

All these sources of natural energy are subject to seasonal variation – the wind stops blowing, rivers run low in summer and sunshine runs low in winter; so you need two or more systems in order to guarantee a continuous supply of power/energy.

There is one natural energy source that never stops – the tide – although at the points of high and low tide it does pause, 'turn around', and run the other way. But high and low tide times vary in different places. High, or low, tide on one side of Anglesey occurs at a different time on the other, the time scale difference being nearly two hours. Thus, I said to myself, as a far-thinking engineering student, get two turbines working, one on each side of Anglesey, connect them together and you have a free, inexhaustible, natural, renewable source of power. Bingo! Free heat, light and power for everyone, once the machinery was paid for and a bit of cost for maintenance and replacement. Nothing like the cost, or danger, of nuclear power or the carbon dioxide (CO_2) pollution threat from the burning of coal, natural gas, oil or petrol that results in the greenhouse effect and the heating up of the world's atmosphere with floods and fog and all!

'Why,' I asked my Dad and the college lecturers, and anyone else who I thought might know the answer, 'why are they not using the energy of the tides to produce usable power?'

'They are trying,' I was told, 'but the technology is in its infancy.' And, up to date (at that time) they were only trying to harness tidal power in estuaries by holding it back with dams and putting in a turbine. A start had been made with prototype propellers, underwater, turning as the tide went by them but only making little power. Not much interest had been shown in this development.

Another system was trying to utilise the up and down movement of waves but insufficient capital was available to finance this idea.

At that time, all interest in renewable sources of energy, as opposed to the then conventional energy sources like nuclear power or gas and coal burning, was in wind power, solar power and electricity from turbines running with dammed up water power and other minor sources like natural gas from municipal waste or sewage, some methane gas from farm manure, and some conversion of forest waste to chippings burned in special ovens to produce heat and/or electricity. This was much more common on the continent in countries like Austria and Norway. Coppice willow was just beginning to be burned in a similar way. Only a total of two per cent of all energy was obtained from those sustainable/renewable sources at the start of this millennium.

Nobody was using tidal energy in any quantity and yet, all round our coasts, the tides ran in and out, up and down, inexorably and, until the moon vanishes away, inevitably; on and on until entropy stills everything, long before which humankind will also have vanished away.

Not my immediate concern – Entropy.

Perhaps tidal energy was not so much in anyone's mind because most of Europe lies far from the sea. But Great Britain is proud to call itself an island and Anglesey is obviously so to all who live there.

To get on or off the place you either come or go by boat to Ireland or you cross the Menai Straits, a tidal sea water which separates Anglesey from the mainland of Wales. A bit further on, over Offa's Dyke, lies England: that home of the Saeson (Saxons), barbaric invaders from Europe who drove the Celts from their ancestral lands!

You can walk, take a car or bus or train over either of only two bridges over the Straits. Or you can sail a small boat across. Now I had been sailing on the Menai Straits since I was a boy and well knew the relentless running and effortless power of the tide. It seemed stupid not to harness it.

So, again neglecting my course reading, but also, to be fair to my course tutor, with his encouragement, I looked up all I could on the subject and set about making a revolving drum which would rotate over and over underwater, pushed by the tide.

I was lucky in having that small canal down by the lake to work in to start with. To have to carry out the initial experiments out at sea or at least out in seawater in the Straits, would have been time consuming and subject to weather interference. By putting my small, experimental revolving drums underwater in the canal, and simply turning them round to simulate the tide change, I could work in relative comfort on dry land and even carry on in the rain.

When it came to it I put up a temporary small plastic-covered frame and it didn't matter if it rained.

It turned out to be a very simple matter to have a drum with a spindle running lengthways through its centre. The drum revolved around this when pushed by water. I put two fins, one each side of the length of the drum, on hinges which clipped solid when told to by a tiny electronic gadget powered by the smallest of batteries.

So, one fin was held solid out at a right angle to the length of the drum, while the other fin, its hinge released, trailed loose in the water, offering no resistance to the tide. Thus the drum rotated, driven by the tidal flow against the solid fin. Hinge solidity was alternated by the electronic gadget whose alternation was triggered by a minuscule computer chip built into the centre of the drum, but controlled and timed by a master computer on land. In the first instance it was a small computer, hand-held, which Dai Jones, fellow student, operated from within our plastic tent, but later, when things were running on a commercial scale, distance didn't matter and the computer could be housed wherever, sending its instructions by short wave radio. Dai was studying electronics and came into the power generation business as equal partner with me when he finished his university degree.

I never finished my course. I left college that summer of 2003 having very much neglected my studies but having a good, solid prototype drum steadily revolving first one way and then the other, as the tide ebbed and flowed, anchored under water out of the way of any boats in the Menai Straits and sending a steady, if small, amount of electricity from its turbine built around the central spindle, along a wire attached to the cable that connected drum to shore.

With all this written up in proper professional manner, its accuracy vouched for by my college lecturers and with the approval and back-up up from my parents, I had gone along in June 2003 to the bank and negotiated a development loan. By 1 September I had taken the lease of a unit on the industrial estate near Llangefni under Anglesey County Council's start-up terms of no rent to pay for the first two years, obtained all possible grants for new businesses and employed a technical college leaver whose wages would be partly paid by the government for the first six months.

I shifted all Dad's workshop machinery into the unit and we started making the first ten commercial size drums by hand.

The drum case itself was made to my specifications by a specialist plastics firm in the Midlands who usually made the strong unsinkable buoys you see in harbours. Much later, when we were exporting our underwater turbines by the hundreds, we set up our own drum-casting unit, importing the necessary raw plastic! Not a renewable material; made from raw petroleum originally.

I suppose that, one day, a scientist will find a substance which will do the job and be derived from a renewable source – a wood tar perhaps – but until then we use what we have to. I am not a purist. And the whole of Anglesey's Assembly has worked on the principle that it is not purist, not dogmatic.

Pragmatic: organic as much as possible, renewable energy sources wherever available, home grown, home made if we can; local ownership encouraged, out with the multinationals. If you own your own house, your own school, your own factory (by having shares in it) then you will take care of things and work with brain and body to improve things.

This is a principle I have held to all my life and I started it from the first day that I took Caradoc Williams onto the permanent staff of 'Anglesey Turbines Ltd' which was the name I gave to that first industrial unit leased near Llangefni.

Anybody working for (but I have always preferred to say and think of it as 'with') – anybody working with me comes on a six month, fixed salary basis. At the end of that time either party can say 'goodbye' and no hard feelings. Good engineers, like good teachers, are born, not made. You can 'make' competent teachers and competent engineers by training and carrots/wages, but everybody, I believe, has it in them to be really good, heart and soul, in some specific activity. Engineers know that square pegs in round holes will not turn smoothly or happily, they wear away fast… stress, anxiety, breakdown.

So I look for round pegs in all my round holes and the wheels will run smooth. I also believe that two heads are better than one and that initiative should be rewarded. Every member of any team I am involved with (every member of any staff of a project) gets a flat rate salary according to the job specification, plus an agreed percentage of the profit of every year, plus shares in the business as it increases in value. A new batch of shares being issued every first of January if the business and the bank allow.

In this way every person involved in any project is not only doing the sort of work they enjoy but can also take their fair share of the profits, by working reasonably hard and thinking as they go and suggesting improvements whenever they can.

Communism? Socialism?

You also need capital to start a business. I didn't and don't care what you call it – Lib/lab/cap?

Personal, local investment of money, plus human energy and the reward of doing a good job for reasonable pay with reasonable working conditions.

David Llewellyn Cliffourd for President! Not chief physical training instructor on a managerial training course as my father had suggested, down there on the little beach when we were talking about what to do with the Plas and its farm, back there when I was sixteen!

I didn't think I would ever be involved in politics or business management training back in those days. But I am still an active member of the Anglesey Assembly and have travelled the world lecturing about motivation and co-ownership in the workplace.

But back in 2003, when all I had was a bank loan, the lease of a small industrial unit and the workshop machinery that came originally from my uncle's engineering business in Manchester, my mind and time were devoted exclusively to fin turbine development. I lived and almost ate the generation of electricity, often sleeping in a camp bed beside the turbines as we were building them. We – me and Caradoc – who I came to call 'Doc' because he could put his mind to any mechanical problem and worry at it, dream about it, fiddle about and make a part or help re-design the whole until the thing worked better than every before.

He became our overseas director, travelling to many countries in many different climates, installing or, later, supervising the setting up of many large scale, underwater, tidal energy, power stations. He and his wife were rich enough on paper to retire long before he did do. 'Doc Williams' our peripatetic maker and fixer.

I hardly noticed the lack of female company that year. Jayne Roberts became our part-time secretary as soon as I realised that my time could be put to better use than filling in forms, keeping records, writing letters or sending e-mails. She was nice and cheerful, hard working and trustworthy, two years older than me with some secretarial experience, already working part time as a farm secretary for two nearby large farms. Short brown hair, laughing brown eyes, reasonable figure and always well dressed, not provocative, not sexy; a very useful member of the team.

Fixed salary, steady increments promised as turbine production improved.

I do not understand the working of the male sexual organs, still less do I understand the working of the female body and mind, even now, at the age of eighty-two, these matters are a mystery.

I had read, as one does, during my adolescence, everything I could about sex and the working of the genitalia of both male and female, I had talked with male friends, and girl friends to some extent, about these things and science books about the working of the human body helped a bit.

From all this I understood: that testicles started working during puberty and churning out, once they had settled down to the job, much as a new machine needs a running-in period, semen.

That there was a small reservoir to store the stuff at the correct temperature before ejaculation and, hopefully or not, as the case may be, fertilisation. At least that is what evolution wanted to achieve. Babies and the continuation of the species. An improvement on its parents or not – as the case may be!

Humans, exploratory and inquisitive beings as they are, had found this mechanical process to also be a source of pleasure, that unlimited baby production was not always a good thing and so invented contraception.

Schools and parents all dutifully explained methods of contraception and science worked away at improving these methods. They did not deal quite so exhaustively with masturbation but it did get a mention and was no longer considered the sin that our Victorian ancestors associated it with.

All that I understood. I had found great pleasure in sex with Maggie and Glynis and considerable disappointment with girl friends during my brief student days.

But what happened to my semen production system during that year when I was totally full-time living and working turbines?

Storage I knew was limited and yet, I assume, like the tides, production goes on inexorably!

I must admit I didn't give much thought to the problem at the time. It didn't even crop up as a problem. I simply collapsed into bed at the end of each day exhausted but satisfied with steady progress in spite of technical or mechanical hitches and never even thought about semen production, copulation or any of the pleasures they bring. Or masturbation for that matter.

I still do not understand the mechanics of the shut-down.

A similar shut down occurred in my life when my marriage ground to a halt although Jayne and I stayed together. I became impotent to all intents and purposes, only being rescued from this sorry state a few years after Jayne and I eventually moved and lived separately, by a very understanding partner plus some expert advice and two tiny little pills from a homeopathist.

Turbine development went ahead with no sexual distraction and I didn't, during that time at least, feel any deprivation.

Strange. Where *did* all that semen go? What a waste!

Developing the turbines was, in its way, relatively simple. You build a machine, try it out down in the small canal, as we did at first and later in the Straits, find out where it is not working or how to improve it, make another one and try that out. Not quite ad infinitum, although it may seem so at the time, but again and again until you get something that really works. Then you have to apply it commercially.

That is the difficult bit. No longer are you dealing with mechanical or electrical certainties but with planning authorities, landowners, banks and business people. All unpredictable, sometimes moribund, often obstructive. Difficult.

At least so I found to start with when I simply presented plans, asked permission or offered to pay for whatever it was I wanted.

However, when I started negotiations by talking about the concepts of renewable energy, sustainable resources, improving health risks by, for example *not* making electricity from a nuclear power station, people began to listen and be co-operative and even enthusiastic. Money and planning rules became less important. I found I was working *with* fellow enthusiasts to a common purpose. Obstacles melted before a very loosely formed team aiming for the common good: a specific improvement to our common environment.

Once I knew that the turbines would work under water, spin the other way when the tide turned and send their electricity production back along the cable joining them to the shore I left Doc pretty much to himself in finalising and refining the design of the beast and set about getting sites to install them.

This is where I ran up against planners and people. Not that planning officers are not people, much as some folk have implied to the contrary, it is just that the aforesaid planning authority and officers are constrained by their rules. Rules that are often laid down by 'bigger' planners further away. When the Anglesey Assembly became a matter of fact, with powers devolved away even from Cardiff and certainly from London, then we could, and did, make rules and regulations that really made sense to the people of Anglesey and the needs of the island, always bearing in mind the needs of the 'outside' world.

I needed two sites for those first, ten, production line turbines; five at each site, producing electricity, linked in series, and sending their power to a common centre.

There is a problem here. One needs to have the sites sufficiently separate to overcome the difficulty, at the point of high and low tide, when no power is produced because no tidal flow occurs. I settled for looking for sites, one each end of the Menai Straits, eventually hoping to have larger production units on each side of Anglesey or even a number of sites in various places all around the coast. This would give a continuous supply because high and low tide times vary round the island. Even better variation around the coast of the whole British Isles giving a totally even, level supply.

Anyway, five fin turbines at each end of the Menai Straits would do for a start. Just to prove to any future purchasers of the fin turbine system that it worked and could give a steady supply.

The second problem was how to use the electricity produced? I could wire everything together with long connecting wires and offer electricity on my own 'grid system' to all the factories set up on the newest industrial estate near Llangefni where we were. But such a local grid system would cost much more money than I wanted to borrow and the loss of electricity along the wires would be more than my ten-turbine source could reasonably loose.

In 1998, in Kyoto, Japan, an international meeting of many heads of state, or their representatives, and experts in the field came to an agreement that the worldwide use of fossil fuels for energy – heat, light, power and particularly petrol and diesel for vehicles – was so polluting the atmosphere as to give even more strength to the concern about atmospheric pollution and the greenhouse effect and something decisive had to be done about it.

It was decided to aim for a 12.5 per cent reduction in the use of fossil fuels worldwide, with the corresponding increased demand for energy sources to come from renewable (sustainable) natural sources.

This commitment by governments worldwide filtered down by the promulgation of directives and ended up, at a local level, by all local governments, in our case by Anglesey County Council, having to improve their waste disposal systems and encourage local generation of power from local sustainable (natural, renewable) sources.

In Great Britain as a whole the large electricity supply companies (as opposed to the makers/producers of electricity like nuclear power stations and coal or oil burning power stations) were to be directed to purchase ten percent of their needs from sustainable sources by 2010.

The difficulty about this was that the cost of producing sustainable source electricity from wind power, solar photovoltaic cells or turbines set in costly new estuary barrages across rivers, or any of the other small-unit local methods like methane gas production or burning chipped forest waste etc., was higher per unit than that produced in the fossil fuel industry.

Either the cost to the consumer per unit of electricity used in the home and factory had to go up or subsidies were required.

The government of the day – Mr Blair and his New Labour – didn't want to do such an unpopular and probably economically foolish thing as to raise the unit cost of electricity and thus universally raise the cost of living. Nor did they want to blatantly fling subsidies around: so they compromised.

In 2001 a levy of 0.2 per cent of their income was imposed by the government of Great Britain on all fossil and nuclear power suppliers to be used to finance the government body that was set up – called the NFFR.

Anybody producing electric power from a sustainable source could sell it to any supplier of electricity in the area and feed it into the national grid. The NFFR came along and had a look at the system, decided how much they approved of it as sustainable, and in the long-run, economically viable source, and then set a price per unit of electricity which the supplier had to pay. This price was to be above market price but would only continue for a set number of years. In this way the government was giving a subsidy but not an umbrella one and each enterprise had to prove its worth; they only got the special price for a fixed period of years. After that they were back in the market place with no favours offered. Sink or swim.

After due application, innumerable forms filled in by Jayne, who understood paper work jargonese, and five inspections on site, we got our price agreed; MANWEB had to accept and all I had to do was deliver.

Siting the ten relatively small turbines at each end of the Straits was not much of a problem. Nothing like the difficulties I met later on with larger groups of underwater turbines in areas where larger fishing boats might have snagged them.

In the Straits there was no net fishing going on from commercial boats. My turbines had buoys floating above them and having only five on each site, local fisherfolk, even if they used a net, could easily see the buoys and not fish nearby.

The drum turbines were set in areas where there was a steady tidal run, information freely given to me by the Marine Biology Research Station in Menai Bridge whose staff were extremely interested in what I was doing, gave me any advice and help they could, and, later, although Anglesey Turbines had to pay them a fee for their services, advised on suitable sites around Anglesey to take advantage of the best tidal runs. All turbines were set deep enough to avoid damaging any passing boats.

They were strongly anchored to the seabed and strung in line across the run of the tide. It depended on the depth of the seabed as to how many we could put on one 'string'. Each produced electricity which was collected in series and the cumulative power ran ashore through an insulated cable set in the seabed.

The advantage of being able to tie in to the national grid at the nearest point to our site meant that we lost little electricity through having to convey it through any great length of cable.

Eventually, of course, Anglesey Turbines Ltd took over the whole grid system on the island: but that was after we got rid of the nuclear power station near Holyhead and by then we were producing much more electricity than Anglesey used and we sold it to the mainland at a very competitive price indeed, until England, mainland Wales and Scotland all realised that they had tidal runs of their own and bought turbines in quantity from us. I had, of course, long before then spent considerable sums of money patenting all aspects of fin turbine design and control and we had cornered the market worldwide. We ended up employing a lawyer full-time, protecting our patents and suing other competitors. But we only did that for a while until it became, in reality, impossible to stop people copying our design. Nor did we really want to go on being obstructionist, capitalist and selfish. By that time we had made enough money to set in motion many other projects and principles that established Anglesey as an independent entity geographically, politically and economically in its own right, with its own Assembly and an island pride in its independence; using the Welsh language within its confines but everybody being totally and fluently bilingual in English; French, German and a few other languages being also available in schools.

But I'll tell you in more detail about the developments in education within the island some other time. At the moment I am on about turbines and, anyway, many other things like education and social welfare, local ownership of resources and money, total removal of pollution from petrol and diesel fumes, a free electric car for anyone on the island, came much later when Anglesey Turbines was well established and its ownership turned completely over to local shareholders and I had nothing more to do with it except as a member of the board of directors.

By the end of 2004 we had the ten turbines running in the Menai Straits, sending their electricity in to the national grid at a price per unit that covered the costs of our original borrowing at the bank, paid the salaries of Doc and Jayne and covered the running costs of our factory unit; we were not yet due to pay rent.

Very nice really. Now I had to sell more turbines.
I failed to do so.

The Doldrum Years

I got married, too young, on 22 March 2005, when I was twenty-two years old, to Jayne Roberts, although I didn't feel too young at the time and perhaps it is flippant and unfair of me to even think or say such a thing. We produced two wonderful daughters during this marriage and the early years of our relationship were all I, or anybody else could have hoped for. Looking about me, at how relationships come and go, rise and fall, stop and start, we did as well as most couples and better than many. Our children have grown into confident adults, secure in the knowledge that each of their parents loves them even though those parents each now have different partners. The extended families are on good terms with each other, meet, not too often, and our combined experiences have not been devastatingly traumatic.

However, Jayne and I did spend eight years in suspended animation, frustrated in our emotional and physical needs, teetering on the edge of expressing, through anger, our disappointment in each other, held together by the wish to maintain a secure environment for our two daughters while they grew up and, let it be said, by the fact that we had made a very nice and unusual home for us all, that we both enjoyed, and each was loath to give up.

When it came to it, we sold the place and each moved elsewhere, but not far away, and we remained in friendly contact. It always saddens me to hear of animosity between separated couples.

Blame. How can one apportion blame? Or even think of marital breakdown in such terms?

If one partner goes off and 'sleeps with' somebody else, it can only be because the partner has not fulfilled them in some way or other. Nobody can help being what they are.

And it need not be sex at all that causes two people who have loved and married to drift apart and eventually separate. One changes as one grows older.

Anyway, I am rambling on. This isn't meant to be a treatise about marriage and divorce, young love and separation. It's meant to be my memoirs as part of the recent history of Anglesey and about my part in its secession from mainland Wales with the establishment of our independent Assembly. Although I can see that, in about another fifty years or so, any real need for us to be so separate will have declined when the whole of England, Scotland and Ireland will have gone organic and fossil-fuel free. We could at least return to be simply a part of Wales. But it is fun to have this independence and our education system is still so superior to the others.

Not my concern – fifty years from now, and entropy that much closer!

Back to when Jayne was part-time secretary to Anglesey Turbines Ltd, and a friendly, helpful part of the furniture. Doc Williams was maintaining the ten underwater turbines; we hauled them up for any servicing required; they are light enough and small enough to handle from the half-decked, outboard-engined boat we got second hand from Dickie's Boatyard in Bangor. The Straits rarely got impossibly rough and when they did we just waited for it to go calmer.

And I set about trying to sell more underwater turbines.

I failed.

At least, for many years, I failed.

For the same reasons that photovoltaic cells were not being set up by everybody on every roof, or wind powered generators in every garden. The cost.

As long as the United Kingdom government was prepared to subsidise, through the NFFR, sustainable electricity generation then units like our ten turbines were, just, able to pay their way satisfactorily. But four years from the time when I was trying to sell our system, the price agreed by the NFFR, MANWEB would have to pay for our electricity, would revert to the mainstream price.

That mainstream price, nearly all of which was for electricity generated from either nuclear or fossil fuels, did not take account of the 'hidden' cost to humanity of radiation damage, either overt as when Chernobyl blew up, or covert by gentle radiation seepage into the environment which, as everybody now knows was considerable and devastating to the health of those effected by it – paid for in money terms by us all through additional demands on the health service. And it did not, then, take account of the cost of the damage to the environment of the release of CO_2 gasses by burning petrol, diesel, coal etc. and the resultant greenhouse effects of flooding and atmospheric change across the world.

In 2008 when it was becoming very obvious that the climate was changing everywhere, for the worse; through fiercer storms and rising sea levels and through a greater awareness, thanks to the media investigation and publication, that radiation from both nuclear power generation and its waste disposal was a very serious threat to all forms of life on earth; then governments, instead of being held back by public demand for cheap electricity, were driven by public outcry to agree to a proper, real assessment of the cost of power from nuclear and fossil sources and so fix the price per unit of electricity considerably higher to take account of these factors.

Then I began to sell my underwater, tide-driven, turbine systems by the hundreds – individual turbines by the thousands. All of us in the firm becoming very well off in the process.

But in 2004, with only my two sets of five turbines to demonstrate and a low price per unit of electricity bought from anyone who bought our turbines the prospect was bleak and I failed to sell any.

Interest in plenty. But, until the price of my installation came down considerably, which it couldn't do at the time because we were so small a production unit, making each turbine virtually by hand; or until the price paid to us, as producers, for each unit of electricity supplied went up considerably, nobody could afford to buy our system. Much as they all expressed interest in the concept of sustainable sources and a pollution free world.

That catch 22 – me to supply a cheaper system which would depend on mass production – resolved itself of course when the unit price per kilowatt went up by popular demand and government decree to a realistic level, then I could compete and mass produce, and do very well out of it indeed. But that didn't happen for quite some time.

Failing to sell even a single turbine, never mind a set of five or more, set me back no end.

I spent money I didn't have on producing glossy promotion pamphlets, and time and travel I couldn't afford in talking to firms and local government officials, trying to sell.

Anybody who had a business anywhere near a coast around Anglesey and Wales received paper information from me. I set up a web site and e-mailed countless firms. Plenty of interest, lots of my time. No sales.

Jayne was a brick! She spent hours and hours in contact with people on the phone and computer. When she realised that there was not enough money coming in to cover anything except Doc's salary and building overheads, never mind the pamphlets printed and my travel costs, she said she'd work for nothing because she approved of the principle of using sustainable resources and 'didn't want any child of hers to grow up in an environment polluted by radiation or get stuck in the mud of a flood caused by rising sea levels or overflowing rivers!'

I took her out to a meal on the evening that she said this and began to find out how supportive, realistic, and steadily sensible she was. And she appeared that evening, for the first time since she started working in Anglesey Turbines Ltd, not in a business-like skirt and top, but a lovely, clinging, shot-silk wine-red dress with shoes to match and her hair held back in diamanté clips.

I looked at the girl properly for the first time! And felt ashamed of my scruffy shoes, slacks and jacket.

We went back for coffee to the cottage she had inherited from her mother; her father, a bank manager, having died when she was still in school. The cottage was down a lane, by the church of Trefdraeth, near Malltreath, a wonderful marshy area over the other side of Anglesey, full of the sights and sounds of sea birds and marsh birds, wild duck and wind, racing clouds, rain, and warm calm summer evenings. We would sit there occasionally, during the next few years; before we had finished building our own house up by the river – the Afon Wen – on Dad's land near where the water fell over a natural waterfall at the top of the farm; exhausted from hefting the straw bales that formed the walls of our renewable energy, well insulated, new family home; or from digging into the hillside to create the lower, cooler bedrooms, or moving soil to cover the roof of the whole thing.

That evening, as the dusk darkened into deep night, there was a wood fire still quietly burning on a pile of ash that only needed stirring and a few more logs to re-awaken and leap into welcoming warm flame while Jayne ground real coffee, the smell mingling with that of the burning wood, and we sat in soft, large, comfy armchairs, one each side of the open fireplace. Jayne told me how her father had dropped dead from a heart attack, with no warning, at the age of forty-two when she was fifteen and still attending secondary school in Menai Bridge.

They had lived in a large house then, as befitted a bank manager. In Menai Bridge, just out of town, up a short drive through small immaculate lawns and low growing flowering shrubs to a gravel front area, garage at the back, steps up between geraniums and urns to the front door. A family home but her sister and brother, both older than she, were away and married already so, when her father died, her mother had sold the place and bought from the ecclesiastical authorities this quiet cottage near Trefdraeth ('village by the beach') church.

The cottage had last been occupied by a couple with the responsibility of keeping the churchyard grass cut and tidy and the inside of the church clean and opened at the right time. The church authorities had changed and modernised its whole system of church cottage utilisation, signed a contract to a gardening firm to cut the grass while the ladies of the parish took turns to 'do' the church.

The cottage had been put up for sale. It had a largish garden, overgrown and neglected, but Jayne's mum, Gwen, enjoyed gardening and Jayne promised to help her so Gwen bought the place, had the roof re-done, damp-proofed the floor, opened up the big old fireplace, installed central heating and a thoroughly efficient, but not too modernised, kitchen.

When her Dad died, sorting things out, buying the cottage and then having all the building work and things done had taken a few years so by the time they had moved Jayne was in her last year of school and then went to University in Aberystwyth to study where, of course, she stayed in digs; so apart from her last year in school Jayne hadn't had to catch the school bus from Trefdraeth to Menai Bridge at the crack of dawn for too long.

Gwen, and Jayne during holidays, had had a lot of fun doing up the garden and growing vegetables, cooking lovely meals for each other in the warm kitchen and driving around in Gwen's car, walking on the beaches and along the old drover roads of Anglesey; usually with a female student friend from college, occasionally a male, whom Jayne would invite for weekends or holiday stays.

And then, out of the blue, three years earlier, Gwen had said she was marrying again, to a man she had met in the village post office. He had been in the area on holiday but also sussing out the possibilities of starting an organic vineyard in the area – a project that came to nothing at the time. He had wined her and dined her and invited her down to London where he owned a house in an expensive part of Islington. He was very well off, a wine merchant with business premises also in Islington. A divorcee, grown up children, and they were off to see the world, buying wine as they went!

Well, not quite as simple as that. They were not married – yet – Jayne said, but were very happy indeed and enjoying life and each other no end. Postcards and letters came from London and Melbourne, Cairo and Connecticut, Bali and Birmingham, and Jayne could have the cottage provided she looked after the garden.

'So here I am,' said Jayne, snuggling into her arm chair, sipping coffee; a different, warm, cosy Jayne from my part-time secretary in the boarded off section of my industrial unit on the industrial estate, dealing with turbines and planning officers, kilowatt hours and units of electricity per second and per pence.

A warm, soft, cosy Jayne in her full, long-skirted, shot-silk dress, shoes shaken off to lie scattered on the rug by the fire, coffee mug in her hand, looking at me over the top of it, telling me about her life.

'What had she studied in Aberystwyth?' I asked.

'Agricultural economics,' she said. 'Hence the other part-time secretarial work for the two local farmers.'

She had hoped to set up a farm secretary service on Anglesey but it was a very difficult time for farmers and nobody else had responded to her advert for computerised account keeping so she had taken the job with me.

'Until farming gets better and the agricultural accounting stands on its own feet. I love it here, in the cottage, gardening, doing those farm accounts, although that's not very cheerful these days. Mum left me her car and I belong to a walking club so we go all over Snowdonia.'

I didn't ask her, then, about male friends because we started talking about what my parents were doing and I found that she was deeply interested and keen about organic food – her garden here was compost based and the produce good to taste – and, as she said, she approved of the principles of using only sustainable resources, disapproved of the nuclear power station here on Anglesey, or anywhere else for that matter, and so would work with me for nothing until things got better.

We talked until three that morning, putting more logs on the fire, drinking more coffee, but staying in our own armchairs. Exploring each other's enthusiasms, pet hates and shared interest in the countryside and I left in the moonless, starry early morning without even the thought of sex or a kiss. Tired, glad to have found someone I could talk with easily, aware of warmth, comfort – and beauty. But no hurry. Secure, gentle, friendly... mature I suppose would be a good word...

She wanted to be shown around my parents' place so Mum invited her to an evening meal the following Saturday night after she and I had walked all around the pick-your-own fields, looked at the cattle and wandered down through the gardens, beginning to look interesting now with the undergrowth cleared and paths inviting you to follow round the next bend. I showed her my turbine in the old turbine house making electricity for the walled garden and restaurant, we had seen the small wind turbine heating the greenhouse up by the farmhouse and also the Pelton wheel making electricity for the house and farm buildings powered by water pipes from the river and back again, and she was as enthusiastic and knowledgeable as Mum and Dad about all that was going on.

It became a regular friendship between my parents and her as much as with me. I would often find her helping Mum in the gardens or cooking a meal for all of us of an evening.

We didn't go out again for a meal, just the two of us, for a long time. Money was very short and I was busy and working late in evenings as often as not.

The people who came picking-their-own were usually very interested in organic ideas and, the whole thing being open to the public now that the gardens and restaurant were in operation, they often walked round looking at our electricity-producing systems. We had put up explanatory notes, under plastic, on posts to explain what things were and interest began to be shown in our small wind turbine.

Plenty of interest in the water-powered turbines but very few people had a stream or a river in their gardens. A lot of wind though.

Large wind-powered turbines were a common sight on Anglesey anyway because there was a wind farm with twenty or so large windmills slowly forever turning in the distance across the north end of Anglesey and, further south in mid-Wales, another herd of slow majestic angels straggling the hills.

People were asking about small wind turbines for their own homes. Were they efficient? How much did they cost? Did they break down in a gale? Dad told them what he could and, if they were really interested, gave them my office telephone number.

At first I told them what I could and referred them to CAT – the Centre for Alternative Technology, down in Machynlleth. But when I had installed those ten turbines in the Menai Straits and when I was getting no further orders, I began to think again about small wind turbines. You *could* buy them in those days but they were expensive.

A small wind turbine was fine for the greenhouse where we had put in that underfloor water tank to act as a reservoir of heat when the wind didn't blow and all we wanted as a bottom line was frost protection. Different for a house where people wanted to be warm on cold nights and needed hot water for a bath. That requires a bigger windmill and a constant supply of wind. No water reservoir back-up is going to hold a temperature to guarantee bath heat when you want it.

You can combine solar panels or photovoltaic cells with a wind-powered system and so, in theory, get the best of both worlds. But in those days solar panels were also very expensive and, anyway, sometimes in winter you get periods of windless days and no sun. No guarantee for hot water all the time.

However, there were a number of people about who were interested enough and prepared to put up with tepid bath water and candles if need be. They also were usually people who did not have a lot of money. But when my underwater turbine project ground to a halt I started having another think about small wind-powered turbines for the house. Perhaps I could design and make one that would be cheap enough for enthusiasts to buy even if they had to revert to mains electricity when the wind wasn't blowing.

Anglesey is an island and the wind often blows. If the wind turbines could be made cheaply enough then perhaps I could survive financially with these supplying my bread and butter while I continued trying to get the underwater turbine system off the ground, if you see what I mean.

A case could be made for a wind turbine giving you 'free' electricity when the wind blew and then back to the mains when it didn't.

Doc and I worked for six months on our small wind turbine, consulting aerodynamic engineering lecturers and students in Bangor University, trying out different materials, different ways of wiring the thing, different sizes of blades, should there be two or three to each turbine...

We got one that fitted the bill in the end and set up a demon-stration model by the pick your own fields. Interest aplenty and orders came in slowly. But they did come in. Enough over the next three years to enable me to pay rent on the industrial unit when it became due; when my initial free rent time ended.

So, with overheads paid for by the sale of electricity from the underwater turbines, and with rent and a few extras paid for by making small wind turbines, what else could I do to justify my existence?

The wind turbines enabled me to pay Jayne a proper salary and she worked three days a week in our office on a regular basis, still doing all we could to promote the underwater turbines as a inexhaustible, totally steady source of electricity but unable to compete with the low production price of grid electricity.

Writing articles to newspapers and journals when we could but watching, mostly from the sidelines, the slow and steady case being made that a true price should be paid by consumers for electricity produced by methods that polluted the atmosphere, affected or threatened the health of whole populations or whose hidden cost – as in the nuclear power case where the cost of building it in the first place and de-commissioning it at the end of its life *and* dealing with its nuclear waste – had not ever been a part of the price of a unit of electricity to the householder or industry. A capital investment by the government – a benefit for everyone!

Well, that attitude was changing. People didn't like living near nuclear power stations or the results of the greenhouse effect caused by carbon dioxide released by the burning of fossil fuels. The greenhouse effect made even governments take notice.

Long ago Margaret Thatcher, as the Prime Minister of great Britain, had attended international conferences in Buenos Aires but not much had changed. However, the 1998 international meeting in Kyoto had everyone saying they would cut down on fossil fuels and aim to use sustainable non-polluting raw materials to produce 12.5 per cent of their energy needs. And governments really did start to do something about it.

Popular feeling and thought went a long way with this – in theory. Different when they found it might mean they had to pay more per unit for their electricity, and governments, at least the British Government in Whitehall, did not dare to raise the price of electricity. They did start a number of schemes to improve the use of what we had got such as putting a two per cent levy (only!) on to fossil fuel users and used this to finance the subsidy to producers like myself using other, sustainable, sources for our contribution. My time for a subsidy would come to an end in two years and unless prices changed my underwater system, like that of many other small-unit producers, would remain too costly to be competitive.

We watched the arguments and contributed to the case for a real, true price for fossil fuels to be charged and for the case against the production of carbon dioxide, from any source, to gain strength.

And hoped!

Meanwhile we made a few small wind turbines per month and I began to think I ought to diversify within the field of sustainable energy and began to find out all I could about solar panels and photovoltaic cells. Let's use the sun as well as the wind.

It soon became apparent that photovoltaics were a better bet than solar panels. Solar panels convert sunshine into heat. You can get all your hot water needs met during summer months with little trouble. Not so in winter; and the panels in those days were expensive.

So were photovoltaic cells – made in Japan or America – but a better bet in theory because they convert light directly into electricity so they produce current even on dull days. But not a lot.

Pretty good in clear sunshine but very expensive to buy in the first instance. Could Doc and I make cheaper voltaic cells? I spent years, on and off, when I had time, thinking about it, finding out, taking advice, experimenting.

Anglesey did, very many years later as you know, set up its own production factory to a very much improved design but only when the price of fossil fuel production had been set at a full realistic level and we could mass produce our photovoltaics and so reduce their price, making it possible for every household to cover their roofs and take advantage of the sun and its light when it was there. Nothing of course during the night! And on a calm night the wind generators didn't help. Batteries were needed; and again in those days, batteries were not very efficient, and didn't hold enough current for long enough, and cost!

I got involved with the production of cheap, efficient, fuel cells – batteries – of all sizes, using hydrogen as their energy source, long before we really cracked the photovoltaic problems well enough to make them free for everyone on Anglesey as we did in 2041, although I had made and sold thousands of them before that happened.

There was a difficult circle which was hard to close using wind and sun power either alone or combined unless you had batteries to cover you during the dark days and calm nights.

Well, we got the cheaper, smaller wind turbines on the market and kept body and soul together with these for a number of years.

The gardens around the Plas improved and became more beautiful, more and more tourists went round them and down to the beach through the woods. Dad's pick-your-own filled all the fields he wanted to use in this way and, with the good staff he gathered round him, went from strength to strength. People marvelled at his crops, their quantity and quality, bought comfrey plants and went off promising themselves, those who had gardens, to go organic; and those who hadn't to only buy organic.

I decided I needed a better way to demonstrate the small wind turbines and with Dad's, and the planning officer's permission, decided to build a house half in and half out of the ground, on the bank near where the Afon Wen entered our farm. Paying particular attention to efficient insulation and getting light and heat from sun, wind and water.

This is when I got married.

The Married Years

Dad's fields were now full and bursting!

The fields he wanted to use for pick-your-own crops were, in a way, working virtually automatically. They were organised on the strip system using the width of three rows of a crop which he standardised as one metre, then came a strip, just wide enough for the tractor wheels, that was permanently covered with a layer of wood chippings; then a metre-wide strip in which were two permanent rows of comfrey plants, then a tractor wheel strip; another metre-wide strip for crops and then an access path of a metre width, covered originally with cardboard and wood chips, kept weed free and topped up every few years with more wood chips. And the same sequence again, right across the field.

The comfrey was cut and either put straight onto the adjoining crop rows or carted and composted.

Now comfrey is full of good plant foods but, being fairly low in fibre, does not supply much humus, neither does it supply much nitrogen. And green crops such as lettuce need a lot of nitrogen. So Dad considered these two problems – the need to build up humus in the soil and the need to supply nitrogen to some of the crops. Everything else in the way of plant food was well supplied by the comfrey.

Comfrey is a very good animal feed. It is also delicious for humans if the young leaves are cooked rapidly in a minimum of water like spinach. It also tastes like spinach and is equally good raw, in a salad.

A marvellous plant, it should be grown everywhere. But it does need to be looked after just as well and as carefully as any other crop. No weeds, plenty of water, and it needs to be fed. It is perennial – the tops die back in winter – but it is very tough and resilient. So you can put manure on top of it either in the winter or immediately after cutting the tops off in the summer.

When dealing with crops by the acre, farmyard manure by the ton or compost by the ton, one needs to think about the labour costs and how to handle the stuff. Farmyard manure – straw mixed with dung and urine – is bulky, heavy and sticky, not easy to spread between growing crops and it gets in the way of planting or sowing seeds if it is left on the surface; and Dad runs his vegetable areas on no-digging principles. You can pile the stuff up, let it heat up and then turn the whole heap over a couple of times and you get a nice, friable, compost that is dry enough to spread around anywhere but it takes time and energy to turn the stuff over. Dad simply spreads it fresh from the cattle yards straight into his comfrey either in winter or after the leaves have been cut and the comfrey then pushes through.

But that means there is no farmyard manure for the crops and they still need humus and nitrogen even when fed with copious top-ups of comfrey leaves or compost.

Chicken manure is rich in nitrogen and the deep litter manure from intensive egg and chicken battery farms is there for the taking. But such intensive battery farming is totally anathema to any organic, healthy way of life. The manure contains chemicals and hormones actively detrimental to humans.

So Dad had decided to produce his own chicken manure. And of course, and almost incidentally, his own free-range eggs and his own chickens for eating. He set up a small workshop in the building which had held his, now my, engineering machinery and started to make poultry houses. These were designed to be one metre wide to straddle the metre-wide crop beds and were about three metres in length. Handles at one end, a pair of wheels at the other. A quarter of the length roofed over with perches and egg boxes inside for the hens to sleep and lay eggs in, the rest, wire netting. Nothing at the bottom so all droppings drop onto the soil. The whole unit is moved forward its own length once a week or pulled by tractor to a totally different row.

Whenever any crop rows were cleared then the chickens followed straight behind, eating any crop or crop residue left and dropping nitrogen as they went, scrabbling in the soil for insects and things – especially slugs!

Slugs are the bugbear for organic growers. But hens (and ducks, of which more later) love to eat slugs. So any crop coming after the hens had been over the ground was guaranteed slug free with extra nitrogen into the bargain. Dad's lettuce began to be famed for size and taste.

Years later we had a small factory unit producing these hen houses when much of Anglesey had become an organic market garden. We continually improved the design, used light-weight materials and ended up selling them as pre-packed, assemble yourself, mobile hen homes that were sent all over the United Kingdom and into Europe. With smaller sizes for private gardens.

Hens, however, need more to eat than a few slugs and insects, cabbage leaves or carrot tops. We daily gave them comfrey from the next-door rows but they also needed grain in some form or other.

Dad grew a field or two of 'corn' (maize) – sweet corn – for two reasons – well, three I suppose. He sold some of the corncobs to his customers as your ordinary sweet corn, to be boiled or roasted and eaten, but this was not the objective.

He wanted the maize cobs to dry, store, and feed to the hens; and the straw from the maize plants to compost with comfrey to give a humus-rich compost for the pick-your-own crops.

And it worked! Racks in a large barn held the maize cobs harvested from the fields in late summer – racks built from home-grown willow! And the straw, composted with comfrey, had produced rich friable humus by the following season.

At the same time as deciding to grow maize by the acre so Dad also put down a whole field completely to comfrey to feed to his Welsh Black herd, for the hens in their mobile homes and for composting.

Now, you cannot keep sending stuff off a farm without replacing it with something else. You can never, in the long-run, get something for nothing. All those lovely vegetables and fruit, those eggs and chickens for the table, even the pedigree cattle and meat sold off the premises, all took stuff away from the farm that, in the long-run, needed replacing. All that food goes off to make energy for the humans who consume it and produce their own waste product – sewage. Farms are not an inexhaustible source of energy. And the energy loss needs to be replaced. In conventional farming this was done by buying in fertilisers.

On this farm Dad did it in two ways.

He encouraged his customers to bring in all their vegetable kitchen waste. Those who had compost heaps of their own of course didn't but by far the majority were more than happy to do so and Dad had a large bin for this stuff just near the car park. All of it to be brought in cardboard boxes to be thrown, box and all, into the bin. If brought in plastic bangs then no plastic into the organic bin but a separate bin for the bags. And everyone who came, all being of organic, useful use of waste, persuasion, brought in their scrap vegetable material; he also welcomed lawn cuttings and general garden refuse.

The bin was emptied daily onto Dad's proper compost heap and duly turned into lovely friable plant food. He just about replaced all the fruit and veg he sold, in terms of organic material, by the waste that came in.

Dad also had a contract to remove all dried sewage sludge from two local government sewage farms and this went straight onto the ground of either the willow plantations or the comfrey field.

In this way he did not deplete the long-term total organic resources of the farm. And in later years, when the whole of Anglesey went organic, when all communal refuse collection and disposal was run on recycle, renewable resource principles then all sewage was composted with all organic waste materials and either turned to natural gas or good compost to be spread on the island's willow or comfrey plantations – free.

Willow!

And you remember I mentioned ducks?

And slugs?

The three complement each other.

You can of course make baskets out of willow, and many people do. There is a steady market for good quality willow wands of varying hue for basket making and craft weaving. Two local craft persons soon found out about our willow and came to cut as they needed and paid a reasonable price for what they took. But this really didn't amount to much over a year and didn't make much of a hole in the willow plantations Dad had growing after a few years. He planted up all our wet land up on the top of the farm near the river with willow and, a few years later, persuaded a couple of nearby farmers to do the same on their set-aside land.

You can make charcoal from willow and sell it for burning in a barbecue. This is economically viable, provides work for one man part-time but does depend on a good summer and people doing a fair amount of outdoor cooking. Some years they did, some years they didn't. You can also use the medium thick branches and twigs to make artist quality charcoal but then you have to have a packing shed and market the stuff in little boxes to artists' suppliers in order to sell any quantity; and even then it doesn't amount to much when you think in terms of an acre or more of willow plantation.

Dad was looking much further ahead when he started with those hundred willow cuttings in the farm garden. But in the early years he did get Les involved in the charcoal production and it had remained a profitable sideline. All the rest of the willow branches at that time went into the shredder and were used to cover paths and keep weeds down.

But my father was aiming at greater things. In South Yorkshire in 1998 they had started an electricity-generating station burning willow.

Electricity from willow coppice is a fully renewable energy source, using no fossil fuel and, with modern, efficient burners, leaves no harmful gasses to pollute the atmosphere.

You need quite an acreage of willow plantation to feed the burners all the year round and it does not pay to have to transport the cut willow branches too far.

Ideally farmers or landowners within about ten miles radius need to grow willow on a proportion of their ground and send it to their local central willow-burning generator. If they put themselves on their own ring main they can get their own electricity. It is then down to comparative costs as to whether a person within the local ring main chooses to buy 'local' or from the main grid. Also, whether they want to continue to support electricity from nuclear power or fossil fuels with the concomitant atmospheric pollution.

Or, as I was doing with my ten underwater turbines, you can sell it to the national grid, leaving all those willow-growing farmers to continue buying their electricity in the normal way.

One of the very great problems with electricity in those days was that they could not store it, except in batteries that only held a very small quantity, as in a car, torch or calculator battery.

It is an interesting concept however to realise that water held in a big lake ready to run through a pipe and turn a turbine is a form of electricity storage, so is coal there in the earth or stock-piled in a heap by a generating station, so is gas underground in the North Sea: stored energy, waiting to be used. But, except for the water (hydro) power stations, you cannot turn it on quickly.

And any electricity board manager will tell you that on a Saturday afternoon for an important football match, or of an evening for a popular television soap opera, the demand for electricity suddenly surges up when millions of people switch on.

Large amounts of electricity could not be stored in batteries in those days so someone had to switch the generating turbines on to full power or switch on extra turbines, to cope with the sudden demand and switch them off again when people went to bed.

You cannot switch a willow-burning generator on, or off, quickly. Back in the early twenty-first century the only way that made economic sense if you were generating electricity on any scale above that of single household units was by making your electricity locally, from local sources like wind, water or willow and selling it to the national grid. Provided your system could sell it at a price that paid the local people who owned the local generator, be it an individual like myself with the ten tidal turbines, or a group of farmers in one locality with a willow-burning generator, or a local syndicate putting up a wind farm in their own neighbourhood, then whoever made that electricity would be paid for it and also be contributing to electricity generation from a non-nuclear or non-fossil fuel renewable source and thus making their contribution to that twelve and a half per cent total energy production from renewable sources as requested by the Kyoto international conference.

It was not until the Anglesey Assembly, through local councils and local people, surrounded Anglesey with community-owned tidal generators, plus more wind farms and water mills where possible, and when the cost of photovoltaic cells became cheap enough to cover every roof to take advantage of the sunshine, with cutting in extra tidal turbines or utilising the large hydrogen storage system for peak electricity demand, that it became possible for Anglesey to come off the national grid and produce its own electricity so cheaply from natural resources that, by subsidising it from the tourist industry, we could supply free electricity to the whole island. That comes later in my history.

At the time I am talking about, Dad was planting up a couple of acres of willow and doing his best to persuade other farmers nearby to use their set-aside land for willow plantations.

He rapidly found that young willow cuttings stuck in the ground with only about six inches above ground, and with no weeds or anything else growing on that land, then the slugs which abound in wet land were eating the young willow shoots and killing off his cuttings.

He remembered, at that stage, that ducks, as well as hens, eat slugs.

One of Dad's, and mine, and many other people's favourite meals, is roast duck. But the duck available then from butcher or supermarket, in restaurant or home, was almost always not organic, usually factory farmed, and pretty well tasteless.

As with the chickens, Dad killed two birds with one stone. Metaphorically speaking, of course; his ducks were humanely killed. It does not do to think too deeply about the fate of each individual slug. Do slugs have feelings? Hopes of entry to a slug heaven? Exciting sex lives and loves? Do they sing songs around a bonfire of nights? Should there be an equal opportunities policy for slugs?

I leave these and similar questions for future generations to answer. Suffice it to say that Dad changed his willow planting and growing system. He stopped bothering about grass or weeds growing in the willow fields. He simply took any old piece of ground and stuck eight-inch willow cuttings in rows all over it. He put a six-inch square of cardboard around the cutting to give it a chance against weeds and turned hundreds of ducklings loose.

Ducks are scavengers and eat most things, although they do not eat willow. So Dad made a series of little ponds in the field as part of the irrigation system which, by now piped water from the river to the whole farm and the ducks were in seventh heaven, free to roam and eat all the slugs they liked. People were encouraged to throw them scraps when they visited. They got some maize towards the end of their happy, if relatively short, free-range life and after a few years Anglesey duckling (because all willow growers on Anglesey followed suit) became synonymous with quality taste and were sent all over the country. Organic, free-range duck farming becoming a better paying proposition than the willow growing which started it. In a way Anglesey got a proportion of its electricity totally free, thanks to ducks. And, if you pursue the logic of the argument, thanks to slugs.

Just to round off this bit about willow: you let it grow for three years, cut it down to a few inches above ground level in winter when the leaves have dropped, tie it in bundles that a tractor can lift, stack it up to dry out a bit with a cover of plastic sheet or something to keep out the rain but let the wind blow through, then take it to the nearby generating station where it is shredded and automatically fed to the burners. Stacked like this in a field it can be taken to the burner any time during the following years as required.

The cut-down stumps grow again and, three years later, are cut again. This can go on for year after year. Cut one third of your acreage each year and you have a steady supply of wood chippings for the burner. An easy agricultural crop, sustainable, and non-polluting. I think we have about thirty smallish willow-burning generators running on Anglesey at the moment supplying their share of our total needs.

From all our different ways of producing electricity from natural resources we now, in fact, produce more than is needed on the island and we sell the extra to the national grid, another factor that is helping us to supply free electricity to the whole island.

But I was telling you about my decision, back in Christmas 2003, to improve my demonstration small wind generators which I would site near the pick your own fields.

Dad, and Mum, were involved in the discussion about this and since Jayne was in and out of our house and in and out of the office, she was involved as well.

Jayne and I sometimes went out for a meal together, but not often since money was scarce. We usually went back to her cottage afterwards for coffee and always talked and talked about our mutual interest in renewable energy sources in general and wind turbines in particular; but, after a while, our conversation tended to broaden and frequently took in the development of an energy-saving house as well as ways of generating electricity and heat.

We inevitably, eventually, ended up in bed together. It was one snowy night in early February. We had talked and talked and she said it was crazy to go back to my home in the blowing blizzard, why not stay here?

There was a single spare bed in her spare room but the double bed in her cosy bedroom was so inviting that we cuddled in there together, went on talking about an energy-saving house and ended the evening by dissipating our spare energy in love making.

Not the violent, erotic antics I had enjoyed with Maggie and Glynis, but a steady, at the time, satisfying, warm, secure making of love that led, before the year was out, to the making of a baby daughter, and a couple of years after that to the making of another daughter and the subsequent making of a home for us all, until they were grown up, and we had grown apart and separated.

House of Straw

We got married on 22 March 2005 and our daughter, Anghared, was born on 16 November that same year.

By that time we had dug well into the bank up at the top of the farm where the river entered our fields. We intended a conventionally upside-down house built into the hillside. It wasn't much of a hillside and we didn't go all that far in.

The bottom layer of the three-storey structure was only a few feet above the fields that lay in front and we soon hit rock. All soil that we removed got taken by tractor up to the top of the bank and dumped, ready to be moved over the roof for insulation when the house got that far. All rock was used to build forward and construct a platform that we reinforced and concreted to form the foundation of the front of the house and a terrace along the length of it. The house faced south-west and we glassed the whole front, the whole three storeys, to form a heat trap.

The next, inner wall, was thick concrete top to bottom, with windows to let light into the inner rooms. That thick wall heated up in any sunshine coming through the glass front, summer or winter, and acted as a night-time storage heater for the rooms on either side.

The bottom, basement, area was one huge swimming pool, heated by photovoltaic cells on the roof, a wind powered turbine set nearby on the top of the bank, or the undershot waterwheel I built into the bed of the river.

I am very proud of that waterwheel.

Where the river flowed over the top of our bank I levelled the rock bed. This wasn't all that difficult because the rock over which the water ran was fairly level anyway and completely solid, being an outcrop of the underlying granite in that area. I concreted it level by diverting the river to run one side at a time during the summer, when water was running low anyway, and I built up reinforced concrete, stone-faced buttresses on either side.

A local iron stockist, with cutting and welding equipment in his workshop, built me a waterwheel frame – long and not of any great diameter, the exact width of the river where it ran between my buttresses. I made strong oak blades to act as paddles and we hung the central shaft on bearings at the top of each buttress. These bearing housings were the clever bit although I say it myself. They were mounted on wooden blocks that rose or fell according to the level of the river, the rise and fall of the whole wheel powered by a small electric engine driven by electricity generated by the wheel itself.

Thus the central shaft always hung just above the surface of the water, rising in winter or during heavy rain, dropping in summer during drier weather, never able to drop so much that the paddles hit the river bed, and we had a constant supply of power in the house. The swimming pool would often get too hot and we had to switch something off; it acted as a heat reservoir for the whole house. Electricity for light and cooking, baths and anything else came from the river turbine.

We found that we didn't really need any of the sun or wind sources of energy for our house but they were there for demonstration purposes anyway. We were lucky; not everyone has a river by the side of their house and so we could show other people what was possible without a river.

We made sure that all the inner surfaces of the house, where we had cut into the bank, were finished with a waterproof concrete facing and then a thick bitumen coat on top of that. We did not want any damp coming through, everything had to be perfectly dry because we intended all the other walls to be made of straw!

A few years previously CAT – the Centre for Alternative Technology – had built a large show room and conference hall for school groups and visitors out of straw bales with a wood frame. We took advice, went to look and built our house on the same principles.

Straw is a cheap building material and a good insulator. We bought top quality, oblong bales at one pound sixty a bale from a farm in Norfolk. Lovely dry, clean wheat straw. Put one on top of the other, with a strong wooden frame construction made of seasoned oak bought from, it must be admitted, a timber yard in England – our local sessile, mountain oak does not produce long straight branches – and you get walls that are sound proof and heat retaining. You can bore holes through the stuff for water pipes, draining pipes and electric wires. You plaster either side of the straw walls and you get a good flat surface that takes paint just like any other sort of house.

Floors are conventional wood and the roof is strong tanellised plywood panels on wooden roof trusses, totally and very carefully waterproofed and then covered with a three-foot layer of soil.

Very warm in winter and we sometimes need to turn on cooling fans in the summertime. We virtually live our daily lives in the 'greenhouse' and terraced area along the front of the house, the kitchen and dining area are on the same level.

Utilities are in the basement as is the swimming pool, bed-rooms on the middle floor and a large sitting/living room on the top floor with a view of the farm, over the Straits and on, away, to the mountains.

I got expert carpentry help for the frame of the building and did the rest myself during the next two years while Jayne, Anghared, and I lived in her cottage. We moved into our new house at Easter in 2007 and Olwen was born three months later.

Compared to the cost of building a 'normal' house – we could not have afforded to do that or buy a new one anywhere else. Anyway, we wanted a house that would run on local sustainable energy and be made, as far as possible from natural materials. And to do it ourselves, to demonstrate the use of local energy production, to sell more of my wind turbines.

This succeeded and sales increased considerably both of wind turbines and a few fresh water turbines to those people who had a river near their homes. We had to put up with a constant stream of visitors though which interfered with our privacy but we made an entry charge for anyone to walk round; the kids became expert guides and we produced an information booklet for sale. From all these sources of revenue our family income became satisfactory.

The stream of visitors became a pain though. The interest in straw house construction with the concomitant natural energy source use was very great indeed and our family life suffered.

The planning authorities had been very helpful and interested in our house and placed no obstructions in our path. On the contrary their officers had made some suggestions for improvements that had made things better and more efficient.

Some fields came up for sale not far from a road near the village of Bodfordd, with the river Cefni running along one boundary. I talked with the planning boys and went to my bank manager – and bought the sixty acres.

I divided it up into twenty-five plots and, working very closely with the council planning officers and the county tourist officer, applied for outline planning permission for twenty-five dwellings.

Capitalist! Despoiler of the countryside! Shame!

Not so.

Each property was to have two acres of garden. I was to install a waterwheel in the River Cefni similar to the one I had built at home. Every house was to have its own wind turbine and all were to have photovoltaic cells on the roof. All twenty-five houses were to be on their own ring main. If they produced more electricity than they needed at any time it was to be sold to the national grid and I knew they would be making more than they needed most of the time. This local group of twenty-five houses was to own all the energy-producing equipment from water, wind and sun, to share the, minimal, running costs of the river turbine; and to share the profit from electricity sales to the national grid. A limited company was formed, solely to produce and sell all electricity above their own needs.

The bank was to play an important part in this. At that time Anglesey County Council – later the Anglesey Assembly – did not have funds for this sort of development. When I had gone to the bank to discuss my loan to buy the sixty acres, they had sent their experts to look at the house I had built by the Afon Wen near Dad's farm. All banks at that time were anxious to appear helpful to natural resource development: the government had directed them to be and it enhanced their 'green' image. Anyway, this sort of development caught the interest and imagination of even their hard-headed business attitude. It was good for business provided the development was a good financial investment.

Anglesey during the 1980s, and before, had seemed virtually to discourage development and tourism, depending on agriculture and service industry to keep it going. Many young people left the area to search for employment and excitement elsewhere. But around 1995 agriculture became a dying industry, largely due to the BSE (mad cow disease) scare but also due to other factors, and tourism became virtually the only way forward. Planning departments became enthusiastically helpful and grants to convert farm buildings into holiday cottages were easy to obtain provided you followed the rules. Any project to promote tourism in the area found its path smoothed and encouraged. So the tourist officer came along with me to the bank meetings, as did a representative from the planning office. The bank was prepared to lend me the money to buy the sixty acres and would also put up the capital for the waterwheel.

The council would run good access roads onto the property and to each house site. Fresh water was to come from the mains and rates were to be paid by each property as usual with some reduction because sewage was to be dealt with on the site. Each house would have its own organic toilet system producing compost just as Dad's pick-your-own toilets did. All other waste water, after passing through a heat exchanger in each house was piped to the communal 'grey' water reed bed filter system, passed on through reed and willow plantations and, perfectly clean by then, eventually found its way back to the River Cefni. A system pioneered by the Centre for Alternative Technology and, by that time, in use in many other parts of the country. All washing powders or liquids or soaps used were to be environmentally friendly.

I was to have a further loan to build one demonstration house and the information centre at the entrance to the estate and to landscape the whole area. The other plots were for sale. All houses to be of wood frame and straw bale construction, free standing with their two acre gardens – all to be organic.

The whole 'estate' was to be dedicated 'organic' and to be promoted, first of all nationwide, and as soon as possible and reasonable, worldwide, as a demonstration 'natural resource' village.

An entrance fee to be paid for folk to look round and the information centre to be made of straw and wood, constructed near the car park on the edge of the estate. Visitors on foot only: leave your car in the car park. Preferably travel by bike or public transport, reduced entrance fee if you did, buses pass the site every half hour. Adequate provision of public, organic toilets and easy access for wheelchairs.

Doc was left pretty much on his own in those days, maintaining the ten underwater turbines and manufacturing a steady supply of the small wind turbines as they were ordered. He had another man working with him by then. Jayne had stopped being my secretary and I took on a full-time girl to run my office with all its varied developments. Jayne carried on with her farm secretary work though and we had a German au pair girl to look after our daughters when neither of us was at home – most of the time in my case. Jayne said she didn't want to stagnate completely by being a housekeeper and childminder all the time.

As soon as the go-ahead from planning and the bank came through I produced sales material for the house plots. The idea was that it was the plot that was for sale, subject to the strict organic philosophy, and new owners were to build their own homes under supervision and help from me. The basic outline planning permission was already in place – wood frame, straw walls etc. – but detailed plans and layout were to be down to the individual, subject to detailed planning permission. New owners were to buy the plot from me but could arrange favourable loans from the bank if they needed to. The bank, of course, was free to advertise how helpful and reasonable it was being to such an enterprise: good publicity for them and good tourist publicity for us. I worked out a price per plot that was reasonable for any purchaser and that would repay my loans from the bank for the whole project. I needed to sell fifteen sites to break even.

In view of the inconvenience to the house owners all takings from the tourists and interested visitors to the village were pooled, running costs of the information centre deducted, and the rest of the money shared by each householder. In a few years, what with income from the electricity sold to the grid and the visitors' entrance fees, every householder was getting a small income that helped to pay off the loan, if they had taken out a loan in the first place, no matter what employment they had already.

The first thing I did on the site was to lay the car park and set up organic toilets. Meanwhile the council was putting down access roads and the Welsh Water Company ran pipes to each house plot. Then I contacted all local papers and wrote articles in all the tourist publicity handouts for the whole North Wales area. I put an automatic pay-as-you-enter gate on the car park and put up a marquee to act as a temporary information centre and shelter if it rained. I kept all the takings at this stage to pay myself a wage and those of a carpenter and his mate while we put up the information centre proper and, next in order, started on the display house.

It took us two years to complete these two structures. All construction processes were made accessible to the public with adequate safety precautions; all visitors had to wear safety helmets for instance and we were closely overseen by the County Health and Safety officer, plus proper insurance against accidents.

Long before the two years were up and the demonstration house finished I had sold every plot and some houses were under construction. I formed a limited company run by a committee of at least one person from every household, co-opted one representative from the planning department, one from the tourist department and invited one representative from the county council and handed over the visitor/information centre and the display house to the company. I remained as consultant, for no fee, to the company and left them to it with the selling price of the final ten sites as my profit.

The year was 2009 and I had some capital to work with. The 'straw' village went from strength to strength and orders for individual house-size wind turbines started to pour in as visitors to both the 'straw village' and our own house saw how effective (and reasonably priced!) they were. I moved to a bigger industrial unit and set up a completely independent wind turbine business with Doc as its managing director. He was to take complete control of this, employing his own staff, still on a co-operative basis with shares of the company – Anglesey Turbines – owned by all employees who stayed more than the initial trial six months.

They were to produce and sell the small wind turbines, continually improving the design, having an installation and/or repair team prepared to travel and set up the thing if any customer required such services. Full maintenance and product guarantees absolutely sacrosanct. Customer satisfaction a prime objective. Nothing too much trouble. Our corporate objective was to utilise the wind to humankind's advantage and to reduce planetary pollution just as much as to make a living for our employees. Myself included.

Doc was to remain responsible for running the ten turbines in the Straits and I kept the original industrial unit. I wanted to see what could be done about producing photovoltaic cells at a reasonable unit price, continue to oversee, as consultant, the development of the straw village and I wanted to look at fuel cells – the long-term storage of electricity. If we humans could get batteries efficient enough to store electricity, powerful enough and holding their charge for long enough to run a car, then we could dispense with petrol and diesel fumes.

Stop the greenhouse effect.

Improve everyone's health.

But this requires a steady, cheap, renewable, non-polluting source of energy – to my mind – tidal power, and, as I have said, efficient powerful batteries.

I made slow and not, at first, economic progress with the photovoltaic cells; they had to buy them from a Japanese firm for the roofs of the straw houses.

But fuel cells were a different thing.

The Fuel Cell and Turbine Years

I think this is where I went wrong.

But who can put a finger on a particular spot in time and say 'that is when it all started.' Or started to stop. Or began to go wrong. And was it my fault anyway?

To what extent are our destinies foredoomed? Why doom? It all worked out for, if not the best, quite a good life for everyone in the end. Richer in many ways than staying trapped in a convention.

I can see the advantage to society in having a secure home, run by two people, one of each sex as a general rule of thumb, in which children can grow up feeling loved and wanted; where a reasonable set of standards is maintained and where the atmosphere is reasonably friendly. If any of those parameters break down then there is a case, after discussion and a chance for things to improve, for the sake of the children themselves as well as the adults, that divorce should go ahead.

I didn't, at the time, realise anything was happening, or not happening, depending on how you look at it. My business was taking off, things were fairly financially secure, I was in a position to develop even further my interests in fuel cells and photovoltaics and natural energy sources in general. The kids were slowly growing from babies into young children, the au pairs were, give or take a few hiccups, very good with them and, anyway, I was hardly involved in this, being at work and away most of the day and often evenings: meeting people, reading things up, visiting research stations, talking to lecturers and students, going abroad to Europe to see for myself what people were doing there. Talking and thinking non-stop about fuel cells and batteries. The possibilities of hydrogen for power storage.

As everybody must know by now, you break down water, which is a combination of oxygen and hydrogen, store the hydrogen as a liquid or gas, and when you recombine it with oxygen under the right conditions, you release energy.

The whole technology was only just beginning to be looked at.

Scientists were talking about a new pipeline system for the whole country moving hydrogen about instead of North Sea gas, or petrol tankers, or electricity pylons. A car driven by hydrogen produces water as a waste product and no carbon dioxide. No greenhouse effect. Interesting.

Jayne at home, running things, running her two days a week farm secretary work mostly from a desk at home, by computer, telephone and fax.

At a weekend, if things worked out that way, if I hadn't worked all evening in my workshop, if I wasn't away, anyway, meeting somebody, if Jayne wasn't tired out from her busy, child-filled day, we might have a cuddle and make love. In a friendly, reasonable, routine and yet reassuring way. Neither of us complained in all those years.

Neither of us expected anything different.

We were married with two kids to bring up and a living to earn. My work was interesting, exciting to me, and improving living conditions for ourselves and humanity. I was making a success. There was money enough for me to develop things... two delightful little children... au pairs to distract the kids... home helps to dust and clean and iron...

Technology could at that time produce electricity from the natural energy sources of wind, sun or water power (let me be careful to differentiate between the use of water to harness power and the splitting of the water molecule into hydrogen and oxygen to release energy, the latter was still in its early exploratory stage), I am talking now about wind and water turbines of various sorts and about solar panels or photovoltaic cells.

These all suffered from the fact that each and every one was an intermittent source: dull days or night-time; calm days with no wind, or tidal peaks and stops as the tide turned.

My underwater tidal turbines, if spaced around the island, could give a steady supply but, at that time, cost too much.

And, anyway, while a steady demand for electricity was what was needed, twenty-four-hour, round-the-clock generation to keep the cost per unit of electricity down, what happened in reality was that there were rapid alterations. A rise or fall in demand that could happen on the national grid, or a local grid, within a matter of seconds, as when everybody switched on to a World Cup match or a popular soap opera. Some of this could be predicted but not all that accurately. And only one or two hydroelectric systems could react with enough speed. Or a nuclear reactor. The latter we did not want but, up to date, had to have.

What we did want was a means of storing electricity on a large scale that could be called on at the touch of a switch, computer controlled, to react instantaneously to a rise or fall in electricity consumption.

Liquid hydrogen does that – stores electricity – for everybody now, on a very large scale, in countries that are nowhere near a tidal coast.

My batteries, plus a renewable energy source, did it for many years until hydrogen technology was in place. But I also wanted electrically powered cars to do away with petrol and diesel fumes. No carbon dioxide: no greenhouse effect. I also wanted no nuclear power stations, no risk of radiation diseases.

I knew my underwater turbines could supply endless and vast amounts of power, if only I could break through the cost barrier or persuade governments to invest as much capital as they had done for the nuclear power industry. But their investment had already been made into nuclear power and nobody was prepared to throw all that money away to start again with a different system. Not yet. Then.

My ten turbines remained underwater. Turning around and around silently, steadily adding a bit of electricity to the national grid: waiting their turn.

If you want to know the technical details about the fuel cells that I finally produced, at first in ones and twos, later by the thousands if not millions, large and small, you will have to look them up in technical journals or in those archives in the Anglesey Assembly government buildings that I told you about at the beginning of this 'history'.

It took five years of trial and error before I felt justified in placing my first electric car on the market. A very lightweight body, seating four plus a good storage boot, powered from two fuel cell batteries, top speed thirty miles per hour, cruising speed twenty-five, fifty miles to go before you had to charge up the batteries. Spare batteries very cheap. Charge up your batteries from any mains supply: do it overnight on the Economy Seven cheap tariff and you got very economic power indeed. Only a fraction of the cost of petrol and no contamination.

Anglesey is only thirty miles from end to end, Menai Bridge to Holyhead. Carry two spare batteries and you can go wherever you like on the island, or inland for a hundred miles or so. Plug in to the mains overnight, the car has a built-in charger, and you can travel the world. But not as fast as you like!

There is a story of a peddler in an antique land, walking to a market two days' walk away. A car from the modern world draws up alongside and offers him a lift, 'Get you there in no time, jump in.'

'No thank you,' replies the peddler. 'What shall I do with those two days when I get there?'

Not a totally appropriate story. But it has a point.

Twenty-five miles per hour, steady, gets you there fairly quickly and accidents will be far less frequent or severe. And if you get there at very little cost and no pollution then it bears thinking about.

I found, however, that people wanted to go fast and I didn't sell many cars. But I did sell batteries, to all the people who wanted their own power supply and were against the principle of using fossil fuels or nuclear energy. With a wind generator *and* battery back-up you could do very well; with solar panels *and* batteries you also did very well. With all three you were laughing. Hundreds of people bought the kits we offered and some of them bought my cars as they could run them for no cost at all from their own electricity supply.

I sold even more large batteries to bus companies. Two of my large batteries could drive a bus for the length of one driver's spell at the wheel. Change drivers, change batteries. Charge your batteries overnight at the very cheap night rate for electricity and you can run your bus service very economically indeed *and* not pollute the atmosphere.

An electric underground train in London has a very interesting pattern to the way in which it demands electricity from the grid. It starts from stop by requiring a great surge of power to get it from stationary at the platform, full of people, to rolling along almost under its own momentum between stations. During that time it makes little demand on power; then a fair bit of power to slow it quickly to a stop at the next station. Lots of electricity, rapid changes in power requirement, all at a time of day when electricity suppliers charge the highest rate per unit.

My batteries cope with instant change in power demand and are charged at the time of day – night – when the cost from the grid per unit of electricity is at its very lowest.

I got a very remunerative contract from London Underground companies and from bus companies all over Europe.

Within two years of putting my batteries on the market I was half way to being a millionaire and three years after that, by granting, for a fee, franchises in America and other parts of the world, a millionaire twice over and Anglesey Batteries had a subsidiary company that was larger than itself – Anglesey Power Units, although we subsequently dropped the 'Units', employing over two hundred local people with a very large factory on that industrial estate near Llangefni.

My family didn't see much of me though.

By then Anghared was nine years old and at the junior school in Beaumaris and Olwen at nursery school. We had a permanent, live-in housekeeper to run the house and Jayne had extended her secretarial business, still based at home but working for a number of small companies. She employed one full-time manager and a number of part-timers who visited the different firms as required. A business person in her own right, Jayne. We had sex together, friendly, gently, securely as I thought, on high days and holidays. Security, familiarity, no sweat.

And me a millionaire.

It had already begun to go wrong.

In a way.

Depending on how you look at it.

Society likes secure family units. So do children.

In those days, up and down the United Kingdom and in Europe, large private companies supplied electricity to the consumer. They bought their electricity from other companies, some privately owned, some like the nuclear power industry, government owned.

I decided, with my millions, to establish my own generating turbines, underwater, in tidal runs, all round the coast of Anglesey and to buy, outright, the supply grid on Anglesey.

There were complications to this of course.

Not so much with the turbines. Doc and I had re-thought the basic design of these and, while the turbine itself remained pretty much the same as the originals with only slight improvements in the construction materials used, we up-ended each turbine so that it spun on a vertical axis and each was secured to the seabed instead of a line of them underwater, anchored at each end.

This meant that each was an independent unit and one could add as many turbine units to a site as one wanted. Each was connected to the other in series, but if one of them cut out for any reason it was of little consequence to total output. A monitor registered any individual failure on a screen in the land-based control room and a boat went out, hauled up the offending turbine and repaired or replaced it.

You increased total production by adding more turbine units. One at a time or by the tens or hundreds. I financed the setting-up of the whole generating complex, making the turbines in my own factory of course and employing my own construction, installation and maintenance crews, with some financial support from the bank, on the strength of my battery business.

Planning permission was not a problem at all. Nobody, nobody at all, liked the nuclear power station at Wylfa, near Holyhead, and I was already a supplier of employment to people on the island. What I was doing could only produce more local jobs for local people. From the start of Anglesey Turbines, when I first employed Doc and all employees after him, I had always insisted on employing local people, preferably Welsh speaking, and training them up to the job.

Buying the electricity grid from the then owner, MANWEB, was a much more difficult problem. They did not want to sell.

That part of the game took eighteen months to sort out. But I was totally determined and went ahead with making and placing my turbines anyway.

In that eighteen months I got to know all the members of Anglesey County Council and most of its officers. They were all enthusiastic about getting their own local electricity generating and supply system, particularly when I proved to them that the cost of electricity supplied to all Anglesey consumers would be a fraction of the price they were paying at that time. I pointed out to them that I was already a millionaire and did not really want any more money. If they would help me to buy, not directly financially, but by 'advising' MANWEB to sell the Anglesey grid system to me then, once I had got my money back, I would hand the whole system over to the county and leave them to it.

After considerable discussion they came back at me with a different proposition. They would 'take over' the grid system, paying MANWEB a negotiated price and paying me for my turbines at cost price. They would run the site construction, installation and maintenance crews. Anglesey Power plc would charge consumers cost price for their electricity and all the people of Anglesey would see their cost of living go down. What a popular county council they would be!

I agreed. If that happened then I would have a marvellous demonstration of the efficacy of my turbine system in producing cheap electricity for a large area. I could sell many more of those underwater tide turbines around the coasts of the world.

They did.

And I did.

Money rolled in.

'What is this life if, full of care we have no time to stand and stare?'

During the next few years the money rolled in for my private company, Anglesey Turbines, on the strength of our being the suppliers of turbines to Anglesey Power plc which was a public company run by Anglesey County Council. I had been able to demonstrate to the world that electricity from underwater tides was not only possible, but was economically viable, positively cheap, and an unending natural, non-polluting, source of power.

By 2017, two years after Anglesey County Council had taken control of the electricity grid system for the county, had bought at cost price enough of my underwater turbines to surround the island with installations wherever there was sufficient tidal run, and had set up their own installation and maintenance crews, I was able to take a back seat as far as that part of my interests ran.

I was thirty-four years old by then, with one daughter, twelve years old, attending the secondary school in Menai Bridge and the other daughter, two years younger, still in primary school in Beaumaris. Jayne ran the house and housekeeper and had her own secretarial business which was now a full-time job for her deputy plus a secretary and an office in Beaumaris, doing quite well thank you.

Money was not a problem. How to organise my time was.

I remember that on the day of that thirty-fourth birthday – a Tuesday, 25 June – I took both children to school by car, a thing I very rarely did, dropping Olwen off at the junior school and going on to Menai Bridge with Anghared and another friend from nearby. There was to be a birthday tea for us all, including my parents, at five that afternoon but I had fixed things so that I was free until then.

Very rarely was I 'free'.

What did I want out of life?

All the big questions.

Nine 'til five to find the answers.

Easy.

June. A lovely, warm summer's day, a few clouds, a bit of a breeze, not too many tourists about yet: freedom.

Alone.

How did I feel about that? Great!

In a way.

No worries about any part of my businesses. All sections were run by managers fully up to their jobs. The underwater turbine production lines running smoothly, orders coming in steadily: wind-powered turbines, a much smaller enterprise but steadily improving, a, very few, electric cars being made and sold, the battery factory going like a bomb, research into efficient, fairly cheap, photovoltaic cells coming along nicely. I was hardly needed any more!

Dad's pick-your-own organic vegetable unit was well developed, producing and selling as much as his ground could grow, his Welsh Black Pedigree herd was still there and winning prizes at shows. Mum's restored historic garden was drawing in tourists and local folk alike, ably managed by Bronwen, married by then to a teacher in Olwen's school.

I was a millionaire with nothing to do!

I drove across the Menai Bridge, Telford's magnificent roadway over the Straits. Hung from cables between two pillars set in the water, it is most beautiful seen from below from a boat, or in the evening light if you walk down from the Liverpool Arms and round the edge of the water, under the bridge. Awe inspiring in the true sense of the words.

All those stones, squared off to individual sizes, graded from large at the base to smaller, higher up. Set in the water and towering up to the roadway high above. The massive suspension chains, way up in the sky, swooping across from shore to tower top, to tower top, to shore. Titans, those Victorian engineers, indefatigable, those Irish navvies. Drunken, we are told, swearing, womanising, terrorising the locals, but building magnificently.

When had I last had time to look at beauty?

With Glynis, years ago when we had sailed our boat in regattas under that bridge; as we walked or climbed the mountains; as we looked and touched and enjoyed our bodies in all sorts of unlikely places for the sensual and sexual pleasure of making love.

What had happened to the sensual pleasures of my living with, being married to, Jayne?

When had I last walked in the mountains, sailed the Straits, wondered at the beauty of things? Been awe inspired?

Turn right over the bridge, on past the road up to the hospital, down the hill to the round-about, miss two then left past big gates, the entrance to Vaynol Estate, and swing up left through a brief stretch of pine forest that feels like Norway and straight on, climbing slowly into Snowdonia.

Bypass Llanberis along the side of the lake, on the other side of which is the vast hydroelectric power station built on the site of the old Llanberis slate quarry. You hardly know it is there, although you can certainly see the lake at the bottom. Underground, using the caverns carved out from the insides of the mountain by the slate miners years ago, are pipes carrying water from a reservoir higher up. The reservoir up there, itself part of the old quarry workings; immense water-powered generators producing electricity at the touch of a button for the National Grid.

They use cheap electricity from the grid during the night to pump the water back up to the top reservoir and make electricity to sell to the grid during the day at a much higher unit price. Seven hours to pump the water up. Five hours full power production as the water rushes back down the pipes and through the generators. Go and see for yourself. Conducted tours by minicoach deep underground. A wonderful renewable source of energy. No pollution.

A pity the UK has not got more high and low lakes near together, I thought as I drove past, But we do have tides all round our coasts.

On up over the Llanberis pass where you can look up to Snowdon and down to Dinas Emrys where there is a mound on which King Uther, Arthur's father, tried to build a castle but the walls kept falling down. Merlin, when asked, pointed out that he,

King Uther, was a fool because under where he was trying to build was a soggy peat bog within which two dragons slept uneasily. No wonder the walls repeatedly collapsed. Uther was to drain the bog and release the dragons. Freed from their underground slumbers, the two dragons, one red, one white, fought overhead until the red dragon of Wales drove the white dragon of the Saxon, English away, and Uther could build his castle. Highly symbolic.

But it is very easy, on a winter's day, with wind howling and snow gusting and clouds hanging low about your ears, to see and hear those dragons fighting and imagine Uther and Merlin standing under the oaks on the mound, water dripping down their necks, snow blowing in their faces, watching the red dragon beat the hell out of the white, seeing it flee across the lake below and away, defeated, back to wherever it came from.

Death to the Saison. Cymru am byth! Wales for ever!

It had been a long time since I had had time to look, and think, and dream. To remember my history and myth. To stop to 'turn at beauty's glance, or watch her feet, how they can dance', as the sunlight was dancing on the lake at the bottom of the valley.

And I drove on down through old oak woods: sessile oaks these, slow growing and twisted, clinging to the mountainside, growing in poor soil, rocky, slate, thin and hungry, never cut down because they were so twisted and gnarled, no good for the 'hearts of oak' ship construction, the fate of taller, straighter English oak trees.

On down to Bethgelert, which has its own story to tell, over the bridge for coffee and home-made biscuits and the quiet comfort of the bar, alone except for an elderly couple enjoying retirement, walking the hills. I bought fresh bread and cheese and apples in a shop next door for my lunch; I would drink water from a stream in the mountains.

If you go out of Bethgelert along the road to Port Madoc, which also has its tale to tell, but turn left up a little single track road that winds through small, sheep-filled fields, drive alongside the mountain stream that pours itself over jumbled rocks and tumbled, fallen, storm-battered alders, up past a moss and mountain ash covered old slate quarry waste tip, now grown wild and romantically beautiful, you can leave your car by the side of the stream and scramble up beside it. Up the hillside and out onto open wind-swept moorland and, provided you are wearing waterproof boots, you can go on and on, taking care not to slip and slide into deeper wet peat pits, on until you come to heather-covered rocky slopes and outcrops, on, up, over smaller summits until you reach whichever peak you choose.

I scrambled up the stream, slipped one foot into deep peaty water while crossing the moorland, drank from a tiny pool among rocks on the slopes and sat, warm and exultant, on the peak I chose to eat my lunch.

But I hadn't really chosen that peak, I had just happened to walk that way. Just as I hadn't really chosen the successes I had achieved in business, I had just happened to be interested in engineering and the creation of useful power from natural resources. But I was now, at the age of thirty-four, on top of what, it seemed, I had set out to do.

I sat up there, with beauty and peace all around me, with a family and a successful business down below me, and enough money in the bank to do whatever I wished.

Alone, up there.

Unsure where to go next, what to do next, questioning myself as to whether I really was a solitary walker at heart.

I scrunched the last of the apple core, threw the tiny bit of stalk away and lay back, uncomfortably on the rocks at the top.

'Too bloody true,' I told myself.

Uncomfortable. Alone. At the top.

Not dissatisfied exactly, not unhappy, not poor. Just uncomfortable…

I wriggled about but failed to find a place to rest at ease. I stood up and looked about me. All those mountain peaks around me, too far off to attempt today but I would get more freedom for myself, I would scale other heights, walk beside other streams, cross other moorlands.

Alone?

I pondered this as I retraced my steps to lower ground, looking for a soft hollow to cuddle down into. Not to sleep but to think about things. How to get myself comfortable?

'To cuddle down into.' There's a thought. There's a concept. I hadn't really cuddled in a proper sensual, sexual sense, with excitement and deep, deep pleasure, since my days with Glenys, and before her, Maggie. And yet, I was very 'comfortable' with Jayne.

Hell, what *did* I want?

I stopped at the bottom of the rocky slopes and cuddled down, warm in the sunshine, into a dip in the heather.

What should I do with my money? Buy a yacht? Build a mansion to live in? I could rebuild the Plas and live there with my family, restore the family to its seat! – A bit anachronistic! Leaving my kids with an albatross around their necks. Buy a house in London and lead the high life?

How about that? And get myself a London mistress? I doubted Jayne would want to move to London, uproot the kids from school, nor did I want that... a flat in London and install my mistress?

Why was I suddenly thinking in terms of a mistress? Why had I an erection while I was so thinking? Sex had been, for years, a dragon that had hardly raised its head, ugly or beautiful, depending on your point of view. Why, now of all times, when I was alone in the warm sunshine, languorous in the heat and the heather, was I attacked by an erection that felt harder and more demanding than it had for many a year with Jayne?

'Down, dog, down!' ...I had serious thinking to do!

I switched tracks and peace returned to the land.

Lying on my back, looking up and away into the blue sky, watching fleecy clouds drifting across, I daydreamed about what to do, in a practical everyday way, with my money and time. How to have fun and feel comfortable. Have my cake, and eat it.

I had an hour or so before I need get up, walk back and drive home to my birthday tea.

What, ignoring for the moment the lack of comfortable cuddles and such, made me uncomfortable about my small world and what might I be able to do about it? How small did I consider my world to be? Certainly bigger than just my own family circle. *That* was comfortably rounded and secure.

The Isle of Anglesey itself. Ynys Mon. Mam Cymru. The Mother of Wales. So called because centuries ago it had been the granary of Wales. At least of North Wales, Anglesey being the only flat land in the area where corn could be grown in quantity. Not any more though.

Grain growing had ceased to be a proposition many many years ago. Any farming had ceased to be a profitable proposition in recent years, tourism seemed the only answer. Cowsheds into cottages, fields to fallow – 'set-aside' in modern parlance; burn your beef cattle, thanks to the prevailing threat of mad cow disease, and the aftermath of foot and mouth. How could I help?

I was already giving employment to nearly three hundred people but I felt that my taking responsibility directly for increasing employment would not be the answer. The population of Anglesey was too big for that. The answer had to come from the people themselves.

What was the catalyst that would best empower people?

And the answer came winging on the wind across the mountains, and had already been flying around in popular newspapers and learned reports.

Education was not what it should be. Far too high a proportion of the population was failing to achieve mastery of the basic skills of reading, writing and number.

I thought back to my own school days. I had been all right, many of my friends had been all right, we had had the benefit of supportive parents and enough money to help where help was needed but I was aware of a whole group of fellow pupils in the middle ability range who did not get the full tuition they needed and knew that those few of lower ability, and those with definite learning difficulties, could have done far better given better resources, mainly more expert specialists and more teachers.

We also had had in our class, as in every other class, a small minority of pupils who were disruptive and made learning difficult for the rest of us and teaching properly impossible for the teachers.

A very good investment for my millions, for Anglesey as a whole, for the whole wide world for that matter, would be more teachers. But I hadn't enough money for the whole wide world.

Start at home. I would talk with the county councillors. Would they accept private money to pay for extra teachers? *Double* the number on the island; just a few more would make no difference.

I would also offer to start an assembly line to produce computers and the schools' software to go with it. We needed our own silicon valley to supply computers to the schools on the island at cost price, to sell further afield to finance the project and to develop programs directly suited to schools needs. To stand on our own feet!

We needed to improve the tourist economy of the island vastly. Our climate could not compete with Greece or Spain for a summer holiday now that cheap air fares and package holidays were the norm. What did we have that others were not presenting?

I stumbled on my feet and headed off, back across the moorland, back down to my car with all sorts of schemes running through my head.

Turn Anglesey into a totally organic farming area, export organic vegetables, fruit and meat to London, the rich south east, everywhere where demand for organic produce far outstripped supply. Dad knew how it was to be done.

Show the visitors how to grow organically on a large scale and small scale. Set up more good, not necessarily very luxurious, hotels and self-catering accommodation.

Invite and show round anybody interested in wind, sun and tide-power generation. We should get everyone on the island investing in their own wind generator, their own roof covered with photovoltaic cells.

By combining wind, sun and tide power the island could sell electricity to the mainland grid and give its own population totally free electricity.

Get rid of the nuclear power station… get rid of petrol and diesel on the island, everybody have an electric car; slow down the pace of life a bit but improve the quality.

Improve health… a total ban on cigarettes… less stress… less cancer…

Utopia!

'What is this life if, full of care we have no time to stand and stare?'

Well, I thought as I got in the car, At least I can talk to the council about more teachers.

Education

So I didn't get a house, or a flat in London. Or a mistress. Then.

Nor did I blow up Wylfa, the nuclear power station near Holyhead.

Instead I took advice from Ifor Thomas, married to Bronwen who was now manager of the Plas Gardens. Ifor was deputy head of the junior and infant school that Olwen attended, that I had attended; he was an active member of the Teachers' Union.

In 1999 the New Labour government under Tony Blair had done a thing that I was hardly aware of at the time but which had proved to be an appalling mistake and from which my children and many other children had suffered, the pupils at school on Anglesey not as badly as some on the mainlands of England and Wales.

At that time every education authority, in every county or borough, had its own officers and offices, run by the council, funded from local rates plus a considerable lump sum from central government. This meant that how much, and in what way, the money designated for education was used varied from authority to authority. Always subject to educational standards and guidelines stipulated by central government, inspected, and therefore controlled, by a separate body of people, the Ofsted Inspectorate and, once every four or five years, each school was subjected to an 'Ofsted' inspection.

Any school that did not come up to the required standard was told in no uncertain terms and re-inspected by HMI inspectors within the year. It was given advice and help, but not extra money, and if things hadn't improved enough then heads rolled and a school might even be shut down completely. Education authorities themselves were subject to inspection and could also be accused of failure.

This had been the state of affairs within education for some number of years before 1999. But in that year two education authorities were acknowledged to have failed and then the Blair government did that fatal thing, which they had done already for the railways and in part to the health service – they called in the private sector.

So, in 1999, Hackney education authority was deemed to have failed, but only its inspection department was privatised. Islington, in North London, was found to be failing completely and the whole education authority's responsibilities were handed over to a private company to manage. They were given six hundred thousand pounds from public funds.

A contract was signed, the private company was to manage all schools, teachers and equipment, salaries and overheads of the administration side of Islington Education Authority as was and, presumably, was to pay its own management team out of the six hundred thousand.

Looking at it as I did years later, on that day in 2017, on my birthday spent in the hills, and the subsequent time out for cogitation and in the light of my own business experience, I could see, what were surely fairly obviously, serious pitfalls.

No mention had been made about any control of the salaries the top managers would be paying themselves and no control was in place as to how the funds were to be used. A profit was to be made out of the teaching of children.

The idea was that superior management would eliminate inefficiency, do away with bad schools, head teachers and teachers. Money would be invested in bigger and better computers. Education would be carried out by computers with teachers playing the part of facilitators. Classes could be much bigger and so less teachers employed. Great savings would be made and pupils would get a better education.

For the next ten years all seemed to be going relatively well in Islington and in the six other education authorities where private companies were given the contract to run the whole education system, Anglesey not being one of them.

The companies didn't sack all that many teachers and more computers were put into their schools. More disruptive pupils were removed from mainstream schools and put into special schools who continued, as they always have done, to try to improve the lot of their pupils, still without adequate funding, but at least mainstream schools did get on with the process of education without impossible interruption from a minority who, in their special schools did get a better deal than the difficulties they themselves met in mainstream.

But the original private companies failed to be much better at running schools than their predecessors. Other companies tried their hand with varying lack of success. 'Teething troubles' were blamed for this. 'You can't change schools all that quickly.' 'All this is a new concept, it will get better.'

The top management of the private education companies continued to get high salaries, teachers' pay remained at its inadequate level so recruitment was not so good and did not attract the best of brains. In many cases schools in these areas became worse, pupils and teachers struggled on.

Anglesey education authority and its schools did better than most; still run by its own borough council, under funded and with too few teachers to get the best for its pupils, just as it had been in my own school days. Kids whose parents had money and were concerned about their children's education, giving moral and financial support, did better, on the whole, than kids who had non-supportive parents. Disruptive pupils, or even simply non-motivated pupils, caused difficulties as they always had done and teachers struggled with too many pupils in their classes and inadequate resources from which to 'enable each pupil to achieve to the best of their potential ability.'

In spite of all this Anglesey schools were pretty good compared to many. Inspections periodically showed up 'areas of weakness' which were addressed and improved in a sort of rolling wave where a few more resources were channelled, from a limited budget, from one department to the next, improving the one under scrutiny but depriving something somewhere else which, in turn would show up as needing help a few years later. Robbing Peter to pay Paul. Struggling with insufficient money and not enough teachers, themselves under stress and underpaid.

This was the picture I got from Ifor, to which I added recollections of my own schooldays, the comments I heard from my own children and the things said on parents' days at the two schools.

I had walked down from my mountain soliloquy wanting to offer money to employ more teachers. Double the number would, I thought, improve matters tremendously, giving all pupils a much better education and therefore a better chance to get the job they wanted.

A 'good' and constructive use of my money.

I wrote to the council with my offer and received acknow-ledgement of my letter, with thanks, but nothing else for a couple of weeks. I remember being quite put out at this. I had expected shouts of joy, welcome, enthusiasm and thanks.

What did happen at the end of that couple of weeks was a telephone call inviting me to an informal – the informality was stressed – meeting with some councillors at the house of Bryner Cadwallader.

I knew Bryn well, he was owner and managing director of his own company running a large farm in the middle of Anglesey, producing pigs rather than sheep or cattle, with his own butchery business to process and market the pork. He had almost gone bankrupt during the foot and mouth epidemic; despite escaping infection, everything was held at a standstill for nearly two years. Now his pigs were run on an extensive outdoor regime rather than an intensive indoor one and were very healthy and tasty as a result. He was well off and had invested his profit from the pig farming, slowly accrued over the years, in an hotel that was not doing too well. He was about the same age as my father, his two sons had gone to school with me and the families were, loosely, friends. He was chairman of the Anglesey County Council.

'We want to talk with you about this business of you giving us the money for more teachers.'

'Who is we?' I asked.

I remember that he laughed and told me to wait and see.

There were six of them waiting when I got there at eight o'clock, after my evening meal. Bryn, of course, let me in and hanging my coat up in the hallway, led me into his spacious sitting room, his two sons not in evidence, married by now and with their own households, his wife not in the room but coffee for us all on the low table in the centre of the room. Quiet affluence.

Already seated in comfortable armchairs in a large circle spread haphazardly around the coffee table were four other men I knew fairly well. Three of them council members I had met, talked with and had dealings with when the council bought my turbines and took over the whole electricity grid on the island. The fifth, Anglesey's Plaid Cymru representative on the Welsh Assembly, Cardiff, Tom Elias.

I was introduced to the sixth, a woman, Marion Stope, Chief Education Officer, the person in charge of Anglesey Education Authority. I had heard of her. Well spoken of, an ex-head teacher, struggling, within a limited budget, to do the best she could for the island's children and teachers.

Whisky, brandy and other drinks stood with an array of glasses on an oak sideboard, a log fire flickered, burning slowly, comfortably in the grate, not needed because radiators denoted central heating and the evening was not cold. But friendly and relaxing. An informal meeting, with informality stressed. But a meeting of powerful figures in the community nevertheless. A bit daunting to a thirty-four-year-old, used to running his own business, a recent millionaire, true, but not accustomed to the corridors of power or meetings with groups of influential, political, important people.

'Coffee, thank you,' in reply to Bryn's enquiry. 'Black, no sugar.'

What was this about?

Education and money, obviously, because Marion was there. But why the others? Why did they not just accept my money and get more teachers? Simple.

But it wasn't as simple as that. The other men had coffee *and* brandy. Marion, like me, just black coffee; and for about twenty minutes they simply chatted about Anglesey in general.

The economics of farming being impossible. Tourism to the island suffering because our climate and facilities could not compete with Greece, Spain or any of the other exotic places. Schools doing all right, just, but not really; but as good or better than anywhere else.

Then conversation switched a bit. I was complimented on my turbines, teased about the fact that I was richer than any of them there, all of them, except Marion, well off in their own right and she got a respectable salary.

The turbines by then were established on the seabed around the island in places where tidal runs were strongest and produced enough electricity to meet the island's needs. A very considerable achievement they all agreed. Anglesey Power plc, run by the council, was in business and running smoothly. In a year's time and because the overheads for their turbines, even with two permanent maintenance and repair teams, were so low, general grid maintenance was as it always had been of course, they would have had enough profit from selling their electricity to everyone to have paid for the capital cost of the turbines and have money in hand at the end of every month when bills were paid.

What did I think they should do with this money? An informal discussion, I was reminded.

My coffee was long gone. I needed a bit of time to think. Why were they asking me? I pretended to look wildly around, in alarm.

'Bryn, how about some of your whisky?'

He grinned wryly in acknowledgement of my need for time and everybody got up, moved around, and replenished their glasses. Gwyneth came in to remove the cups and coffee pot with the promise of more later and we re-seated ourselves in different chairs, talking between ourselves quietly about nothing much for a few minutes until Bryn, our host and informal chairperson, brought us back to their purpose.

'Well, Davydd, young man, you're on the hot spot. What shall we do with our profit from your turbines and electricity?'

We were all Welsh speaking and this whole evening we spoke in Welsh. Council meetings were conducted in English but among ourselves in this and in the many informal meetings we had later, we spoke Welsh. The phrase he used for 'young man' had nothing derogatory in it, rather an implication of envy and opportunity. I replied in the same idiom.

'Diolch yn fawr, hen wr.' ('Thank you very much old man.') Nothing sarcastic or derogatory, rather, respect for an elder.

'You *could* give electricity, at cost, to all Anglesey consumers,' I suggested. 'But I'd rather you put your profits into education at all levels, infant through to teenage students and adult education. Give everybody a real chance of "achieving their fullest individual potential".'

He nodded.

'And how would *you* use extra money?' asked Goronwy Thomas, councillor and owner of a chain of garages throughout North Wales, born and living on Anglesey. He addressed his question to Marion.

'Ooo... dream time,' she smiled, sitting back in her chair, speaking slowly with eyes closed.

'Many more teachers of course, as Davydd has proposed, but also, a computer in every classroom, a resource room with more computers and even more electronic equipment, many more books, plenty of pencils and paper and things like that.' She paused. 'Proper repairs to all buildings. Build more schools to hold more, smaller, classes. Proper, ample, specialist resources like cookery stuff, metal work, carpentry, engineering.' She blinked and looked around at us all. 'Not, I think, our own university, but much improved adult education facilities. Have I got any money left after that lot?' She relaxed and waited.

'Maybe, in time,' replied Bryn. 'For now, Mervyn wants to introduce *his* ideas.'

Mervyn Evans, whizz kid of the 1980s, London banker, dealer on the international stock exchange, computer and exchange rate expert. Made his first thousands, later millions, out of fractions of one per cent rises and falls in currency values. A mansion with extensive grounds on the Anglesey side of the Menai Straits. Son of a coal merchant in Llansadwrn, Anglesey. Retired. One of our new type of councillor. Out of my league. Or so I thought then. Wife dead five years ago. Children grown, left, and with kids of their own. Time on his hands. An active, influential member of the council.

'Well now,' said Mervyn, at ease, eyes twinkling, surveying us all with benevolence, a lynx in lamb's wool, abundant white hair and whiskers, rotund and relaxed. 'I'm an old man now, time to sit and think, make friends, enjoy. There's good brandy you have here Bryn, a little drop more, os gwelwch chi'n dda, if you would be so kind, diolch.'

'But still influencing people,' I thought to myself as he continued.

'I have made a lot out of the capitalist system,' he admitted easily, 'but I think humanity will have to do better than that.'

He paused looking at Marion. A slim career woman, single, good-looking and well dressed.

'I've been talking to Marion about schools and,' with a glance at Bryn, 'to your electricity boys and girls. Let's turn this evening into a think tank session and free wheel, as my American advisers might say. His benevolence vanished and the lynx looked out. 'Marion, tell them what you think about what Blair and the governments after him have done to education, especially the privatisation part of it.'

'Totally irresponsible and idiotic,' she sat up, eyes flashing, animated and attractive in her anger. 'Every penny they took out from education as a business run for profit meant less money for the classrooms. You can't do things like that with education, or health for that matter, they are not things anyone should make a profit from. It's not working anyway, even in boroughs where a lot of money was put in by private investors, they are taking their capital away now and the profits are being swallowed up by poor management and rising costs. The kids and teachers in those boroughs are even worse off than they were before!'

'Just so,' said Mervyn. 'Now, Bryn, you asked young Davydd here what he thought should be done with the profit from our turbine-generated electricity. I want to suggest to you that we should look at electricity and education and public health and lots of other things from a different point of view. As far as funding is concerned, I mean.'

He glanced around, sharp, acute. The very successful businessman apparent in every word. 'Look, as Marion has said, nobody should make a profit from teaching children, or public health, or anything else really, if you think about it. A proper salary for a proper job, yes. But a lot of money to one person, just because they thought of an idea, or are good managers of other people, or have money to invest and demand a percentage of the profit for doing nothing towards directly improving anything? Marion is right, that's immoral.'

'I suggest a non-profit making company be formed called Anglesey plc. A subsidiary company being Anglesey Power plc. The profit from electricity generated to be ploughed back into education and Marion can have all those things she asked for. I think we should demand of central government that our education authority here on Anglesey be privatised, not because it is failing, but because we can run it better ourselves as a private, non-profit making company – Anglesey Education plc.

Proper full salaries to all employees, increased salaries for all teachers to get quality back into schools. With the money Davydd wants to give us plus money from Anglesey Power, and I will add as many thousands, a million even, to what Davydd gives you; we will have the best schools and adult education in the world.'

He sat back grinning, triumphant, sure he had carried the meeting.

As indeed he had.

Gwyneth appeared with more coffee and sat down with us, more drinks were given to those who wanted them and we stayed there until the small hours excitedly, even in our maturity, planning our own Utopia.

Utopia

All public services and utilities were to be privatised as non-profit making companies. All staff were to have good, reasonable salaries. Within Anglesey prices charged for these services or goods would be at cost plus five percent. This five percent would go towards paying for better education in all its aspects, more doctors and local health facilities and form a pool of money to finance research and investment in capital development.

I was prepared to hand over Anglesey Turbines as a subsidiary to Anglesey plc provided I retained a salaried seat on the board as a consultant but only receiving money commensurate with contribution.

I suggested that I be head of Anglesey Research and Development, at a reasonable salary, there were a number of schemes I would like to start going.

Anglesey Power should form a subsidiary of its own to promote the wind, water and sun power generation of electricity that would be added to the under-water turbine production giving a surplus of electricity that we should sell to the mainland grid.

That subsidiary company, Anglesey Wind, Water and Sun should have a factory producing its own wind turbines (I would hand over my own wind turbine business free of charge) and it would make its own turbines for use in rivers and streams (very few in Anglesey), a small number of hydro-power dams should be constructed where possible with their associated turbines, and we should make our own photovoltaic cells and solar panels. My own research into improved design for all these things should be intensified and improved designs put on the market. Their products to be sold at competitive prices on the open market but to go to householders on the island at cost plus five; free installation and repairs by a central team paid by Anglesey Wind, Water and Sun. All profits to the general kitty of Anglesey plc.

Another subsidiary to Anglesey plc to be The Anglesey Electric Car Company.

My company, Anglesey Batteries, to be handed over as well to the common pool. I wanted to be free of the responsibility of running anything, would be glad of consultant status in any project, especially, at the moment, electric cars.

I also wanted to be involved in the promotion of tourism and agriculture within the county... how about more police...

Why not turn Anglesey into a completely organic island, a show place for the world, exporting organic meat, fruit and veg?

Develop our history. My mother's show garden was a Victorian/Edwardian place of beauty and interest (all her gardeners worked in costume). Why not develop historic show places on authentic sites, in costume?

Everybody was throwing ideas now. They came thick and fast...

Have all our enterprises open to the public.

Vastly improve hotel accommodation and catering as well as the holiday cottage concept.

Cater for wildlife conservation and preservation and observation of our natural habitat.

Reduce all pollution. Close down Wylfa, the nuclear power station near Holyhead. Get our electric cars going and forbid petrol and diesel on the island.

No smoking anywhere, no drugs anywhere...

Set up our own brewery and wine making using vegetables and fruit and the leaves of trees for wine instead of grapes... grow our own grapes...

All at cost plus five to the islanders. Market prices for top quality goods to the rest of the world.

Passports to our own citizens. Secede from Wales. Change our county council to the Anglesey Assembly with a representative sitting in the Welsh Assembly in Cardiff, a Member of Parliament in Westminster and another in Europe.

The rather absurd suggestion that we should mint our own currency brought matters to a close and we all trooped off excitedly, enthusiastically, tired, to bed with many thanks to Gwyneth and Bryn for their hospitality.

I crept into bed beside a sleeping Jayne and was asleep immediately.

And got up, full of beans, before any of them. 19 July 2017.

A lovely early morning. A slight blue haze over the water as I looked down to the Straits below me: boats, motionless on a gently falling tide, masts immobile, sail-less, moored; beyond and rising into the distance, the hills and mountains of Snowdonia, faint and far, far distant in the midsummer early heat.

I felt immeasurably freed from responsibility, remembering that I had, in effect given away all my businesses. I did not need, anymore, to be bothered about the management of people.

I glanced at Jayne in bed beside me, sleeping soundly, confidently and, as far as I knew, contentedly, in our bed. No passion stirring. Secure. She had the management of our household well in control, as indeed she ran her secretarial business, confidently, securely, competently, contented.

I was not contended managing people. I could do it, and quite well too. People liked me, did, on the whole, what needed doing, situations seeming to dictate what was required, rather than my conscious decision; I felt myself to be a pawn in the process. Somebody had to be there, a catalyst, between what needed doing and the person who would do it. A boring position to be in. Essential, it seemed, in the scheme of things, that management should be a lubricant to action, but a catalyst remains unchanged in the middle of the process. Essentially boring.

But research and development – that was fun!

Shirt, pants, trousers, sandals, bathroom, downstairs, quietly.

I was halfway through cooking breakfast for everybody before Mary, housekeeper, appeared. 'Let's have 'em all up quick, Mary. It's a lovely morning and I want to get them to school in good time. I'm off to the hills for the day, don't count on me to be back for any food this evening.'

She grinned at me, an outdoor girl herself, and went off to the unenviable task of getting teenagers out of bed for school.

Jayne appeared, tousled, washed, but no make-up, in her dressing gown and bare feet, still warm and soft from sleep.

'You're a bright spark. Late in and early up. What hit you?'

I put the breakfast on hold, would do the eggs when the heads arrived, and poured coffee for us both. We sat at the breakfast table knowing that we had at least twenty minutes before heads, or tails, were likely to descend on us. Voices: 'just another five minutes,' 'its too *early*,' 'leave me *alone* will you,' in expostulation.

We grinned at each other, Mary could cope. And I told Jayne about the meeting last night; that I had virtually given my businesses away. 'Good,' she had said. 'Now you can get on with what you like doing. And you don't really need to worry about money, I'm getting almost enough from my own business to run this house and feed the kids.' Unperturbed, confident, matronly at home, efficient in her office, the passion and panic of adolescence long past. Was I getting as middle-aged as she?

'I'm taking the day off, into the hills, I need to sort out clearly in my own mind what I should be doing next, long and short term. We talked a lot of castles in the air last night but possible realities as well. I need to get feet back on solid ground and draw maps, plot possible tracks and define objectives.'

The kids tumbled into the kitchen and the daily, not always that friendly, family fracas commenced.

I left a message explaining – no – explicitly stating, absence on the office telephone, dumped the kids at their respective schools and headed, once again, for the sanctuary and exquisite peace of the hills.

I drove steadily, relaxed, unthinking, southward towards mid-Wales. The whole of a long summer day before me, a gentle heat haze still suspended. Cattle, ankle deep in water, as I crossed, just beyond Port Madoc, Madox's embankment that carries road and slate railway over the estuary of the river Mawddach with its reclaimed acres and acres of flat rich silt farmland. A narrow-gauge train, full of tourists, just ahead of me on the parallel track, pulling upwards along a magic railway line through fairyland, through ancient twisted oak woods and wonderful tiny waterfalls to Blaenau Ffestiniog and the underground goblin caverns of vast slate quarries.

I drove steady distances, hardly aware of passing miles or time, living with the trees and fields and woods, not thinking, being.

Coffee, with home-made shortcake, in an old pub in an old street in Dolgellau. Sitting, comfortable, in a big, old, wooden armchair in the dim parlour by a smouldering fire of, mostly, ashes; a fire to combat damp rather than warm the customers.

Warm, damp, dim now, Dolgellau, I mused.

Delicious shortcake.

Once a thriving market town, centre of an agricultural economy, slowly dying; farming disastrously dead now. Its architecture serene and unspoiled, its largest hotel in the centre of town shuttered and neglected; a double-fronted shop with turret between, probably once the main general stores, teetering on doorposts that sagged sideways, all but falling into the main street, slats of wood nailed across gaps with printed, fading council notices warning of 'Danger' and 'Keep out.'

But; gold had been found in the area in Roman times and mined in Victorian times, 'used for the Queen's wedding ring' or some such, we are told by the publicity for the golden tourist centre. And for many years you could go down the original gold mine and pan for gold yourself until the tunnels became unstable and there was not enough money then to make it safe.

They built a motorway-type bypass around Dolgellau in the 1980s and it is pretty and well nigh forgotten now. But peaceful!

Back to the car. I would find the gold mining area and sit and dream, draw up plans and plot a course. Sleep in the sun…

On along the road to Machynlleth, turn right towards Barmouth and stop for early ploughman's lunch in a pub by the side of the estuary. And then, replete, and watered (beered?), I struck up into the hills along a track, much overgrown, down which the quarrymen used to walk to their houses in the valley. An apple and a carrot in my pocket and the whole summer day, endlessly in front.

Walking slowly, idly letting ideas drift in and out, just as gulls and gannets idly rode the hardly moving waters of the estuary, dropping away behind me through the trees. Up into the endless stretches of heather and moorland, the almost-mountains of the area stretching beyond and far away. Too far for me to bother with today.

Up above the tree line, over the occasional loose stone wall, were untidy heaps of quarry waste. Not the vast piles of slate slabs of Ffestiniog or Bethesda, small, molehill tumbles of diggings done by one or two men only, grass grown, long neglected and deserted because no nuggets were to be found in that little patch. But there had been gold found there. There probably was still gold under there. And, further on, a negligible-looking cave entrance, blocked by balks of timber, led up to by a level trackway and with recognisable substantial spoil heaps tipped out in front of it, was an indisputable, real but old and now unworked, gold mine.

And nothing and nobody anywhere near it. Just a few sheep and the blue sky. Not even a rabbit.

I found a dip in the springy, short, sheep-grazed, grass and lay on my back, shutting my eyes to the glare of the sun.

Another breed of Titan those miners of gold and slate, as great in the underground tunnels and caverns as the builders of the Menai Bridge or those who struggled against storm and tide with horse and cart, tumbling rocks from nearby quarries to block the river Mawddach at its estuary mouth near Port Madoc, forging a road and railway across mud and sand, rescuing acres of ground to grow grass and fatten cattle.

Who was I to worry about energy and its production? The world would roll on. I was no Titan. Natural selection and geophysical forces would mould the world in spite of any individual human effort.

And yet, we, descendants of those Titans, were so polluting (I opened one eye and looked at the clear blue sky above me, disbelieving), our world in our demands for ever more, cheaper energy, power, electricity.

Worry about energy? Wrong word! I was *interested* in energy. In its production from natural renewable sources. I was an engineer with an interest in helping develop a non-polluted environment.

Research and Development plc, a subsidiary of Anglesey plc, me to be its director drawing a proper salary therefrom, retaining a seat on the board of Anglesey Turbines and Anglesey Wind, Water and Sun. Enough money for my family's needs, more than enough since Jayne was earning plenty as well, we could get our two children through university and live well. No problems there.

I would need a free hand and considerable capital for this research and development. To whom would I be answerable? Who would be running Anglesey plc, the parent holding company?

What were to be its objectives?

At that informal meeting the other night had been one paid county officer – Marion Stope – education, and one member of the Welsh Assembly – politician. The other four had been retired wealthy businessmen, plus myself, wealthy but not yet ready for retirement. All those four were not so aged that they wanted to put their feet up. I needed to meet with them again. Soon.

What were the things we had brainstormed? I pulled paper and pencil from my pocket, sat up and, scrunching my carrot, noted down what I could remember of that evening's suggestions:

Anglesey plc. A non-profit making holding company to develop the whole island for the benefit of its inhabitants. Communism? Socialism? Whatever...

Subsidiary companies: Anglesey Education plc. To receive financial input from myself, Mervyn Evans and anyone else prepared to contribute in order to enhance the quality of education for all ages on the island. Further financial input directly from Anglesey plc said company to derive its income from Anglesey Turbines in the first place and from all other subsidiary companies as they in turn become contributing units.

Anglesey Turbines plc. Now paying very well indeed by selling underwater turbines around the world to anyone who had a coastal tidal run. Continually improving our design by always having a development department and so keeping ahead of our competitors. I would leave that research where it was but, in my capacity as a director, add to their work by getting them to look at the design and installation of turbines way out to sea in the deep water currents of the world.

Anglesey Wind, Water and Sun plc to be independent of me. The wind being the smaller size of wind turbine suitable for individual houses or small groups of buildings, not large-scale wind farms. Leave that to the firms on the mainland already in the business and, anyway, we already had one installation right across the top of the island and people didn't seem interested in having more.

The Sea part of the company was not doing anything yet but it sounded good to have the triumvirate and I could visualise that a time would come when we would put a dam across either end of the Straits and have a hydroelectric generating station at each end. Maybe even, before I was dead, dam each end of the English Channel; we had co-operated with the French to build the tunnel so why not a dam or two?

The Sun part of the company would now get immediate attention. I needed to get my Research and Development to work on those photovoltaic cells. I had been playing about with them since 2009 but costs had been high for them then and I had gone for the development of my fuel cell batteries. High time photovoltaics really got some attention. Solar panels I still thought to be not worth following up, needing as they do full sunshine to produce a reasonable amount of energy. Not much good for Anglesey's climate, fine for the desert and clear skies. Leave that for others.

Further areas suggested for development by Anglesey plc had been tourism and agriculture under which headings had appeared:

Turning the whole of the island organic and exporting the produce.

Developing sites of historical interest.

Developing conservation of wildlife and enhancing access to sanctuaries etc.

Making organic wines and beers.

Reducing pollution.

It was the latter heading that I felt most interested in. Reducing pollution. The group had mentioned cigarettes and drugs with the concomitant need for increased policing but I wanted to tackle petrol and diesel fumes since, worldwide, they threatened the atmosphere by the greenhouse effect of their carbon dioxide emissions. This led me directly on to:

THE ANGLESEY ELECTRIC CAR COMPANY

I stopped scribbling my list there and lay back down again, marshalling my thoughts.

I had produced an electric car back in 2014 and sold a few to enthusiasts. They had been fairly expensive to make, I had little capital in those days, and anyway, I now realised, I had tried to sell in the wrong market; also, by then, things had changed.

Way back in the 1980s a chap called Sinclair had made a lot of money from designing and marketing a small computer in the early days of computers. He had then put on the market a revolutionary small car which held one individual who had to 'sit' lying down on his back, intended for use in cities. This was before everybody had woken up to the danger to health from breathing in exhaust fumes, before anyone became convinced of the effect on the world's environment of the greenhouse gasses and before congestion on the roads in cities had reached its present appalling state.

In the year 2000, when the Lord Mayoralty of London was up for grabs as an important political post, transport within London had been a very hot potato. Congestion through trying to pack too many people into each carriage, not enough trains, breakdowns, and high ticket price on the underground; too many private cars blocking up streets, obstructing buses of which there were often not enough, the cost of fuel and pollution from exhausts; all had been getting progressively worse.

The government at Westminster had passed the buck on to the Lord Mayor in the case of London, and the Mayor and council of all other boroughs and counties in the country. Each had tried over the years to combat the problem.

Some inner cities allowed no cars in at all, some surrounded themselves with an inner city boundary and charged a toll for entry, some charged a very high price for a parking place.

The use of my large batteries on underground trains had made it possible to run them more cheaply; this had partly been swallowed up by repairs, maintenance and improved rolling stock. The price of an underground ticket *had* come down a bit but not enough to get people out of their cars and into the trains.

It seemed to me that the time was right for a small electric car for commuter use, run off my car batteries and charged each night from the mains. It would not solve the parking problem although smaller vehicles would help to some extent, smaller cars would also cause less congestion, electric cars would certainly cut pollution considerably.

I decided to go ahead with producing a small four-seater car on a full commercial scale. Run from two batteries charged at night from cheap electricity, a range of thirty miles per battery. A small, utility, cheap car. Made with a plastic moulded body. Not for use on the motorway, just a family or young person run-about, very strong reinforcement so that it would be unsquashable, safe and non-polluting.

I had in mind what we had said at that meeting. 'No petrol or diesel on Anglesey.' To do that I needed to persuade the population of Anglesey that twenty-fives miles an hour was the fastest they ever would need to go on the island.

To do that would need the carrot of either very cheap or free electricity and therefore free car-running costs. And the change to a cheap car.

I would mass-produce cheap, safe, small electric cars, sell them to commuters and anyone else who wanted them, and with the profits, sell very cheap cars to the people of Anglesey.

I could see all sorts of difficulties and objections to this but that was as far as I was prepared to think at the time. I needed to talk to the others.

Up, on my feet, and, enthusiasm rekindling energy, I walked on, over a tumbled stone wall, pushing knee deep through heather and rushes, the ground underfoot dry now but wet, I knew, most of the year, in cloud most of the winter, soggy from being flat upland marsh, peaty and poorly drained in dips between rocky outcrops. Mountain sheep country, too high and too wet for forest, one and a half sheep to the acre. The huddled farm buildings hiding in the valleys below, hundreds of acres to a sheep farm and a poor living at that. No living at all these past years, the price of lamb and mutton being disastrously low, farmers wives bringing in a better income than their husbands could by giving bed and breakfast accommodation to holiday visitors, barns converted to weekly let holiday homes, daughters running pony trekking groups, sons and daughters leaving home to be nurses or doctors or teachers in the cities. The more remote mountain farm buildings becoming deserted, too far from a proper road or mains electricity for even the most eccentric or foolhardy of escapers from modern life to even attempt to rescue, rebuild and live away from it all.

I followed a sheep track winding over the rough ground, leading round the hillside that held the deserted gold mine, deeper into the hills but dropping gently down to areas of slightly better grazing, cotton grass, sedge, sphagnum moss in soft wet patches. Not many sheep about, at this time of year – they are high up searching out the sweeter mountain grasses. I saw a group of small wild-looking ponies away across the moorland, scrambled over a boundary wall that had collapsed into the heather in places, the boundary now being maintained by wire netting and two strands of barbed wire, difficult to climb over because all the wooden posts were rotting at the base and wobbled when touched, impossible to put any weight on so I had to walk a long way following the boundary until I came to a corner in the middle of that moorland where the fence turned at right angles on itself and there was a substantial post with strong oak props keeping it upright against the pull of the wire.

I walked on, down the slow slope of the curving hillside finding more sheep tracks where the going was easier, heading for a dip in the skyline where trees began and through which I would find a farm or forest track of some sort to bring me back down eventually to the road, my car and an evening meal in a hotel somewhere.

The Plas Druiddion, a five star country house, almost a castle in its spacious grounds, spreading lawns leading down past lumbering cedars and sprawling hydrangeas to the wavelets lapping with soft kissing sounds against a low stone wall that bordered the waters of the Barmouth estuary.

I had found the place by chance on my way back from the hills, and, large schooner of sweet sherry in hand, had drifted down to the water's edge. 'Salmon steak in a deep rich mushroom cream sauce with peas grown in our own garden, ready in twenty minutes, sir,' awaiting me when I would return to the bar and the dining room.

I sat on the wall and dangled my feet dangerously near the water, sipping, watching the sun dropping down to the sea's horizon away to my right, a large glowing ball of fire seeming to move faster as it sank lower, shot across with thin streamers of cloud turned purple in the evening, misty summer heat.

Another lovely summer day tomorrow.

I took my empty glass back up to the bar, chose a half bottle of dry white wine and went in to my solitary seat at a table by the window, sitting down in time to see the sun touch the earth rim and slide, very rapidly it seemed, away.

Jayne and I had slipped, quite rapidly it seemed, away from the rather passive passion of our evenings in her cottage before we were married. A gentle, steady passion, not the hot rampant sex of those earlier escapades of mine but a more secure, yet also sexual relationship that meant a good basis for bringing up a family. Had I subconsciously had that in my mind when I asked her to marry me? Security. For me and my children?

A prawn and avocado starter with lettuce and creamy mayonnaise was placed before me. Not many people in the room yet. A family of four, the children, two girls, like mine, about the same age as mine and well behaved, in a far corner, talking excitedly, subdued, why dining out on an ordinary school day? An elderly couple, two tables away, ordering their meal; two men in dark lounge suits, tall glasses of beer between them, talking fast and quietly. A very thin, tall girl (eighteen, twenty?) in a flowing summery silk long evening dress sitting, waiting, 'my husband will be down in a minute, thank you,' to the waitress.

Should I bring Jayne and the girls here? They loved the 'Sunshine' Chinese restaurant in Menai Bridge – and so did I! Extremely good cooking there, better than any I had found in London or Birmingham on business trips to those and other cities. Poons of Covent Garden, fantastic of course, but our Sunshine in Menai Bridge was – is – very nearly as good. So was – is – the Chinese restaurant in the square in Caernarfon. I couldn't see the kids wanting to travel this far. Didn't think they would really appreciate the difference in quality of a place like this as compared to, say, the Vic or the Liverpool Arms in Menai Bridge, or the Bull, Beaumaris. Good food in all those places. I often went there myself with business colleagues or on family evening meals out. But the kids preferred Chinese and Jayne and I were more than willing to accommodate their tastes.

Then bring Jayne herself and leave the kids with Mary, housekeeper. Stay the night… weekend… recapture honeymoon time…

Research and Development

But when I suggested this a few evenings later, after supper, when the kids had vanished up to their rooms to do homework and listen to loud music on their CD players, she, politely and kindly, put the idea off. 'I'm so tired these days, darling and there is so much going on in the office. Perhaps later, in the autumn maybe, when the colours are showing on the trees. Thank you all the same.'

Deflation.

No honeymoon. Not even a fuck that night.

I rang Bryn and arranged to spend another evening with him and Mervyn Evans, retired banker and stock market millionaire. Soon. To talk about Anglesey plc and a practical Utopia here on earth. Forget sex. Deal with reality.

I went over to Bryn's place, invited to an evening meal – 'Bring Jayne too, there will be a few others and we can talk around what we were discussing the other night.'

I asked Jayne, but she chose not to come with me.

Gwyneth, Bryn's wife, had catered for ten. Roast local lamb deliciously cooked with rosemary and garlic, roast potatoes and parsnips, green peas and lovely gravy. Apple crumble and cream or fresh fruit. Eaten in the cool of the evening, outside, at a long table on their paved terrace. Wine, beer, fruit juices and candles under the trees at the edge of the lawn, another glowing sunset lighting, far away across the fields of Anglesey, the summits of the mountains in the distance, reminding me of recent holidays with the family in Provence, so warm it was, except that were was no all-pervading scent of dry grass and herbs and there was no swimming pool at the edge of the terrace.

But a carefree, holiday atmosphere, among friends and no hurry.

And yet, we were serious, talking quietly about serious things. The candlelight growing brighter as the evening sunglow diminished, candle flames wavering and burning tall in the still air. Wine glasses, emptied and refilled among spoons and forks that still littered the table, cigar smoke and ambitious ideas floating around in the dusk.

Ten of us, the same people as last time plus four other members of Anglesey county council.

Ceinwen Gryfydd, a middle-aged widow, active in local politics, whose husband had been a property developer on Anglesey and in North Wales, he had died of a heart attack four years before.

Mari John, infant teacher, single, thirtyish at that time, an ardent conservation enthusiast, very concerned about whales as well as Wales.

Rhys Howells, farmer of 120 acres of good land in the middle of Anglesey, traditional beef and sheep farm. Doing very badly now and wanting to do something about it. A recent council member I learned.

Idris Pugh, farmer of 200 acres over towards Brynsiencyn. Also sheep and cattle fattening but with a wife who had turned their large farmhouse into a, now well-known, first-class, expensive and rightly so, bed and breakfast. Always booked in advance, three local women to help. The farm open to tourists especially at lambing time. Printed leaflets giving details of nature walks around the farm and associated woodland. Financially, doing all right. Daughter, a teacher in Coventry, son with a degree in Agriculture from Bangor University, an honours degree in economics from London, married and helping his father on the farm.

'Helping,' exclaimed Idris. 'Running the bloody place, isn't it. And nothing left for me to do and not much say for me either!' Proud of his children and very active on the council.

He was next to me as we sat round the table and asked in detail about my father's willow project, which he hadn't heard about and which he promised to go round and find out all about. 'Plenty of "set aside" and wet patches on Anglesey that we could use to better effect, especially if we can make electricity by growing willow in ground that isn't much use for anything else.'

Mari Johns, infant teacher and conservationist, sitting on the other side of me heard the mention of electricity generation and joined in. 'Will it cause a lot of smell when you burn the willow? Not as bad, I suppose, as having the nuclear power station at Wylfa, near Holyhead threatening us all?'

'No smell,' I replied. 'There's a willow-burning power station over in Yorkshire that's been running for about fifteen years now, go over and have a look if you are worried about that. They have been talking of decommissioning Wylfa for years. What with the turbines giving us electricity from the tides, if we could get a lot more photovoltaics on roofs, plus more wind generators so that we could feed a lot of electricity in to the mainland grid, perhaps we could force them to shut down the nuclear power station.'

After hearing more of my ideas Mari was one of the most staunch supporters and an active speaker on the council in developing not only our willow burning power stations but also all other natural resource sources of electricity generation.

During that evening it was suggested to me that I might like to become a member of the county council or at least take the first step by putting myself forward as a possible candidate. I declined, not wanting to use my time in such a fashion, important as it is. It wasn't until nearly twenty years later that I did become elected as a member of the Anglesey County Council and, as you know, leader of the Council in 2045 when I was sixty-two. We changed our constitution in 2053 and became the Anglesey Assembly, very much independent of either the Welsh Assembly in Cardiff or Parliament in London.

I left that evening convinced that Bryn and all those who were there were fully committed to Anglesey plc, that it would go ahead guided, pushed and controlled by expert, experienced and fully motivated people, with full backing of the council and its officials and giving priority, to start with, to the improvement of education within the island.

In this 'history' of mine I am going to tell you about all the different aspects of what we have done here in Anglesey. As the people said who asked me to write these memoirs, there are minutes and records in the archives for anyone who wants to know the recorded details but I will tell you how it all appeared to me and how I was involved in nearly everything that went on. So I will write a chapter about education. I've already told you nearly everything about the underwater turbines, I'll tell you about how we developed our tourist industry and 'leisure complexes', to use a horrid phrase to describe an important part of our economy. I'll write a whole chapter about electric cars, no petrol allowed onto the island, and our photovoltaic cell economy. Another chapter about how the whole island went organic and our exports of fruit and veg, lamb and beef, and succulent, wonderful, tasty organic duck and chicken. Another about our hotels and cottages with their concomitant healthy, first-class catering so that people come from all over the world to see how they, in turn, could live a healthy, less stressful, active, enjoyable life not glued to the telly or full of fast food.

And, in between, bits about me and my family: how, once the girls had grown up, Jayne and I separated to our mutual advantage, about Val and how she shook me out of an early middle age; how she died and how I found Elen; how we matured together to garden, eat and drink, and make love even in old age, after our fashion.

I am a very lucky and happy man you know.

More Research and Development

I didn't wait for Bryn and the others to set up Anglesey plc formally as a company; I left them to organise a solicitor and go through all the legal aspects, which they did although it all took the best part of a year to sort out.

The work I had done over the years was in files and a few boxes of equipment stored in our original office and workshop on the Llangefni industrial estate. I shifted all the stuff left over from electric car, wind turbine and battery development away to their respective factories and set to work on photovoltaic cells, sending for details and ordering one of each of everything that was on the market at the time.

While waiting for them to be delivered, which wasn't all that long since there were stockists in England of material made in both Japan and America I went down to London and visited again the Institute of Mechanical Engineers in Birdcage Walk, London where I found a vast amount of historical and developmental detail about photovoltaic cells. I imbibed all this over a period of a full week, becoming an Affiliate Member in the process and wrote a resumé of what I learned, a copy of which is in the Anglesey Archives as well as in the library of the Mechanical Engineers, available to all who ask.

What was of equal and possibly greater importance to me, personally, was the seven evenings and a few of the afternoons during that week when I began to appreciate the galleries and concerts available to those who had time for them in the capital city. Any capital city I suppose, and I have visited some in these latter years. Cardiff cannot compete although it tries. Llangefni, the main town in Anglesey, hasn't a hope even though we have declared ourselves virtually independent. Bangor, as a cathedral and university city, does its best but is unable to compete with London, Paris, Rome, Vienna, New York, all of which I have spent time and money in, none of which can give the peace and beauty, the tranquillity of Llanddwyn Island on Anglesey or the space and majesty of the mountains of Eryri, but all of which have their own individual claim on the arts and architecture.

One of my greatest delights when walking in any city, that I discovered during that week in London, is looking at chimney pots. You can go from street to street in any city searching out the particular buildings of fame and special beauty, differing according to country and when built. I get even greater pleasure from looking up as I walk, avoiding lamp posts or not, as the case may be, and seeing all the variety of chimney pots on every building in every street, an endless succession of twists and turns, tall ones and short, reds and purples, cream and sooty black. One could write a book about them – perhaps someone has. I find them fascinating and endlessly varied.

Not very much fun in the rain though!

Anyway, chimneys apart, London during that week offered me the first of many pleasurable evenings attending concerts and a few afternoons looking at paintings, not to mention fantastic meals in prestigious restaurants. The one that sticks in my mind from that first 'cultural' visit to London was an early evening meal in Poons of Covent Garden. Wonderful Chinese food with an unending succession of dishes, cooked before your very eyes behind glass in a kitchen in the centre of the dining areas. A feast for the eyes, ears and taste buds and followed by Dvorak's New World Symphony at the Festival Hall... what more could any man want?

A companion, female, and a large comfortable bed afterwards. Not necessarily for immediate sleep.

I wished Jayne were with me; I told her about the concerts and galleries I had been to, even mentioned the chimneys, which was perhaps a mistake, a rather esoteric pleasure not necessarily appealing to everyone; asked her to come with me next time, proposed a special trip not associated with any business needs, but, again gently, she put me off. Her own business was busy, she wanted to spend her free time with the kids before they grew too old. 'You go and enjoy these things when you are down there, we will go sometime together but not just now.' And there it was, a gentle rebuff. And, again, no reassuring sex in bed that night either even though I made a few preliminary moves.

'Sorry darling, I really am exhausted.'

So I wrote my assessment of the state of progress in the development of photovoltaic cells and concentrated on designing a cheap mass production system.

By that time a lot of work had been done experimentally and the most promising line seemed to me to be in having slate-shaped units with which one could roof a whole building or part of a roof, depending. The concept was already in place, photovoltaic 'slates' were already available – at a price. I set myself to improve the energy production capability of each slate and to improve the method of roofing either existing roofs or new ones.

Remember that photovoltaic cells produce energy from the action of light on their surface, it does not have to be direct, clear sunshine although that is the most effective. What had stopped their universal acceptance and use had been their cost, both as unit slates as opposed to standard slates or tiles, and their installation cost which required a specialist knowledge and skill.

It took me two years and a team of five people to get those 'slates' right and cheap enough under mass-production conditions before I was ready to train installation teams ready to go anywhere and roof anything. By that time Anglesey plc was a legal entity and I handed the whole caboodle, just as I had handed the turbines and the batteries as a viable business, over to them to publicise and use. The company they formed, 'Anglesey Energy Roofs', offered new roofs or part roofs to anyone on Anglesey at cost plus five and, of course, at a competitive price to the rest of the world.

The concept of using natural resources had, by this time, been fully accepted throughout the world and coupled with wind or hydro power, plus my batteries for storage, the three natural energy sources could be exploited, without atmospheric pollution, to the full and sales rocketed. They established a large new factory up near Holyhead at the end of the motorway. Which wasn't a motorway by then anyway but I'll tell you about that some other time.

Mixed in with my work with the team on photovoltaics I spent quite a lot of time on two other projects, one directly related to the diminution of pollution – electric cars and taking full advantage of their unique qualities, the other being education in all its aspects on the island.

It was while I was handing over the photovoltaic cell development to Anglesey plc that I first met Val. An energetic, athletic woman in her early thirties, solicitor to Anglesey plc, a junior partner in the firm of solicitors based in Llangefni, moved a few years ago from Manchester – 'to get out of the smoke'. Welsh speaking of parents from Caernarfon. Very much on the ball and dealing with the hand over and formation of a new company with competence and verve. A pleasure to work with although most of our contact at that time was on paper. But her presence registered.

Education. Let's give a whole chapter to all the aspects of what we have done about education on Anglesey. I'll jump ahead of the details of other things like our forbidding the use of petrol or diesel anywhere on the island and the concurrent adoption of electrically powered cars everywhere, jump ahead of how we closed the newish motorway across the island and stopped *anyone* bringing their car onto the island, and how we managed to get all the lorry loads of stuff ferried to and from Holyhead and the mainland without causing a national strike by lorry drivers, thus clearing our skies and streets of pollution.

So – start a new chapter and I'll talk about Anglesey Education plc.

Anglesey Education Plc

There are a lot of different aspects to what we have done about education on the island but let's go back to what I have already told you and take it chronologically from there, only mentioning in passing, for the moment, all the other things I was involved with at the same time.

You will remember that I decided, up on my mountain top, well, hillside really, in 2017 on my thirty-fourth birthday, to hand over all my businesses to Anglesey plc, to run Research and Development on their behalf and to donate a million pounds to helping education on the island; that Mervyn Evans, retired financial wizard and banker had offered a similar amount, our intention, initially, being to double the number of teachers in schools on the island.

Well it wasn't as simple as that when we came to look in detail at the variety of difficulties schools face all the time. Mervyn volunteered to act as co-ordinator for, what started out as we thought, a simple fundraising exercise and the handing over of the money to the education authorities to be used for extra teachers' salaries.

Soon after that initial meeting at Bryn's house when the main decision had been to go ahead with forming Anglesey plc as a holding company for a number of subsidiary companies, Mervyn asked me to join him one evening with Marion Stope, Chief Education Officer for Anglesey. Between them they were going to round up a few head teachers for an informal discussion to find out roughly how many more teachers were needed and of what sort, and how much money, in total, we should aim to collect.

I came away from that Friday evening get-together with Mervyn, Marion and those head teachers, my mind reeling, appalled at what we, as parents and as a society, expected of teachers and schools, amazed that anyone would want to do the job no matter what the pay and glad that I hadn't gone for being a teacher myself. And Mervyn, when I spoke to him on the phone early the next morning agreed with me. 'There is much more to this than I thought,' he said. 'Can you come over again today, we need to go into this much more thoroughly. I'll ask Marion to come as well.'

I finished my coffee and toast, left Mary, housekeeper, to cope with those two teenage kids, still asleep in bed, exhausted after the rigours of a Friday night no-school-next-day, Jayne had already left for her office so I told Mary where I would be, 'ring me rather than Jayne if there are any problems, I'll probably be there all day,' and off I went.

Another coffee with Mervyn while we waited for Marion who had to drive from Aberfraw, the other side of the island, but was on her way.

We sat in Mervyn's comfortable arm chairs looking out across well-kept lawns to that beautiful view across the Straits and on away to the mountains, a view very similar to the one from my father's fields and my own sitting room two floors up in our unconventional house built into the hillside above Beaumaris, except that his view was slightly marred by a tall building on the skyline, one of the high-rise blocks of student accommodation plonked there by Bangor University.

'Why did they build it there?' I asked him, sipping the hot liquid and looking.

'Nobody gave a thought to the view from this side of the Straits,' he replied. 'Everyone, myself included, agrees with the need for proper student accommodation. Anyway its not so bad, beats living in a city whatever.' Then he went straight on to what was bothering us both.

'From what those head teachers were saying, it's not just more teachers that's needed for our schools is it? I've been awake nearly all night spinning things around in my head, being a banker and making money is easy compared to what those teachers have to tackle.'

'I thought the same thing myself, before I went to sleep. I'd much rather play with batteries and turbines than try to cope with all the conflicting demands made on a teacher. Listening to them last night there was one aspect of their job, among many others, that struck me as impossible. Think of the different groups of people within our society who impose, and quite rightly for the most part, their expectations on a teacher.'

'I was worried about the money side of things,' said Mervyn, 'they simply haven't got enough money to do what is demanded of them, but go on, explain how you see the difficulties of conflicting expectations.'

'Well, starting from what I suppose we should call the top – the government. And even there, Mervyn, you get a conflict over priority, who is the more important? Pupils, government, parents, fellow teachers, your own head teacher? I supposed, rationally, everyone should be working for the good of the pupils and I am sure they all would claim to be so but if you then look at the reality the mind boggles. You get instructions from the government about a National Curriculum that *must* be followed. As I understand it that is a farce in itself, the detailed contents of what was put out as the bees' knees when first printed out and sent to schools got changed and cut down a few years later so that teachers had to re-think, and then think again, and again, about what they were teaching day by day.

'There were, and still are, differences of opinion about what should be taught in schools and how. Ofsted inspectors come round to check up that it is being done according to government dicta. Parents, those who are articulate enough to have a say, also have their own agenda, head teachers are in the middle, trying to satisfy both sides; the kids, of all ranges of ability and different first languages, have to cope.

'How would you like to have an Ofsted inspector sitting in your classroom every five years or so, critically assessing what you were doing? Particularly if there are one or two disruptive kids in the class who are only too glad to show you up?

'A few disruptive kids in a class puts every other child at a disadvantage. My own child, Olwen has had this difficulty and it's a good thing, from our own selfish point of view, that we can afford to get a tutor to give her extra help. Not all parents can do that by any manner of means.'

Mervyn nodded. 'My grandchildren all get extra tuition for some subject or other,' he agreed as Marion arrived at the front door.

Fresh coffee and biscuits for her, but no more for me thanks, and we got straight to the nitty gritty.

'Davydd and I need your expertise,' said Mervyn when Marion was settled in her chair. A good-looking, tallish woman, confident, well dressed in a grey skirt that covered her knees when she sat, white starched blouse and purple, colourful scarf loosely around her neck, pale mauve cardigan loosely over her shoulders, tights presumably, sensible brown shoes, conservative make-up but undoubtedly put on with considerable care, dark-brown hair done up in a bun but long, one could tell, glistening and soft. I wondered what it would be like un-bunned and flowing over bare shoulders and breasts, a very good figure although ten years older than myself. A reassuring, capable and not yet sexless woman. 'Why,' I wondered momentarily, 'was she not married?'

'Davydd and I were talking about the conflicting demands made on teachers, from the government, from local authorities like yourself, from parents, other teachers, head teachers and from the children themselves,' said Mervyn.

'Very stressful,' nodded Marion. 'The whole job is stressful in many different ways. Lack of money for resources, too many children in class, having to cope with the difficult ones, not having enough time to deal with everything they are expected to do and everybody saying "you took on the job, you are paid for it, you are held responsible" ...and in my opinion,' she said gravely, 'no human being can possibly do all that teachers are expected to do; not as well as is asked of them or as well as they demand of themselves. The stress is high. Just as it is for young doctors in hospitals, or any doctor really. And policemen, and perhaps politicians.

'The stress of too much to do and not enough time to do it in. And, mostly, they are genuine, very hard working people who want to do the best for their pupils and cannot. That's the terrible thing. As things are they cannot do the best for their pupils.

'And we, as an Education Authority, have not got enough money to solve these problems. We do what we can with what we have got and what the government allots to us as our portion of the rates, we have our inspectors, who act more as advisers, to help; we give extra training to teachers where we can, we all need more and better resources – that is always ongoing – and yet, in spite of all this, teachers everywhere are doing a reasonable job within the circumstances and here on Anglesey we are doing better than most education authorities. Mind you, we do not have any inner city conditions, nor many pupils who cannot speak English.

She turned to us, smiling, but serious. 'How would you like to be a teacher? We need people like you, with experience of the world to teach our pupils. Come on, both of you, come and be teachers.

'You'd be fantastic,' she said turning to me. 'And you, Mervyn, could advise our head teachers about handling their finances – getting a gallon out of a pint pot – I should say how to get five litres out of a one-litre container, to be politically correct. I don't suppose many kids know what a gallon is these days although too many know about a pint. That was a fight and a half to keep pints and not half litres in pubs.' She grinned, looking expectantly, and somewhat accusingly, at us.

We grinned back, a bit ashamed, in unison. 'No thank you, we do not wish to be teachers, thank you very much.'

'But perhaps,' said Mervyn, 'we can do better than that. Davydd here has already handed over one million of his ill gotten gains and so will I. But, after last night's talk we can see that money will not solve all the problems and that's what I want to ask you about. As you know, my wife, Iris, died five years ago, my children have kids of their own and I am retired from banking. I had thought Iris and I would enjoy our retirement by sitting here and playing with the grandchildren, taking world trips and seeing places and people we didn't have time for before. But she got cancer and went... too soon.'

He paused, grinned at us sadly, and went on, 'So, here I am, still relatively young and healthy, I don't want to travel round the world by myself, I think I could do better than just advising head teachers about how to stretch their pounds. I'll come, full-time, as your financial adviser and organiser to Anglesey Education plc if you will have me and if you will sort out, with your entire school staffs, what needs to be done about education. And I don't just mean getting more teachers.'

'Why Anglesey Education plc, why a company?' I asked. (Remember that this meeting with Mervyn and Marion occurred just after the first informal meeting where I had simply proposed giving money to double the number of teachers.)

'Because,' answered Mervyn, lynx eyed and alert, 'the English government will not let us do all the things I think we are going to have to do. They cannot afford to put enough money into all schools to change things as I think we are going to need to. They have, however, established the precedent of allowing local education authorities pay a private company to run their education within the borough and that is what we will do.

We form a non-profit making company, Anglesey Education plc, and we make a bid to Anglesey County Council to run their education office for them.'

'Jumping the gun a bit, aren't you?' I asked him. 'We haven't yet established how much money will be needed or for what exactly and will the teachers or the councils agree to this revolutionary step?'

Mervyn smiled, roundly and confidently. 'How do you think I made my money? By sitting still and waiting to check up all my facts and details or seeing the whole thing in the round, leaving the details for others to deal with later, moving fast before others grasped the nettle or the opportunity; seeing things before they did. That's what I'm doing now. We heard lots of details last night. Lots of separate legitimate moans about different aspects of a virtually impossible job as it stands now. All those will need sorting and dealing with. More teachers for sure, but many other aspects of school management like curriculum content, balancing expectation from all interested parties, resources and so on and on. All details, important details and not small details at that, which Marion, her head teachers, myself and any others who are needed, can sort out if given the authority. But if we try to do it within the present set up we will fail.

We need to know that we have the local power and the money to carry out what I think will be quite radical reforms of schools within the county. Which means changing the rules. And, at the moment for us here, the rules are enforced, if that's the right word, by Marion and her Education Officers under direction and law as laid down from England's central government. We need to use the right to go private which they have given to failing education authorities – which *they* have used as a cop out from having to do something directly themselves about failing schools – *we* can use that right, go private ourselves and make damn sure we get a better education for our children and a better, less stressful, job for our teachers.'

Marion nodded her agreement. 'We can tell you what we need in the schools,' she said 'no doubt about that, but to get a consensus or even a simple list will require time from head teachers and classroom teachers, myself, and my officers. How will you convince them that what you propose to do will really happen? Are *you* sure you can do it? Will you be able to persuade Anglesey County Council even to apply to go private? It's a very big step you know.'

'Marion, provided I know that you agree in principle to the idea then I am sure it can be done. The present situation is almost intolerable. For the last twenty years teachers have been clamouring for and taking early retirement, many have had breakdowns from overwork and/or stress and recruitment to the profession has been poor. You know there are not enough teachers both because the pay is poor and working conditions stressful and because not enough people want the job, again, poor pay but also because society does not value good teachers sufficiently highly.

I'll make them the most important people on the island, given the go ahead. They are. Without good teaching where can anybody get? We need good teachers, good doctors and good homes, without which, as parents, we are failing our children… well, what do you say?'

'Mervyn, I agree with you, totally. In principle, you are right. In practice and before I can do much to help you I have to know that the money will be there and that the council will agree to go private. And remember,' Marion said with a lop-sided grin, 'I may be voting myself out of a job if you go private.'

'Not you,' cut in Mervyn, 'we'll need you for years to come. You're doing a good job as it is and all your colleagues acknowledge that. Don't think I haven't done my homework about the people who are involved with this. On you too,' he said turning to me. 'We will need more than your money from you, you know. I want you to stand for the council for a start.'

Well, Mervyn invited us to lunch, cooked by his housekeeper in the mansion by the Straits and we stayed all afternoon and on to an evening meal. He rang the head teacher of John Hughes, the secondary school in Menai Bridge who joined us for the meal, 'for a couple of hours only,' he said. 'It all sounds grand but far off. Can it really be done? If you only give me a few extra teachers I'll be more than grateful.'

He and Marion went home at about nine that evening while we, not having to be at work first thing on Monday morning and not feeling stressed about anything, being able to use our time as we wanted to, Sundays were not our only free day if we chose; we stayed on in the twilight, full of the roast duck and green peas, sipping brandy, sitting in comfort, looking at the mountains as they vanished under the twinkling starts, laying rough plans for tactics over the next few years.

And it did take years.

Mervyn immediately registered a non-profit making company 'Anglesey Education plc' as a charity with us both putting a million pounds into an opening account and with him being chairman and myself a director, both unpaid. That meant that we could immediately meet Marion and her fellow officers on the Education Committee and offer to pay for extra teachers. That proposition had to go before the general county council meeting where, of course, it was gratefully accepted.

In the meantime, Mervyn had canvassed the few other really wealthy people on the island and had a further three million or so in the coffers. He then went public as a charity and set up action groups all over the island to collect money in whatever way they could. Getting those action groups together and informing them as to what the charity was up to meant addressing public meetings and writing articles in all the local papers which kept me and Mervyn, as directors, very busy over the following year. After that the local group leaders knew what we were aiming for and did their own organising and publicity. By that time everyone on Anglesey knew what we were up to and things had moved on from charity collection boxes anyway, although they will always play a part since it involves the whole community in directly contributing to, and therefore feeling an integral part of, one aspect of their children's education. Direct parental participation and responsibility being a keystone of our education philosophy. And not just in finding money either, as you will see.

Once the company was officially registered as a charity, formed to provide more teachers for Anglesey schools which took us until the end of 2018 as I remember, Mervyn was then able, with justification and a confident expectation that many people would attend, to call a public meeting of all teachers and school staff, all education office staff and anyone else who cared to come, to discuss just how the money collected was to be spent.

Should we simply double up on every teacher there was? What really were the priorities as far as teacher employment went? Should we, at this stage, increase all the teachers' salaries? And Mervyn also fully intended to broach the question of how to meet the other needs of the education system and to even mention the idea of taking the whole education system of the island into the hands of the people of the island.

What came out of the meeting was a remarkable consensus. The teachers did not ask for an immediate increase in salary, much as they would have liked it and much as they felt they deserved it; they asked for more teachers and they appointed a committee to draw up priorities as to how many and what sort of teacher. That list of priorities was to be publicised throughout Anglesey, not just to the schools, they wanted every single person on the island to know what was going on.

They requested that consideration be given to other issues: smaller classes, better resources, repairs to buildings, maybe a few new schools completely, better adult education facilities, retraining, and, perhaps not surprisingly from a responsible group of people, what could we do to improve the prospects of employment on the island?

That last question resulted in my forming another committee and has kept me busy all the rest of my life – still does although there is no unemployment on the island now and we welcome, within reason, our share of refugees of all languages, religions, customs and colour.

Mervyn got what he wanted from that meeting. A happy acceptance of the money for more teachers and an implied mandate to tackle all the other issues.

As a result of my being asked to form a committee to tackle the unemployment problem and as my own interest seemed to be moving towards political involvement – local politics, not national, I put myself forward as a candidate to be councillor for the Beaumaris ward and was elected in 2019. I was subsequently co-opted, as a non-voting member, onto Anglesey County Council and became a County Councillor in my own right five years later in 2024. And Leader of the Council, as you know in 2045, helping Anglesey to become pretty well independent of both Cardiff and Westminster in 2053 when we called ourselves the Anglesey Assembly.

One very important question that was asked at that meeting was how we intended to finance all this. 'Five million,' it was pointed out from the floor, 'would not go very far towards paying for the double the amount of teachers never mind anything else. Did we think Cardiff or Westminster or the National Lottery would cough up?'

Mervyn, from the chair, asked Mr Bryner Cadwallader, from the floor, if he could perhaps point us towards a possible answer.

Bryn stood up and gave a concise and brief reply, promising to write full details to the local papers with individual copies to anyone who asked for them, 'leave your name and address before you go from here tonight.' Briefly he informed them that Anglesey Power was already in profit. Anglesey Turbines was doing more than very well as were other subsidiary companies, all handed over, thanks to the generosity of Mr Davydd Cliffourd of Beaumaris, here, to Anglesey plc, a non-profit making company set up precisely for the purpose of financing Anglesey Education plc and all it intended to do for the teachers and pupils on the island.

Cheers and general jubilation nearly brought the roof down. Bryn stated that accounts for Anglesey plc and its associated companies would be published yearly and freely available both in the company head office and the county education office.

A good beginning towards building confidence in Anglesey plc and all its aims, not only for education but also, hopefully, for anything else it might propose – like, I thought to myself, the abolition of the use of petrol or diesel on the island coupled with everyone having an electric car and producing, by one method or another, their own electricity. And turning the whole island into an organic-farming community. All projects requiring the building of a great deal of confidence.

Further Education

With Anglesey Education plc established, and at that stage answerable only to Mervyn and myself, we were able to start things moving quickly.

The education office was, of course, only too delighted to be getting extra teachers and we told them to go ahead as fast as they could recruiting them. We left it to Marion and her staff to sort out with the schools, who, what, and how many. All we asked was that, at this stage, all expenses incurred in relation to these extra teachers be listed and sent to us. We handed one million straight over to the education office, just to be getting on with.

I left Mervyn to sort out the office and financial organisation side of everything, only asking that I be allowed to be present at any planning meetings when other projects were under discussion.

None of the new teachers were due to start working until the start of the academic year – September 2018 by which time we had realised that a lot more money would be needed quite quickly although how much, we had no idea.

Mervyn had accounts drawn up to show how much Anglesey plc with all its associate subsidiary companies already had in the bank with a forecast of income for the following year. These figures were very encouraging indeed – you will find them in the minutes of the company meetings – and Mervyn went to the bank manager well prepared with them. We wanted the facility for what was virtually unlimited borrowing for the next few years on behalf of Anglesey Education on the strength of the value, present bank account and projected income of all those companies.

Well, he didn't give us the unlimited right to borrow money, but, in view of our previous record of reasonably rapid repayment of monies borrowed in the past by myself in my various company developments, and with the accounts as presented by Mervyn, plus the fact that it was to improve the educational opportunities for pupils of all ages on the island, he agreed that we should go ahead. But he asked that a member of his staff be allowed to attend our board meetings.

Since, at that time, the board consisted solely of Mervyn and myself we were happy to accommodate him. Particularly when he hinted, without saying anything directly, that it would be he who would attend. We knew he lived on the island and had young grandchildren in junior school there. 'Nuff said. Co-opted, non-con.

Again, he retained on behalf of the bank the right to publicise their commitment to helping investment in local industry and general welfare. Fair enough!

Between 2018 and 2040 Mervyn and I saw the face of Education – the way in which it was delivered, by whom and about what – change out of all recognition. You will find all the details in council minutes and records kept by Anglesey Education plc. But I propose to tell you, in a more informal way, of the things we changed and why, not necessarily in their right order but as I remember and as I consider their importance. The difficulty is that things intertwine and react to each other and some things were developed during the same time period while I can only write/talk about things one at a time.

Anyway, in 2040 Mervyn died and I resigned from the board of Anglesey Education, leaving others to carry on a, by then, well established and highly respected education policy which was frequently visited by other folk involved in the educational world and followed by others as and when they could persuade their governments to invest the money. Marion had married Mervyn a few years after they started working together, after Anglesey Education became a plc in 2020. She retired eight years later and they went off round the world on that extended cruise Mervyn had intended taking with his first wife. They remained consultants to the firm until, as I have said, Mervyn died in 2040, but Marion continued to take an interest in all that was done.

All three of us can really claim little credit for what was developed over those years for education on the island. The only credit we can claim was that we organised a cash flow into the system which no other government was prepared to countenance at that time. The rest came from teachers, parents and pupils themselves. The needs within the educational field are obvious to anyone who cares to look. To meet those needs does require money. On Anglesey anyone can now see that such investment repays itself one hundred fold and more, not in direct cash terms though, so a capitalist approach to the problem will not solve it.

I am often asked to which political party I belong – Plaid Cymru, of course. But this does not convey much to anyone outside Wales. I like to quote to them something I read many years ago, which hardly answers their question but applies indirectly to many of the things I have done in life and I ask that they think around it.

'When I give food to the poor, they call me a Saint.

When I ask why the poor have no food, they call me a Communist!'

If you ask the right questions of yourself (a difficult task in itself in the first place) the answers may be uncomfortable and what you then do about the answers you come up with may be difficult indeed.

For instance. Is nuclear power a necessary thing?

The world needs cheap (is it cheap?) unlimited power... Is the price we pay healthwise, are the risks we run, worth it?

Are you getting uncomfortable answers? Is finding the money to do away with nuclear power difficult indeed?

And you can ask these sorts of questions about many other problems... Famine in the Third World...

You can be called a saint and give money for food, or you can ask the question 'Why have they no food?' – the answers to which may lead you to a form of communism, much as we have here on Anglesey, where all public services are run, not for profit, but for communal good.

What we did about education:

Double the number of teachers, right across the board as a first priority. From which a number of things directly followed:

No class to contain more than fifteen pupils.

Requiring virtually double the number of classrooms!

Over the following next few years we built three new secondary schools and five new junior/infant schools plus many preschool local groups. All these new buildings were of the wood frame, straw bale, construction, fully up to health and safety, particularly fire safety, standards, all of which problems had already been solved, certified and regularly inspected first of all, way back in 1988–99 when the CAT in Machynlleth built their structure as a display and lecture hall for the Centre Alternative Technology and subsequently by my own team in our 'straw village'.

Whenever we could we got pupils and parents to help with this construction under the supervision of our own team of experts.

Concurrent with this building of school classrooms etc. was the development on the island of an entire self–contained 'straw village' with shops and a pub, village hall and all sorts over near Newborough, designed as a new housing project in itself but also as a tourist attraction and information centre for others the world over who wished to build in a similar economic and low-energy-demand way.

We also removed all responsibility for any buildings from the shoulders of all head teachers. They had been landed with this when budgets were devolved from local education authorities onto individual schools. Head teachers, who were highly skilled educationalists but with no training in budget control or experience of dealing with building contractors, were expected to deal with leaking roofs or blocked drains out of their total allocation of money for running the school. Plus anything they could raise from local industry or parents etc.

I remember one newspaper quotation of the time… 'It will be a great day when our schools get all the money they need… and the air force has to hold a bring and buy sale to get a new bomber!'

We let our head teachers get on with organising teaching and formed our own buildings repair team within Anglesey Education plc.

Another of the things that was done around the 1990s within the education system of England and Wales, and Scotland too for all I know, was that schools were expected to keep within their mainstream classes nearly all difficult pupils. Many special schools were closed down to the detriment of any class who had within it a pupil who simply disrupted and made difficult the education of other children. It became almost impossible to exclude an impossible pupil. Not fair to the others in the class, and not fair to the disrupter either.

His/her needs were certainly not being met.

We built two small, special schools on the island and employed, or trained, a team of special needs teachers and psychologists whose remit was to get the pupils happily back into mainstream classes, or make any arrangement they, as a team and with full consultation and agreement of parents and pupil, felt was the best thing for that individual. In the full and complete knowledge that within our further education system anyone, of any age, could resume or start their education at any level. Nobody was to be deprived of the opportunity to develop to the best of their ability. At the same time nobody's education was to suffer from the distraction caused by a disruptive pupil and, very important, teachers were not to be frustrated in the use of their skills to teach rather than contain.

We employed a parallel team of social workers specifically to help the families of special needs pupils – the disruptive ones or those with learning difficulties. Pupils with physical special needs were given every help necessary to continue their education within the mainstream. Our special needs social workers worked in very close collaboration with the main group of social workers and we never bothered about which department paid for whom, or where any departmental boundaries lay – we left it to the individuals on the staff to sort that out and anyway all salaries for social workers were paid for by Anglesey Health plc from 2046 onwards when we built our own hospital and took over the responsibility for the running costs of all doctors and health needs of the island. Of which more in another chapter.

Special needs – a maximum of six pupils of mixed age and sex per 'class'. Sometimes individual pupils were placed elsewhere – work experience, adult classes, anywhere that suited them best.

In those early years we formed a team of specialists to help all schools deal with basic literary and numeracy difficulties and all pupils soon caught up. After a few years, thanks to having more teachers/smaller classes, this was no longer necessary. Every teacher had time to help every pupil properly and there was no problem about the basic skills of reading, writing, spelling and number.

We set up another separate company to design and build computers and their programs specifically for school needs. That meant that they did not have to be as complex as commercial computers and so could be cheaper. Our programs were directly aimed at curriculum needs. We sold these computers and their programs to English-speaking schools all over the world since they were cheaper and yet very effective within schools' needs and we put these computers into every classroom. We also used mainstream computers as well of course and so had the best of both worlds. It goes without saying that we set up our own web site and had our own reference library within it.

In every school we employed two deputy heads. They were not expected to take responsibility for any one particular class but often did quite a lot of teaching in any class, so relieving class teachers for further training etc. although we also had a team of supply teachers on hand to do this because we considered a deputy head was really too skilled to be used simply as a supply teacher. Each deputy head had a separate role. One was to be responsible, under the head teacher, for the educational needs of the school and the co-ordination of all individuals concerned with this aspect of school life.

The other deputy head was responsible for the social needs of the school. And this was one of the most innovative and revolutionary improvements that we made during all those years. One that lead to the direct involvement of the whole community in the education of their children, cut down truancy, misbehaviour, and increased the effectiveness of our education very much indeed.

First of all, in the very beginning – in 2018 – as a condition of our (Mervyn and I) giving any money to education, we demanded that video cameras be installed in every classroom, which we paid for. At first the teachers didn't want this to happen at all. 'Worse than an Ofsted Inspector looking over your shoulder all the time. We are professionals. Don't you trust us?'

We replied that it was not a question of trust. That they *were* professionals. That in all other professions colleagues worked in the same room and were directly, observably, responsible to each other, so why should teachers be the exception? And that, anyway, the object was not to check up on the teacher but to observe the pupils. No disruptive behaviour could go on behind the teacher's back and, most important of all, there would be incontrovertible evidence for parents *and the offending pupil* to see.

This measure alone resulted in far better behaviour in classrooms.

But then we did a far more effective thing.

It had long been the practice that a 'lady helper' be employed within some classrooms to 'hear the children read'. We extended that principle. Vastly.

We asked that grandmothers, retired grandfathers, unemployed mothers with a bit of time to spare – anybody with a bit of time to spare, come into the classrooms to help any and every pupil. On a voluntary basis. And we spent a lot of money publicising this.

We went further. We demanded of every unemployed person that they spend a specific, quite considerable amount of time each day, helping in a classroom. Our aim being one adult to every pupil.

It was the responsibility of that school deputy head to organise and supervise this part of the school.

This measure caused a lot of anxiety within the teaching profession and within the hearts of all parents concerned – 'you will be letting all sorts of perverts gain access to our children.' But, of course, this was not so. So many adults around all the time totally prevents this and, with the vetting, supervision and training organised by those deputy heads we have had no trouble on that score during all the years since we started this and our pupils really do achieve to the very best of their ability.

Having a fully educated young population who can see that they have the prospect of full employment ahead of them, doing something they like and are well trained for has had a beneficial effect on the level of petty crime within the island. That, coupled with other police and social measures which we set in place after we became independent of Cardiff and Westminster, has resulted in a safe and law abiding, satisfied and happy community – almost Utopia!

Just to round off this chapter I need to tell you that our adult education programme offers courses covering all aspects of tourism, the arts, crafts and skills: mechanical, electrical, building etc. etc. required by the island population. If tuition is needed, then it is supplied to the highest standard and it is the responsibility of the adult education department to see that their students get employment. Setting them up in their own business if needs be and supervising and advising as necessary.

You will ask why isn't everybody coming to live here? A good question.

Transport

In the autumn of 2020 I handed over the research and development work my specialist team had done on photovoltaic slates to the newly formed Anglesey Energy Roofs plc, which then became an independent company under the aegis of Anglesey plc like all the others, and I ceased to have anything to do with it. Some of my specialist research team went with it, others, the ones involved with our electric car development, stayed.

I then found my life running very easily. Photovoltaics gone, the basic design of our car developed and we had six prototypes, hand built and nearly ready to run on the roads.

About three days a week I found myself involved with matters educational and the pattern of three days to education was roughly what went on until my retirement from that field of operations in 2040, except for an intensive six months when we set up a small factory making the video cameras which we installed in each classroom – and in many other places all over the island, including shops.

Too much like Big Brother? Not so. I've already given the rationale for their use in classrooms. Their universal use in shops is obvious, cost had been the difficulty for many shopkeepers until then. We positively encouraged tourism and went all out to make Anglesey a safe place for everyone. In a way, our policy of ensuring that petty thieving simply could not succeed was part and parcel of our road safety and secure streets objective.

In the early 2000s, particularly in cities, but also in small towns all over the United Kingdom – and elsewhere – mugging of elderly people and the not so elderly also, was becoming endemic and very frightening to anyone to whom it happened.

Senior citizens became frightened citizens. Which is not the way our elders should finish their lives.

In just the same way as teachers had become devalued within our society, so had the elderly. Kids could be rude with impunity.

Once we had got many more teachers into schools we were able to improve the social behaviour of pupils both in and out of schools. Teachers or social workers could follow up anti-social behaviour and the pupils no longer felt that they could get away with things with ease.

A few years after getting more teachers we also got a lot more policemen and women on the beat and *they* also had as a priority the following up of anti-social behaviour.

Many more strategically placed video cameras helped very much indeed. The cameras available at that time were relatively expensive, so, following our fairly well established by now, policy of making things for ourselves on the island and selling them to ourselves at cost plus five *and* giving employment to our population, we set up a small camera factory solely to produce video cameras for use in class, shop or street.

I spent an intensive six months with our Research and Development team designing this simple camera and then setting up a nice little, highly roboticised, production line. They sold very well all over Europe. Strong, cheap, not good-looking, effective for one specific purpose only so not worth thieving. A good little business in itself.

Anyway, apart from that six months I started living an easy and interesting life.

Roughly three days a week with education, sitting in on meetings, often conferring with my daughters as they were growing up through the system and could shed insider light on things, often talking with teachers and head teachers informally, getting well known by many pupils in the playgrounds – which we were able to improve according to their suggestions rather than those of adults. I enjoyed all this and you could hardly call it work.

So, in 2020, there came a lull in my life, a peaceful interlude that I look back on with pleasure but also, pervading it, an indefinable (at the time) sense of loneliness which, perversely, I also enjoyed.

Those six prototype cars were nearing completion, my team had the job well in hand, I was hardly needed, we would have to start publicising and selling them soon but in the meantime I was free.

And, as always when I am free, I headed for the hills.

Anghared was fifteen and Olwen thirteen, both at secondary school in Menai Bridge. Jayne's secretarial agency took up all her time and Mary Roberts was still our housekeeper. Jayne and I rarely met. When we were both at home of an evening, which was not often, she was either glued to some soap opera on the telly – 'pure, mindless relaxation,' she admitted, or she had brought back work from the office. The children were usually up in their own rooms, hopefully doing homework, certainly with music blasting until told to cool it. A different species but with friends enough for us not to need to worry. Anghared was showing an interest in art and also in maths. Olwen kept changing the colour and shape of her hair.

I curled up in a corner of the couch when at home, in a room away from the telly, reading books and listening to music. Going to bed fairly early and out of the house before eight usually, off to Research and Development or, during that period of peace, away into the hills.

I also started taking long weekends in London – preliminary work on selling the electric cars was my excuse. And I did… a bit…well… not really.

Sex had taken a sabbatical from my life. Slowly but surely Jayne had become less and less… interested? …co-operative…?

Never one to take the initiative sexually, she just wasn't interested any more. And it was not the menopause.

Talking about it with her, many years later, long after we had separated, we found that it was a mixture of things. And neither of us put any blame on the other.

It was, we agreed, insidiously inevitable. In a way we should never have married – basically we are two different sorts of people who could never supply what the other needed and yet we have produced two well-balanced and happy children, both now married and with children of their own and better matched to their partners than we ever were.

Anyway, we found, over the years, that Jayne was a very independent person indeed, fully secure within herself, not needing the reassurance of physical contact; her body not demanding sexual stimulation, happy to pursue her business independence, frustrated by the, as she came to see it, boring demands of a household of two girls and a largely absent husband. She married again five years after our divorce to a very successful accountant working in the head office of a prestigious London firm of lawyers. His children were also grown up and away. They have a large flat in Bayswater, attend many concerts, art gallery private views and are regular playgoers. Much quiet entertaining at home among a large circle of friends with similar interests and, Jayne assures me, a steady, undemanding, but satisfying, sex life.

Whereas I have realised that I need lots of reassurance in the way of frequent (getting less so as I grow older) sex, and lots and lots of hugs and touches, continual physical contact.

That late summer and autumn I walked Offa's Dyke. Staying in pubs of an evening. Not trying to go for miles and miles. Ambling and looking, feeling the roll of the hills, the quiet and shade of the woods, talking to farmers, avoiding people. A quiet pint, an early meal and early to bed.

Retreat.

Impotent. Although I didn't, during those months, put it to the test. Just no reaction and no interest. And not bothered about it either.

I simply did not want to complicate my life by getting involved with anyone else. I was frightened to. I did not want to upset those two girls. I put it all down to approaching old age and tried to go gracefully.

And enjoyed the unhurried long weekends which were often not weekends but three or four days mid-week when nobody was out and about on the hills.

When it came a bit wet, sometime in the early autumn, remembering the pleasure I had had at a concert and looking at chimneys in London, I drove down there, staying in a quiet hotel in a side street near Green Park.

So, as you can see, Jayne and I, in 2020 and for the following four years, were definitely drifting apart. We were both very concerned not to upset the girls and we were very good at organising the household between us, agreeing about their education, taking them on holidays and running, in their teenage years, a private taxi service for them, their friends and their boyfriends. Mary Roberts, housekeeper, was with us for those years and invaluable. The girls loved her.

In October that year I went to a Friday evening concert in the Royal Festival Hall to hear Mendelson's violin concerto and there, alone and sipping a pre-concert glass of wine was Ms Valerie Griffiths, lawyer, to whom I had written and from whom I had received a number of letters about transferring my companies to Anglesey plc. We had already met a few times in her office in Llangefni for me to sign documents.

Val: wonderful, secretly voluptuous, romantic, beautiful and eternally sensually loving. Exciting and adventurous. Always seeking. Effervescent, independent and elusive. Dead now, these thirty years, but I remember and can see her still. Elen knows all about her so we can talk freely. They knew each other before I met Elen.

We are older now but Elen has all those qualities... and more... I have been a very lucky man.

But Val, in the foyer of the Festival Hall that evening, seemed only formidable and efficient. Dressed in a black trouser suit, white shirt and formal, loosely tied, flouncy black tie. Black shoes with a slight heel and hair held loosely back by a black ribbon tied in a large bow – the only hint of her latent flamboyant style of dressing when on duty. I observed her from across the carpeted, thickly peopled, front of theatre, not wanting to intrude if there was a partner somewhere, hugging my solitude and freedom, not wanting to have to make polite noises, unwilling to leave the peace of my own space... But... I waited a little longer and nobody came to join her, we already each had our concert tickets which were bound to be in separate seats so it need only be 'hello.'

The first bell went indicating ten minutes to start of concert and I went over. She *was* alone, had been to court that day and was due there again on Monday, could well be there all next week. Yes, she would join me for a drink in the interval, a nice long, cold, ginger beer and lime. Os gwelwch chi'n dda... if you would be so kind, and we always spoke Welsh together after that –

a useful privacy when out and about in England. And we Welsh have a healthy sense of humour so it didn't matter if any other Welsh person overheard us, they joined, unashamedly, in the fun!

And Val and I had fun. Lots of it in the fifteen years of the rest of her life. She is buried on that little island near the Menai Bridge where there is a little church and graves and nothing else. Gales blow over it and birds sing and nest in the spring... Val...

I left her then, went to order her drink and my beer for the interval, and went in to the concert.

Dark-brown hair with a hint of copper, down to below her shoulders when loosed. Deep, dark-brown eyes that could flash with anger or melt you with languorous longing, depending; as I found, later. Does it matter – the features of her face?

Beautiful. Everyone said so. Striking, the opinion of men, but these things, nice as they are, are extra and not always what they seem. Beauty really *is* in the eye of the beholder and it was not long before I didn't really see her any more, not as an artist or photographer or stranger would see her. She just became herself and to me she was pure joy. To touch and look at, be with and enjoy.

Enough. One man's love affair is like any other I suppose, magic for the two, commonplace to outsiders. I will dwell no longer on our own special magical entity.

All I was aware of then, as I took my seat, was this formal dark-haired woman, about my age, about my height, who I had met only briefly in her office. We would make polite conversation, me about electric cars and she about, perhaps, the case she was there for, we would meet for our drink in the foyer at the interval, talk politely and then – 'Nice to see you, perhaps you will be dealing with the electric car legal stuff when all that gets under way? Good night.'

I settled in my seat to listen.

But it wasn't like that. Things never were, with Val.

We collected our drinks, she perched on a stool, kicked off her shoes, took off the tie and stuffed it in her briefcase along with the black ribbon, shook out that lovely hair, grinned at me and demanded to know what brought me away from the hills.

I explained about chimneys. She told me a bit about modern paintings and we agreed to meet outside the Museum of Modern Art the next day at twelve, it being a Saturday. We would have an early pub lunch and she would show me some of the stuff in the galleries of Bond Street, perhaps collecting a few chimneys on the way.

I don't remember much about the details of that afternoon. We behaved like teenagers; me aged thirty-seven with two teenaged daughters and a wife; she thirty-five, and no ties at all.

We had seen enough paintings and walked enough in the London streets by four that afternoon and I asked her to come with me for a meal – 'Out of the city away from people and petrol fumes.'

I remember she stopped in the middle of the street when I asked her that, paused, looking at me questioningly in the face, seeking something, then nodded.

'Okay. Let's go find some quiet.' Then she took my arm and hugged it, laughed a lovely gurgle laugh, 'Let's explore. Let's drive out into the countryside somewhere and have a meal. Let's take our stuff and stay somewhere… only… separate rooms if you please, and I pay for myself.'

She had come down by train, I, in my car. I collected my belongings and paid my bill being due back on Anglesey by Monday morning, we got her overnight bag and she told them she would be back the following evening and off we went.

Straight up the M1 with no particular place in mind, just the quickest way out of London. Woburn sounded nice, the country-side, fields and trees, and by seven o'clock we had booked in at the Bedford Arms on the corner. Two single rooms, at the back, away from traffic, os gwelwch chi'n dda.

A few minutes to drop our stuff in our respective rooms, tidy up and then book a table. She came down those stairs as I was doing that, hair free and flowing, still in trousers but a light-blue silk scarf loosely over her shoulders, jacket held by one finger, swinging and a bounce in her step.

'To watch her feet, how they can dance.'

And 'time to turn at beauty's glance' I told myself.

Time, enough, I also thought to wait…

'til her lips can…

Enrich the smile her eyes began.'

We strolled round the old town – not much more than a crossroads really but expensive antique shops in the High Street and an interesting-looking Fine Art Gallery that we would visit after breakfast next morning. Not saying much but her hand tucked into my arm, walking slowly, looking. Peaceful, in contact, arms and the occasional brush of a hip.

That meal did not go all that easily; we were still exploring ourselves in relation to each other. We had large sweet sherries each while ordering what proved to be a very good meal, I forget what wine, and ended it with Irish coffee in the lounge, which slowly emptied as we sat and talked. A late stroll by the church and each to our respective beds. 'Good night, see you at breakfast, about eight thirty.'

She knew all about the different firms I had started up, she was enthusiastic when I told her more than she had already heard about what we were doing for education and she approved of my electric cars and no pollution.

I heard, briefly, about her law course in London, her work for a firm of lawyers in Chester, her wish to return to North Wales with its freedom of sea and sky, mountains and space and her junior partnership in Llangefni; business law, her particular speciality.

I heard a bit more detail about her parents, separated when she was sixteen but both still living in Caernarfon, much to her mother's distress because he was an alcoholic. An older sister, married and living in Liverpool, teaching and married to a teacher, three kids.

Her father had behaved appallingly during her adolescence, beating up her mother, hitting the girls, drinking any money he could lay his hands on. Her sister had got away as soon as she could and her parents' divorce went through with a lot of unpleasantness. Her father was still to be seen, drunk on the corner of the square in Caernarfon, swearing at Val or her mother if they ever passed by, forbidden by court order to go anywhere near the house. Val had a cottage now in Dwyran, Anglesey, a quiet place, away from the main road and away from Caernarfon.

But she found it difficult to trust men, had had plenty of affairs, starting early at sixteen, but none lasted, 'Too boring; expecting too much of her time, all getting too serious once they had had sex with her.'

'So I am fancy free and glad of it,' she smiled at me across the table, over her glass of wine, 'I don't intend to get involved with anyone. The difficulty,' she continued, 'is that I prefer the company of men, I work well with them in my job… but they often ask for more… and then they get serious… and their wives, if they have one, get jealous… and it all has to stop. But what the hell am I supposed to do? I don't *like* going to concerts by myself. I *prefer* going for a walk with a male companion, an evening meal is more *fun* with a man, damn it!'

I said very little, really, in reply to all that. Just told her what she already knew, that I was married to Jayne, with two daughters but spent quite a lot of time away from them these days, walking, enjoying my somewhat solitary state, the occasional concert, and left it at that. I didn't *want* to get involved.

We met for breakfast, visited the gallery, had a brief look at the grounds about Woburn Abbey and by unspoken mutual agreement returned to the car and off to… wherever…

A walk across fields to a wood over a stream, leaves beginning to turn, a bit cloudy, birds, late bees buzzing, muddy shoes and a ploughman's lunch in a pub that was too crowded. Not saying much, both of us, I think, wary. Not wanting involvement. But her hand was firm in mine as I helped her over that stream and, again, she slipped her arm in mine as we walked from the pub to the car after lunch and we drove silently London-wards.

Near Hitchin at a village called Ayots St Lawrence is where Bernard Shaw lived. We paid and looked in the summerhouse where he had worked then walked along a path by another stream to what looked, at a distance, like a small castle but which proved to be a mausoleum. Strange. Some local landowner, Sir Somebody or Other, and his wife. One tomb in a small tower at each end, connected by a covered terrace. Not together. We got there, Val and I, read their names and that they had not been on speaking terms for the last years of their lives. Laughed to each other… and kissed. A long deep kiss with bodies that moulded and clung. And then we stepped apart, grinned and walked back to the old, smoky pub for grilled trout and so, back to London.

I dropped her off at her hotel and drove back up the M1, M6, A5, turned right in Menai Bridge, and home to bed in Beaumaris by half past two in the morning. Into the office and electric cars by eight thirty. But I had her home phone number.

Deeply concerned.

I had a wife and a home that I valued highly. And I had two daughters who I was very proud of and loved. And who loved and trusted me.

But I *desired* the company of Val. The touch, the feel, the look and laugh of her. At ease, we had been, together.

Why did Jayne and I no longer have this?

I ached and longed for touches, hugs, kisses, companionship. Looking back on things, Jayne had never been a toucher, sensual. My children hugged me – sometimes – but it's not the same. Wonderful when they were tiny and I could hold and cuddle them, change nappies and bath them, feel soft skin and sing or talk them to sleep.

'You're a better mother than me,' Jayne used to say, breast-feeding and the pair of them beautiful.

Jayne never acknowledged her own beauty. Val knew exactly what effect she had, coming down those stairs.

I remember making special efforts in the following weeks to be home a bit earlier, tried to persuade Jayne to come with me to a concert in Manchester or Liverpool or London. But she didn't want to. Never had been all that set on going to concerts, symphony concerts. Preferred her own record collection or the telly and a curl up in a chair. Not a couch where there was room for two, a comfortable large chair. And go to bed to sleep.

I tried being more amorous, brought flowers home, cooked meals for us all.

'Thanks, Dad, you're being really great these days.'

'Lovely meal darling, I'll just finish these papers.' And go to bed to sleep.

I talked to her about it, one evening when both the kids were out. Diffidently I told her that I seemed impotent these days, pointed out that I hadn't been getting much practice lately, did

177

she mind? Should we be doing anything about it? Did she miss the cuddles and hugs?

'No,' she didn't. She had had enough of those from the kids growing up. She was beginning to feel emancipated, free from bringing up children, free from anything that clung, like hugs or cuddles. Grown up. Adult. Herself. And her body no longer needed sex. No more children, thank you. No more bother with contraception. She didn't mind my being impotent. A good thing really, then we could both rest easy, grow into middle age and old age gracefully...

I tried to explain that my need to touch and be touched, feel and be physically close to somebody, like my pleasure in walking the hills, was a hunger and a need, like food.

She said I must be an arrested infant, needing cuddles. I was an adult wasn't I? Grown up? Independent?

But I have found that I am not. Not even now at the age of eighty-two. I still need physical love, contact. To be given freely to me, and for me to give. Elen and I have that. Val had that quality. Jayne preferred to walk by herself through the jungle.

She told me she still loved me but, that if I wanted sex and such, I should get a mistress – half in fun and half in earnest. For now, she was tired, it was late, where were those girls, lock up after they come in, good night.

And that was how it was for the next four years until the girls had grown up and Anghared had a job in Aberystwyth, Olwen by then was in her second year in college – a mixture of fine arts and media studies in Warwick and Jayne and I, amicably, divorced.

I got on with the electric cars.

A long haul.

You know what they are like... We've all got one or more in our family these days. They are cheap enough, they run on the electricity produced by each household with its own, free, mixture of wind, photovoltaic and battery-stored power. Plug in and charge up overnight. Draw from the mains underwater tide turbine electricity if house batteries run low. Plug in anywhere on the mainland and charge up. Maximum speed twenty-five miles per hour (kilometres per hour, these days!), seat four... small boot... you know...

But difficult to persuade people that pollution from petrol and diesel exhaust really was so much of a threat on the island.

But I wasn't the first on the market. In the year 2000 I remember cutting out a newspaper article about atmospheric pollution, and the world warming up as a result. It pointed out that in the United States a gallon of petrol was cheaper than a gallon of bottled spring water but informed us that car makers were doing considerable research into cutting down emission of greenhouse gases and said that the first experimental hydrogen filling station, complete with forty experimental vehicles would appear that summer in America, with the first commercial vehicle expected in the showrooms in four years time. Well, they did appear eventually and many more are now on the roads using liquid hydrogen as a power source, giving off water as the only waste product, reducing pollution, but not cheap!

To get liquid hydrogen available at a filling station costs. The engine itself is no more expensive than a conventional petrol one and the vehicle goes at conventional speeds.

My advantage is/was very cheap power but limited speed if you required any distance before recharging.

The whole thing ground slowly along. We continued to produce a few cars on a limited production line, selling some locally, more in cities where some people used them as second cars to commute within the city boundaries.

Towns and cities continued to get more and more congested, buses and cars jostling for space, an inadequate underground train system packed to overflow and accidents at peak travelling times, pollution becoming more and more apparent in hot summer weather. Road rage and abuse increasing to a frightening extent.

But, Westminster alone around that time was making well over one hundred million pounds a year from parking charges – according to a newspaper report – so, in some ways there were vested interests in leaving things as they were.

It was only in 2023 that the Lord Mayor of London, newly elected, did as he had promised to do in his manifesto and imposed a twenty-mile-an-hour limit, cars and lorries, on the whole of London.

At the same time (they were working together for a change) the government added a further ten per cent tax on all fossil fuels – petrol and diesel – in a bid to find funds to help to pay for the proposed Severn Dam.

This had been talked about for years. A vast dam across the River Severn estuary. Not rising particularly high, but very long. A hydroelectric scheme that would use the dammed-up tidal rise across the whole estuary to generate electricity as the tide ebbed, a series of generators set up at intervals along the dam. Hitherto opposed by environmental interests, not least being the bird world preservationists and also hindered by the usual difficulty – that tides only flow for half the time. They ebb for the other half. Fine, you can generate as the water flows either way but at high and low tide – nothing. No flow of water, no electricity. They proposed getting over this by building very big liquid hydrogen storage tanks on the mudflats, covering them with soil and grass for the wildlife, electrolysing the water to hydrogen and oxygen during night-time, release the oxygen, store the hydrogen and then use it as a power source to get electricity, getting oxygen back from the air and releasing water as a waste product, using that electricity when the tide was not moving. Very environmentally friendly, a natural, renewable resource. Very expensive to build. Not a split nucleus in sight.

Measures were aimed at getting people out of cars into buses, and more and better underground trains were promised. It was also projected that twenty miles per hour would cut down accidents by fifty per cent. They had figures to prove it.

I spent a lot of time in London, employed six drivers, men and women, to drive and exhibit our cars, spent money on advertising, appeared on telly interviews, and began to sell cars. Main selling points: NO pollution, cheap fuel, less accidents but still your own wheels. Demand began to build up.

I, confidently, gambled and we set up a full production assembly line.

Other cities followed on and three years later I handed over all sales and production to Anglesey Cars plc. Parent company again Anglesey plc and nothing more to do with me. Val handled the legal side and Research and Development became a small unit indeed.

By that time – 2026 – other things had happened in my life.

My father had died the year before, with no warning – a massive heart attack while he was out in the field superintending his willow plantation annual cutting.

Divorce

In 2022 Anghared was seventeen and had left her sixth-form college intending to go to Aberystwyth University to study maths, a course that included a large portion of Computer Studies, way beyond my comprehension. But first she was to take a year out and travel the world with Margaret – Marge – Jamieson, a friend from college, plus two other lads they had met that year who Jayne and I hardly knew, although in the last few weeks before departure we saw quite a lot of them, and the whole four lived in our house for three days before they left.

I must admit, looking back on it, it all seemed very low key. They took everything into their own hands, organised injections, visas, passports, open-dated tickets… everything. All through the internet, all information about what to do, where to go and who to contact supplied via the computer by youngsters who had done it before. I had a web site in the office, Jayne had her own at home so we would be in instant contact by e-mail and off they went. Vanished for a year! Australia first stop, a long stay, working in a number of jobs and then slowly wending their way back through India, South Africa, jump to Italy and up through Europe. I followed their adventures as though reading a book about strangers.

The girls split from the boys soon after flying to Australia so that didn't last long. Anghared had confidently told Jayne and I that she didn't need any sex or contraceptive advice, both girls were fully armed and, I gathered after their return, were now fully experienced! 'It's all right, Dad, don't worry.' And off she went to university and I didn't worry… much! But what can a parent do? I remembered my own escapades and hoped for the best.

Jayne's attitude was that we were there if needed, just shout. And occasionally Anghared shouted from university during the next three years, either over the internet or while at home. She always consulted Jayne who always seemed to know what to do.

Jayne always told me about these things. Anghared knew I knew. I was spectator in this marathon but well aware that I was valued and we watched various boyfriends come and go.

Odd…!

Being in almost the same position myself!

One relationship ending, albeit slowly. Another fighting to find its feet. Feeling, at the age of forty, no wiser than Anghared at eighteen, feeling all the anxieties and deep emotional insecurities of being in love – whatever that might mean; a whole compendium of complexities that it doesn't help to try to understand or analyse, one just goes round and round in ever-decreasing circles until vanishing in a cloud of incomprehension – or bursting through the layers of introspection into a clear sky of bewildering happiness.

Bewildering because, in my case, perpetually plagued by concern for those two girls.

Anghared, I felt, was old enough to understand, Olwen not so. Jayne and I presented to the world and to our children, a couple who were functioning amicably and well. Many of our friends and the parents of many of our children's friends had separated and divorced, not always easily. I had seen how upset the children of those relationships had been. How, in many cases, it had deeply, adversely, affected them. Some got over it and coped, some didn't. Jayne and I did not openly fight or be unpleasant, I felt it incumbent on me to stick things out until Olwen should be old enough, until I knew she would understand and be able to cope with the situation. Possibly until she left university. Until then Jayne and I would continue to present a united front and I would either go without my sexual, sensual reassurance, proper companionship, shared fun, or I had to be very careful and conceal such activities. Or rediscover a full, satisfying relationship with Jayne.

And as I have told you, when I tried she carefully, comprehensively and kindly, said she didn't want that. And I slowly, over the next few years, realised that absolutely, really, and truly, she just wasn't made my way and I wasn't made her way. No blame, no guilt. Just that was the way it was.

How to manage things for everyone to feel as secure *and* happy as possible? Jayne and I held things together until 2027, until Olwen was twenty and living with her own boyfriend in Manchester, working in a hectic environment designing costumes for television. Anghared, the elder of the two, not yet married, a research assistant for computer studies, doing some lecturing at Aberystwyth University.

Then we divorced, sold our unconventional house and Jayne got her own, smaller one, down near the sea in Beaumaris.

I wanted to move into the cottage with Val but she would have none of it, so I bought a fully improved and modernised small old farmhouse up on the hillside above Red Wharf Bay, secluded and peaceful with a considerable garden, not far from Research and Development, not far from Bangor and a quick train to London, and the girls sometimes brought boyfriends to stay and, eventually, husbands and children.

That considerable garden was mostly a field with overgrown encroaching hedges, a large lawn with flowering shrubs around it, and a small patch of scrub oak and hazel woodland with a stream running through it. In the early years of my residence there I did little but cut the grass when it got impossible. In later years it has given myself and Elen immeasurable pleasure, hard work and joy.

After Jayne had told me firmly and finally that she wanted to be left in peace to get on with her way of life I spent a few months in limbo. Plagued by concern for the girls, angry in a way, with Jayne – and myself – burying my doubts and desires in work and walks in the wind, going for miles along deserted beaches, through forestry plantations and up onto mountains. Not climbing them, mostly devouring them at speed on paths and over moorland or sometimes wandering lazily by the side of some stream, listening, looking, seeking salve and solitude.

Until, on one wet Sunday morning, I rang Val at her cottage and invited myself over for coffee.

Trousers and a high-necked pullover, a touch of lipstick, bare feet, loose hair held back by a black headband. Coffee and toast in the small conservatory, her late breakfast... 'Have some with my own home-made Seville orange marmalade?'

I had two thick slices, causing her to toast more and we caught up on activities. Me, electric cars, and she her legal work, in general terms, not to abuse confidentiality. That didn't take long.

We sat a while in silence, watching the rain suddenly blowing in from the sea in a vicious tree-bending squall, drumming on the polyvinyl roof. Me, wondering what to do or say next. Wondering why I was there really! Why *had* I come?

'Come inside the house,' said Val, getting up from her chair, 'I'm going to light a fire. It's too noisy in here with this rain.'

We took up breakfast things, dumping them in the kitchen.

'Choose a CD, something cheerful like Strauss waltzes or something, while I light the fire.'

No questions from her as to why I was there.

The fire caught and burned up. 'Here, read the papers.' She threw them into my lap. 'Stay to salad lunch, how's Jayne and the girls?' But she didn't stop for a reply, went off to slice lettuce and tomatoes, refusing my offer of help.

I didn't read the papers. I looked at the books on her shelves and when she came back we were able to talk about her interests – the history of Wales, the history of the slate quarries of North Wales, Welsh harp music and songs. The countryside and coasts of Anglesey, plants and, to a lesser extent, birds. And cooking.

No mention or sign of a partner.

An early glass or two of white wine, an early lunch and, with clearing skies, we drove down to nearby Llanddwyn for whose car park she had a season ticket, left the car and walked all the way along the beach and round the island at the end. Very few other people about, hardly talking, often walking separately as something caught somebody's interest and the other walked on. Companionable, undemanding, easy.

I drove her back to the cottage for tea and buttered crumpets by the revived fire. She had a load of legal papers to read through that evening, ready for the next day, so I went back home.

But I could come for breakfast next Sunday, if I liked and we would go up into the hills, she would show me one of her favourite deserted slate quarries over near Waenfawr. 'Ask Jayne if she would like to come too,' said Val as I left.

But Jayne didn't want to so Val and I had breakfast – eggs and bacon, plenty of home-made, wholemeal toast, local butter and her home made marmalade and off we went, up into the hills, well fed.

A lovely, clear day, late autumn and not many people about. The colours of the leaves turned reds and orange and yellow, beginning to spin down in ones and twos, not yet the full swirl of cascading colour whenever a breeze plucked at them.

Val in walking shoes but boots in the back of the car with my wellingtons, waterproof climbing jackets, just in case, but only wearing white shirt and v-neck woollen jumper, mountaineering trousers and colourful socks as she got in beside me. A hand momentarily on my thigh… 'Let's go…'

We parked and walked up through wet, badly drained fields, over walls of slate waste, past tumbled dumps of more waste that had, by now, scrub oak and ash, hazel and bramble, self seeded and growing wild in the crevices among moss and ferns. A damp overgrown sheep track winding upwards through the slate slabs that, after a while, joined a smooth, straight incline sloping at a steep angle up to a ruined cable house with rusted narrow-gauge iron railway lines half buried under more moss and ferns.

When we got up to the cable houses there was the drum, tilted to one side, one end come off its bearing, coils of thick metal cable tangled and twisted, a hazard to trousers and skin, very rusty and spiky where the finer metal wires of which it was composed had broken and sprung apart.

In front and below us now was the great quarry hole. Its sides weathered away and crumbling, a scree of loose slate colonised by small trees and yet more fern and bramble down which, Val decreed, we were to scramble. Here and there round the perimeter of the quarry hole, terraces where miners had delved deeper, working the face back where quality material was found, leaving sections to jut out as natural outcrops where the stone was not good enough. Even here the occasional ash sapling had found a crack to germinate and grow.

The bottom of the quarry, part rubble filled, part pool of stagnant water.

We scrambled down into the gloom, holding on to the saplings and tufts of grass, slithering over wet slate as water oozed its way from above to drip on down into the depth below, sliding faster nearer the bottom and landing, together, in a tangle on a heap of mushy, muddy, rotted leaves and stinking black ooze. Val on top of me, laughing her head off, gave me a great ultra-passionate kiss, wriggled her body on top of mine and was off and away to wash what she could in the water of the small lake at the base of the quarry face.

We pushed our way round the edge of the water, gazed up at a fine thread of stream falling from way up on the rock, the constant drip of drops seeping through mosses and over stones all around us and birds twittering in anger at our disturbing their haven. A mixture of nettles and wild geranium growing in the leaf-mould, richer, debris of the quarry floor.

A magic, half underworld, green, wet and peaceful site which must have rung with the clamour of hammer, the crack of explosion as rock was blasted and the rattle of windlass and more distant railway trucks moving the rough slabs. Saplings, rubble and birdsong.

And when we were back in Val's cottage she showed me photographs and books about the old quarries; history and lives, families and communities, totally dependent on slate dug from open quarries like the one we had just visited or from caverns deep underground as anyone can see if they visit the Llechwedd Quarry at Blainau Ffestiniog, open to the public, deep underground.

We spent many other days in that late autumn and early winter visiting other deserted slate quarries and I, in my turn, learned about the lives of quarrymen, the economics of slate production and the details of the slow decline in demand for slate until, nowadays, very little is used on roofs, a situation I have done nothing to help since I, and Anglesey Roofs plc, are doing all we can to persuade people to cover their roofs in photovoltaic 'slates'.

The quarries are show places or closed down and getting over-grown. Forgotten testimony to long-gone skills, way of life and community cohesion. Slate quarry villages re-filling as the older inhabitants reach old age and die, the younger ones moving away to find work and life in towns and cities except for a few who commute; young rock-climbing people forming 'relationships' and living in the houses, crafts setting up and, often, failing or moving on. Holiday cottages 'to let' in many cases. Communities no longer with a common cause.

But living conditions in those times were hard, wages shockingly low; no one would argue for a return of the bad old days. It is too easy to build a picturesque image of the slate quarries in their hey-day.

Val and I enjoyed and explored off and on, among other visits to other places, the haunting, romantic beauty of the slate quarries of Wales, part of our own romantic love affair.

For the next five years I lived a double life. Staying based at 'home' with Jayne and the girls. Usually in the same bedroom as Jayne, although, years before, we had installed two three-quarter sized beds, side by side, for comfort and space, so not in the same bed. Never any physical contact, no hugs, no kisses; but a friendly co-operation in running the household, shared expenses and the girls, young women by now, having a home and two parents as a base.

No questions asked as to where or what the other was up to and, as I have said, a void for me until I rang Val that Sunday morning and joined her for late breakfast. After that we increasingly spent time together, usually a Sunday, sometimes of an evening during the week but Val had a heavy workload and we were both wary of commitment. No sex and a rare touching of hands.

Breakfasts and walks in the mountains or by the sea. Long walks, companionable and easy. Lunch in a pub, and back for an evening meal cooked expertly by Val. Quiet music and Val working at her papers; back 'home' to fairly early and unquestioned-by-Jayne bed for me.

Platonic.

Who was this Plato fellow anyway?

More like impotence on my part. And from what Val had said in the early days, she had had enough of men jumping into bed with her and then demanding all of her time and life. So we stayed companions and not lovers.

Until one very wet Sunday early in November.

I drove over earlyish, as usual, for breakfast, through driving rain, leaves squishy and squashed under the tyres, windscreen wipers swishing madly from side to side, branches bare and bending in the wind. Val was still in bed when I arrived so I lit the fire, boiled eggs and cooked the toast, made the coffee and took it up to her, sitting dishevelled and half asleep still, in half of the king-sized bed.

'Come on,' she said, patting the bed beside her. 'Join me.'

I took of shoes, socks and trousers and clambered in.

We ate our breakfast, hardly talking, half listening to music on the radio, Val still half asleep, me lulled back to being half asleep, warmed by the kitchen and comfort of the bed after the cold drive over. Val moved the tray of things off the bed and snuggled down beside me.

'Come on, cuddle down for a while, let's have a lazy day.' She put a hand on my arm, gently tugging.

I hauled off shirt and pullover and wriggled lower in the bed, pulling the duvet up over my shoulders, turning towards her as she turned and curled away, so I moved close and we fitted together, a curve of bodies, warm and soft, her bum fitting into my tummy, my arm over hers reaching down to hold her hand. The back of my hand nestling, warm and soft, against her breast.

And we lay there, quiet for a while, listening to the wind and rain and quiet music. At least I assumed she was listening. For my part I was in a curious state of mind and body.

Acutely aware of her physical presence. Sensitive to the slide of the silk of her nightie against my skin, conscious of the close contact of our legs and feet. My fingers gently touching and caressing hers, being caressed and gently squeezed in return. My mind aroused and longing to caress her whole body from top to toe, breasts and belly, back and front, exploring every inch, and wishing for her to do the same to me.

Starved for years.

She wriggled and pushed back, against me, gave a little gurgle of a laugh and began to turn. 'Come on, turn over, I want to talk to you and hug *you* for a change.'

We reversed positions and I could feel the warmth of her breath on my neck, the soft heat of her breasts against my back, her lap warming my bum and our legs and feet again entwined.

Her hand momentarily reached over to squeeze mine and then, the stretch being uncomfortable, her hand dropped to my belly and began soft circular caresses round and round, enlarging the circles until she touched thicker hair lower down, kissed the back of my neck and murmured, 'Nice?'

'Of course, wonderful.'

'Good. Turn on your back and don't talk.' I did as asked and her hand moved lower, down, pushing into the top of my underpants, finding my balls and penis, soft and full but not a proper erection, and she encircled them with her hand, squeezing gently.

After a moment or two... 'What's the matter, doesn't this excite you?'

'Of course it does. That feels wonderful, I love your touch, I want your kisses, I need your caresses. But... I think I am impotent. I haven't had a proper erection for years. Jayne and I stopped having sex long ago and I haven't slept with anyone else since before we were married.'

'Oh you poor man!' Val sat up in the bed. Fully awake now, and interested. 'How do you manage? Masturbate every few days?'

'Not even that, or at least, not very often and I seem to be able to get an ejaculation even without a full erection. But it's not the same thing.'

I lay there, stretched out in the bed, thinking back about how little the lack of sex and bothered me over those years but aware, at that very moment, how much I wanted to make love, fully, with Val. And yet... no erection... so how could I?

I said as much to Val. I told her how beautiful and seductively entrancing she looked in her white silk nightie – which she promptly removed.

I told her how beautiful and seductive her breasts were and she leaned over to place a nipple in my mouth. 'Go on, bite.'

And I did, pulling her over on top of me, except that she didn't need much pulling and she kissed me with a long, deep, tongue searching kiss, pressing the whole length of her body against mine, moving her thighs, seeking a response. Then, coming up for breath, 'Remember when we fell on those wet leaves at the bottom of the quarry?' she asked with a wicked gleam in her eyes. 'I wanted you to fuck me then. Come on, let's do it now.'

'But I can't!'

'Try. Come on, I'll do all the hard work.' She grinned, sat back on her heels and lifted her breasts, showing off. 'Nice, eh?' she took a nipple between each finger, pinching. 'Look, they are getting bigger and harder. Now for your cock!'

She removed my underpants expertly and took my penis between both hands, moving up and down, exposing the glans and licking the tip. Gently, incessantly; encouraging. Talking to me.

'I want you, I want you. Now; inside me, hard and big and deep inside me. Fill me with sperm. Come on. Up you come, up you come. There's a good boy, up; come on, up... ooh lovely... now, come on, inside me, now, I'm all wet and ready!'

And it did stay hard enough for long enough for Val to scream with joy and pleasure with her orgasm and I lay, still inside her but small and gone away; no ejaculation.

We lay there, aware again of the wind and rain and the music, until our breathing subsided and I moved off her to lie beside her, holding hands; still, quiescent.

'Well,' she said at length, 'that's all right then. Thank you.'

'Only just,' I said. 'And not really properly.'

'Never mind,' she grinned happily, her hand again between my legs. 'At least you got in there and I had a lovely time.' Her hand again gently squeezing, my cock again filling, my desire arousing, but not enough to gain a full hard erection.

And that was the pattern of things for about another two months.

Many times we made love, in all sorts of places, in all sorts of ways, using fingers and tongues, exploring, caressing, seeking, exciting; always she achieved her orgasm, seeming torn apart by the ecstasy of it, not always from my penetration, quite happy, when I failed, as often happened, to get an erection hard enough to push in, to climax from the use of tongue or fingers. Always saying 'It doesn't matter how we do it, it's lovely, let's do it again.'

Wonderful, erotic, beautiful, vital Val...

My cousin Pete, from Manchester, when we were boys had both hands covered in warts when we were about eleven. Doctors tried various ways of removing them, including some special ointment to 'burn' them off. Nothing really worked until his mother took him to a homeopath who talked, and more importantly, listened to him for about an hour and a half, gave him two little white pills and said the warts would go away in about a month.

And they did. Every single one of them. Pete showed me when they came to visit. Holding both hands out instead of hiding them out of sight as he used to. A changed boy. Confident and happy!

I remembered this and found a homeopath's telephone number in the book. Yes, she was a homeopath...

A she...? Oh well...

Could she please help restore me to a full erection.

Silence.

'Would you please repeat that,' her voice calm, doubtful.

I did so, adding my name and age and address.

Still doubtful, calm, enquiring. How did I get her phone number? Could I please tell her a little bit more about myself? Not my problem, just about who I was.

After a few more explanatory sentences she butted in. 'Oh, I know who you are! You're the man who wants us all to buy an electric car! Yes, all right.' And she booked me an appointment for half past nine one morning the following week.

When I got there she explained that her initial hesitation was because the request was unusual, coming from a man, and she was scared of it being a hoax or some sort of sexual come-on.

Both of us feeling reassured, I was seated on a rather hard small couch with her opposite in a more comfortable office chair.

She told me: the consultation was open-ended, she never knew how long things would take, there was no hurry and I could always come another time if needs be. Could she please record our conversation since she always needed to go through everything again in order to understand things properly and could she also take written notes as she went along? Thirty-five pounds an hour, to the nearest quarter, roughly.

Everything was totally 'in confidence' of course.

Very professional. And of course she could.

'Now, please tell me whatever you like, so that I can understand what the problem is.'

Quiet, confident, undemanding. Middle-aged. The small consulting room, part of her family home, books in the hallway a mixture of all sorts including school textbooks I had seen as I passed through. Sensible dark-blue jumper, cardigan and trousers, sensible black shoes and socks, hair greying a bit, cut neat but not old fashioned. A friendly, warm face and voice. No threat. No direct questions. Just, 'Please tell me whatever you like.'

I had not realised what emotion had been hidden away inside me. I cried when I spoke of the drifting apart of Jayne and myself. I recovered and cried again and when speaking of my concern for our two children. I spoke of my work, Jayne's work, my lonely walks and the pleasure that also came from that loneliness, of my enjoyment of the beauty of things and I told her (with Val's permission and encouragement, but naming no names) of my involvement with another woman and of the difficulty of my achieving a full erection, and often no ejaculation.

I ended, after what had seemed like half an hour or so, but which was really nearly two hours, by saying that if she concluded that I was simply getting too old for all this then that would be all right. Val and I had plenty of fun and pleasure with things the way they were. But if she *could* improve matters…?

'Yes,' she said, she thought she could. Please would I call back in three days to collect a few pills. She needed time to listen again to what I had said, go through her notes and then decide what to do about it.

I paid for the hour and a half, which was all she would allow me to pay, and returned in the three days' time.

She gave me two small white pills in a small plastic tube. 'Take one today. Just put it under your tongue and let it slowly melt away. And another in one week's time. You should see some improvement in a few weeks. You may feel more emotional than usual for the next few months. Come back and see me again if you want to in about six month's time.'

And that was that!

Whether it was Val's personality, technique or determination, or whether it was the effect of the pills, or my own desires taking command again, I do not know, perhaps a mixture of all those things.

Anyway. Slowly, the thing came back and I was able to satisfy all Val's demands and achieve my own full measure of pleasure before another year had passed. And I still can. Not so often now I am over eighty, and Elen is also growing, gracefully, older. But we still enjoy each other's company, personality and body.

As I have said, I am a very lucky man.

I did go back to see that homeopathic lady about a year after that initial consultation. Took her a box of chocolates and half a dozen bottles of wine. Gave her Val's best wishes and thanks and my own heartfelt appreciation.

She laughed, 'Good,' she said. 'Come again if you ever need to. But I doubt you will. We'll drink to your good healths and new life, my husband and I.'

Elen knows a lot about homeopathic remedies and healthy eating. Do you? I recommend to everyone that they find out about these things. Good health is very important you know, and you only have one body, one life. Look after it!

Agriculture

My father died from a sudden massive heart attack in the November of 2025; this was five years after I had begun seeing so much of Val and three years before those girls were grown up enough to handle a divorce between Jayne and myself.

He had been out in his willow plantation supervising the annual cutting of coppice ready to be transported to the 'green' power station at Rhosgoch here on Anglesey.

Back in 2002 this had been an electricity-generating power plant using gas from under the North Sea for eighty per cent of its fuel. The other twenty per cent came from willow coppices, miscanthus grass, forest waste and rhododendron. The rhododendron supply had dried up over the years as repeated cutting and grubbing up by conservancy teams had reduced this invasive weed to virtually nothing.

Rhododendron can colonise mountainsides rapidly by seeding. Once established it creates a complete ground cover, preventing grass, heather or young tree growth and it had been encroaching along the mountain valleys of North Wales for many years, destroying by enveloping, pasture required for sheep, cows, goats and ponies. The conservancy agencies had tried to contain it by cutting it back but it simply grew up again rapidly and they didn't really have enough money to fund a serious attack on it. The rhododendron had been winning the battle and steadily advancing until the power station had started operations and paid for the cut-down rhododendron branches; they paid just enough to make it financially possible to employ foresters to cut down and grub up. They didn't pay enough to make it a viable proposition to actually grow rhodies as a crop for fuel.

But willow and miscanthus grass *are* a viable crop.

Miscanthus grass needs reasonably good soil and if manure is added to the ground you get a very heavy crop indeed. The stuff grows over six feet high and produces a lot of fibre. Cut it dry and you have a good fuel to burn in a special furnace to produce electricity. By 2002 quite a number of Anglesey farmers had contracted to grow, and the power station had contracted to buy, miscanthus grass.

The stuff had certainly grown, but cutting and keeping this material dry enough to burn usefully had proved not so easy in our climate. Willow, however, was a much better bet.

Dad had been a pioneer in starting his willow coppice, had wanted it for shredding and mulching his pick-your-own pathways, plus some sales for craft purposes. But when the Rhosgoch power station began to take shape and very many more acres of willow were required, he found himself to be the local expert. He was also in a position to supply thousands of eight-inch long cuttings.

At the beginning the power station found it difficult to get many farmers to start willow coppices. This was an alien crop to all of them and they got no money back from their investment for the first two years. Willow needs three years to produce coppice growth thick enough to be worth burning.

However, farming at that time was in a terrible state, beef cattle was impossible to sell at an economic price due to the mad cow disease scare, the foot and mouth epidemic and subsequent legislation, enforced burning of suspectedly infected pigs, sheep and cattle gave poor compensation and fat lamb prices were very low. Anglesey until then had, historically, not grown crops, only grass (except that, back in the Middle Ages, it had been a grain-growing area – Mon Mam Cymru – The Mother of Wales).

Farmers had been at their wits' end to find some source of income. Grants were available to pay half the cost of fencing against rabbits and establishing a coppice. The farmer had to fund the other half. A few enterprising and desperate farmers had been able, with assurances from the power station company, to borrow enough money to set up coppice areas and Dad had been there to advise.

The fact that he also strongly advocated running ducklings in these plantations – where rabbit fences kept any predators like foxes or dogs out – meant that the farmer could get some income from the sale of fattened ducks for the table. Dad already had contacts in London for the organic duckling he produced in his own coppice plantations.

At first it was the farmers' wives who took care of the ducklings; Dad arranged to collect them when they were ready for the table, to process them in his own buildings and market them in London.

It wasn't long before farmers realised that organic Barbary duckling were a better proposition than beef or lamb or willow; run willow and duckling together and you had quite a good thing going.

Some farmers in North Yorkshire and others in Norfolk had formed their own marketing group to sell their own particular 'specially good quality' lamb or beef products. A small group, which rapidly grew larger, of farmers on Anglesey set up their own co-operative to produce and sell to the restaurants and butchers of England and anyone else who wanted to buy, top quality, very tasty, free range, organic Barbary ducklings.

They also started running chickens in the coppice lands on the same principle, they were able to ask a slightly higher price than the ordinary table chickens produced in ways that were becoming less and less popular with the public. Their product certainly was of a far higher quality, taste and health wise, organic and no trace of fertilisers or chemicals.

'Anglesey Table Birds' became as well known as Cornish Cream before many years were out. Dad became consultant to the co-op; they built their own collection and marketing establishment in the centre of Anglesey, near Gaerwen, and all Dad's duckling and chickens were sold through them.

At the same time public confidence in beef and lamb meat had recovered and a separate co-op formed to market that.

But it all had to be organic. Public confidence was not restored to 'ordinary stuff'. Too much media coverage had been given to the use of chemicals in agriculture with the resultant health scares for people ever to feel really secure about chemical farming. There had also been a great furore over growing even experimental GM – Genetically Modified – crops.

So all willow-coppice areas were grown under certified organic conditions and the ducklings and chickens marketed as 'organic'. These poultry were fed on home-grown feed like maize and oats. Comfrey was grown among the willow and the birds ate innumerable slugs and other insects. All food fed to the poultry had to be organic itself so all these farms soon became completely organic, as did the beef and lamb producing farms.

With their own organic marketing co-operatives set up it wasn't long before their marketing directors were suggesting greater diversification and many farmers began to grow fruit and vegetables for the English markets. Organic, health enhancing, non-carcinogenic, and very tasty.

And now, here in 2065, Anglesey Organic produce is synonymous with good quality and taste; we cannot grow enough of what people are completely confident is the best.

Somewhere along the line, I forget quite when, the farmers of Anglesey agreed to allow no genetically modified crop growing whatsoever within the island, which, although I am not convinced is for totally valid reasons, has served to be another good selling point.

Our ever-growing 'crop' of tourists comes here for our good food as much as for any other reason and departs laden with what they know are absolutely fresh fruit, vegetables and meat although, as you know, we now have refrigerated containers going daily into England selling ultra-tasty and healthy produce that is in the shops the next day.

Anglesey agriculture is a thriving business once again and the countryside has changed from when I was a boy. Willow coppice covers all poor and wet land, regularly cut in a three-year rotation to supply fuel to our power station. The nuclear power station at Wylfa, near Holyhead was phased out in 2022 and all nuclear contamination removed. The Rhosgoch willow power station is fuelled only by willow and no longer needs to burn gas from under the sea.

The willow coppices provide shelter for all the good quality agricultural land under vegetable and fruit crops, the grassland has only Welsh Black cattle grazing on it and also produces the earliest and tastiest lamb anyone could wish for. Areas of comfrey grow for animal feed or compost production – miscanthus grass proved to be not so good as a fuel but is ideal as a source of fibre for compost making.

All Anglesey's sewage treatment units are now compost-producing establishments using miscanthus grass and comfrey grown on contract by farmers to mix with treated sewage and producing very good compost. Sold to private gardeners, exported to garden centres in England and used on farms to produce better crops.

Polythene tunnels are also now an intensive method of production, well hidden behind coppice and windbreaks of planted, but natural, species of oak and other indigenous trees, early lettuce being a particularly good product grown in our compost enriched soil.

We are especially fortunate in that underground water flows across Anglesey coming clear and unpolluted from the mountains of Snowdonia. With that on tap and free electricity from wind, sun and battery storage, just as Dad and I did all those years ago with my mother's first greenhouses, protected crops are a very viable proposition.

We have become a second Evesham and are once again Mon Man Cymru – the Mother of Wales.

When Dad died I asked Les to take over as manager of the farm so he moved into the farmhouse with his family. Bronwen had been managing the Plas gardens for years, with Mum supervising but now virtually retired. Mum moved to a cottage down in Beaumaris near to shops and doctors and no need to drive her car unless she wanted to. She died in her sleep in 2031, aged seventy-one, frequently visited by myself, Anghared and Olwen. She always kept in close contact with Jayne and could never really understand why we separated; her own marriage had been, sexually, sensually and from a companionship point of view, a very rewarding one; not understanding that Jayne was not so inclined.

Research and Development stayed very small and I spread myself around. Still about three days a week involved in various ways with education. Doing as much as I could to encourage every household to produce as much electricity as they could for themselves, mainly by installing photovoltaic slates on every bit of roof area, working with the factory to reduce the cost of each slate. And being more and more involved in all aspects of council work. I had been elected a councillor the year before Dad died and was finding myself in great demand as our policies of doubling up on teachers, social workers and police numbers began to show results.

Council work began to take up more and more of my time and I put my small team in Research and Development on to finding out all they could about the advantages and disadvantages of constructing two hydro-electric dams, one at either end of the Menai Straits. They were to prepare a pilot feasibility study.

By the end of 2027 they had enough stuff ready for me to take it, first of all to the Board of Directors of Anglesey Power plc, and then to introduce the concept to the County Council.

Anglesey Power directors knew that I knew what I was talking about and said 'Go ahead.' The council voiced many more concerns and asked that public meetings be held so that everyone would know what was proposed and could voice their objections, agreement or amendments, as the case may be.

It took two years of constant public meetings, small group discussions, a lot of publicity in the press and the formation of a committee before proper plans were laid before the council, accepted and yet another company, 'The Menai Strait Water Power Company', was in being.

All Research and Development staff moved to the new firm and I closed the premises down that we had used for so many years. Everyone moved to new offices on the side of the Straits opposite Caernarfon.

We intended building one dam across the narrow part of the Straits somewhere between Port Dinorwic and Caernarfon, and one across somewhere between Menai Bridge and Beaumaris. Our surveyors got to work to identify exactly where.

At the end of those preliminary two years a strange fact had come clearly to light.

Everybody was in favour of building these two dams. By then everybody was fully aware of the need to produce power – electricity – from a natural, renewable source and do away with the need for nuclear power stations or the burning of fossil fuels, be they either oil or coal.

But many fully justifiable concerns were expressed.

At first these were knee-jerk reactions from people who didn't really know what we were proposing to do on the ground/in the water.

'How high was the water going to rise when the dams were built?' And the answer was, of course, 'No higher than it already gets at high tide.' There would still be a rise and fall of the tide within the confined area exactly as before. All we would do was force that moving tidal water to enter and exit through our hydroelectric sluice gates where our turbines would be installed.

A much more intrusive effect would be that boats could only enter or leave the enclosed area at the times of high or low tide through 'gates' in the dam. This, we acknowledged, was unavoidable, perhaps not too high a price to pay for cheaper electricity and no greenhouse gas emission.

The nature conservancy folk were, at first, alarmed that we would be altering the natural habitat and disturbing wildlife for ever. But when they realised that would not be the case, they took the wider view that we would be doing our bit to help reduce atmospheric pollution and that if the whole world would turn to natural, renewable, non-polluting resources then everybody – humans, animal, bird and plant growth – would benefit.

I was one of the members of Anglesey County Council who worked closely with this development and it took a lot of my time. Construction work started in 2027 and we held a grand opening in the summer of 2032, five years later. All details are available in the official archives but I remember the date particularly well because that was the year in which Jayne and I became properly divorced, sold up the family home, both girls now living with their partners in Aberystwyth and Manchester respectively and I bought my small farmhouse up above Red Wharf Bay. Still remaining in a full, close and friendly relationship with Val but each of us at our own base. Very independent, Val.

The construction of the two Menai Straits barrages encouraged all those folk who had been advocating for years that a dam be built across the Severn Estuary; a far bigger enterprise than ours but involving all the same principles and objections. I accepted a consultancy position on their development board which paid me a useful salary for the next eight years. This got augmented by other consultancies in Europe, America and even further afield that brought me in a steady income until I retired in 2050 from anything that meant travelling on business, by which time I was sixty-seven and well settled with Elen up on our hillside.

Tourism

Val died in a stupid car accident that should never have happened.

The years between my divorce from Jayne and Val's death were extremely happy ones for me. Anghared and Olwen were leading lives of their own, there was no bitterness between Jayne and myself – we occasionally went out for an evening meal, keeping a friendship going and talking about the two girls and our mutual friends. Now that we were separated Jayne seemed to take a greater interest in what I was doing and those meetings were something I came to look forward to.

Val encouraged this although she never went as far as to suggest that we made up a threesome. She said it made the whole thing less threatening for her. Totally committed relationships filled her with a sense of claustrophobia. She did not want to live in the same house as any man. She did not want children and young people hardly ever impinged on her life, although one caused her death. But she also never wanted to go out with any other man after we had met.

'You are "safe",' she used to say. 'I can get away from you, in terms of both space and time, whenever I want to. And so it is not often that I want to. If I couldn't, I would feel stifled and trapped.'

And once I had regained a full-erection capability – which took about six months and those homeopathic pills I told you about – then our sex life was infinitely varied and often repeated.

Val loved to cook exotic meals, spent money on wine, and enjoyed going to classical concerts. We frequently went to London, Manchester or Liverpool for a concert, stayed for a night or two and explored those cities. We more often travelled the length and breadth of Wales searching out its history, enjoying its beauty, walking its rivers and streams, climbing hills and mountains, always discovering a bit of magic wherever we went and taking our own magic with us. She was an unending source of fun and innovation. Never the same, not wanting to be bored by repetition, needing to be wooed in our love making some of the time, taking enterprising initiatives herself as often as not. A wonderful, and beautiful, woman.

Liking to be in her own home, demanding the best of meals and hotels when away. We revelled in each other's company and did not seek the companionship of others, avoiding business lunches or expense account dinners whenever we could. I was devastated when a young man, high on some drug or other, smashed into her car on the motorway as she was returning early one evening from Chester where she had been attending a case in the assize court.

I didn't get involved in the police case against him. I hadn't been there, we weren't married. There was no reason to. I did attend the funeral. I had met her mother, not her father, so I kept to the back of the few who were there and I then plunged myself into council work.

Her cottage was sold and I virtually simply camped in mine. I got a woman from a house down below me by the sea to keep the place clean and lived on baked beans and egg and chips. Often buying take-away food from wherever and going for long, long, lonely walks around the coast of Anglesey and up into Snowdonia. Walking to exhaust myself, not letting myself think, not enjoying where I was, crying for no apparent reason on occasion, sobbing and stumbling along. Wallowing in my deprivation.

The Severn Dam was my salvation, that and the steady development of our tourist 'industry'. They had started construction work down in the Severn Estuary and many other countries were interested. I became a roving consultant during the four years it took to actually complete the construction. I took a permanent room in an hotel near the site where I got good food and wine and considerate care and continued to roam and be consulted about environmental planning aspects of similar installations worldwide for many years after that.

In 2040 the Severn Dam was completed, Mervyn died and I retired from the board of Anglesey Education plc.

This was because I was getting much more involved with the development of tourism on the island and since that covered many other areas of interest, I was no longer able to devote the three days a week to education.

Anglesey had had a Tourist Officer for many years – way back to the 1980s; there had been three of them over that time, all women, and their importance and that of the tourist industry had been vital to the economy of the island.

Even before they had been appointed, people from Lancashire had regularly come to the beaches and cottages for their holidays, back to Victorian times. That had been a thriving time for Anglesey, agriculture was the main occupation of the inhabitants with drovers taking cattle, pigs and geese down along the old drovers roads to the markets of London.

In the early 2000s agriculture had hit rock bottom, thanks to mad cow disease and people's reluctance to eat beef – the foot and mouth epidemic hadn't helped – and the tourists preferred to fly to Majorca, Greece, anywhere it seemed, to find sun or excitement, taking advantage of package holidays and relatively cheap air fares.

Not so many wanted the rather risky weather of North Wales. However, those tourist officers had steadily done a very good job and Anglesey boasted many well equipped holiday cottages, converted self catering apartments in old farm buildings and hotels that continually, over the years, improved their cuisine. Many of the farmhouses offered bed and breakfast of the highest quality with home cooking that was, and still is, out of this world.

I first became aware of 'tourists' and 'tourism' when my mother opened her gardens at the Plas. Because she and her team had reconstructed the old Victorian/Edwardian gardens as they had been and because they dressed in authentic period costumes Mum had got a lot of good publicity in the press and on television. She also produced a pamphlet describing the gardens which was to be found in all the tourist offices, hotels and wherever, and gardening magazines ran articles about the place with the result that interested people came in their thousands especially to see the Plas.

Having got there of course they visited the castle in Beaumaris and walked round the town and wanted to know more about what was to be seen on the island. Many of them visited Dad's nearby organic unit, often buying beef or duck and invariably expressing interest in my windmills producing electricity for the greenhouses.

Once Jayne and I had built our house nearby they wanted to see round that and also the turbine I had set in the Afon Wen. And after the straw houses were developed we directed them over there.

This 'straw house' village had generated great interest among all enthusiasts for self-build and the use of natural resources, again the project had received media attention and a whole different host of tourists regularly visited that place, often people from other countries who were interested in, and had heard about, this self-contained, self-built village which sold its excess electricity to the main grid and made a profit!

Some of our historic sites realised the value of dressing in costume and quite a number of farms opened themselves to the public where you could spend a day, or a week, seeing what it was like.

All our electricity generating systems were fully open to anyone interested and highly geared not only to producing electricity but also to generating interest and sales of turbines, windmills... In fact all our factories opened to the public – the electric car factory where anyone could test drive a car, the school computer production line where anyone, especially teachers from other areas, could test our programs.

By about 2040, when I began to be more involved with all this, there was hardly a place on Anglesey that was not of interest to a visitor. Back in 2005 a complete coastal walk round Anglesey had been negotiated with landowners and the whole island is a bird watcher's paradise, particularly sea birds and waders.

When the whole of the Isle of Anglesey was designated 'organic' we really began to be inundated with visitors for all the reasons I have given you, and others I can't think of at the moment. Very good for our island's economy but a bit congested on the roads.

And it was with that road congestion that I got more involved.

Nearly every household was producing its own electricity by then, mostly from photovoltaic slates on the roof, augmented by wind power where possible, stored in batteries and backed up by our very cheap electricity (to islanders only) from the underwater tide-powered turbines.

In 2045, seven years after our two dams in the Menai Straits started producing power, we decided that all electricity supplied to anyone on the island was to be free of charge. The whole island was anyway, by then, an exporter of electricity, many people being able to feed from their own supply into the grid for which they were paid; we were getting good input from our initial underwater tidal turbines and, once the hydroelectric power generation came on line from the dams in the Straits, we were selling a great deal of electricity to the mainland grid.

Enough to steadily pay off the debt incurred in building the dams and their turbines, making it possible to give free electricity to anyone who needed it on the island.

And then we could really revolutionise our economy and political status!

For the five years before he really fully retired, (he had opted out of banking officially many years before that,) Mervyn, and all of us, had become incensed and frustrated by the way the large banks had closed down many of their smaller branches throughout the island making it very hard for elderly folk and anyone not on the internet to get to a bank. They had done this, starting way back in the year 2000, 'in order to cut costs'. At the same time they were annually announcing great profits for their investors. What it amounted to was that they were not prepared to subsidise, to some extent, their smaller, outlying branches in order to help the local community, preferring to maintain their high profits. There is no doubt that the smaller branches were not producing the same high rate of profit due to many people banking direct, either by phone or by computer.

But we on Anglesey ran our businesses not for financial gain, although we paid good wages; we ran them to create employment. It was, mainly, the council who underwrote socially useful enterprises, not consortiums out for profit, although until the end of 2039 any borrowing required was done from the main banks.

By 2038 too many people of Anglesey (and all over the United Kingdom), mainly elderly or those not on the internet, were inconvenienced too much by the lack of a local bank. Our enterprise managers were also a bit grieved that the interest they paid on loans from the main banks was going off the island into pockets of capitalists making money by investing money.

Anglesey County Council decided to open its own bank and asked Mervyn to mastermind the process. 'Banc Mona' – The Anglesey Bank – was not out to make a profit. It would make charges enough to cover running costs *only*. It would lend money only to enterprises based on Anglesey and operating in Anglesey. Its capital would come from monies held as savings from all who had an account with the bank, on which of course normal interest would be paid to the account holders just as was done by any bank, and the County Council would stand as guarantor, as required by international banking rules.

Essentially it was a bank set up to benefit the people of Anglesey, as a convenience for local communities and as a place from which existing or new enterprises could borrow money at a rate that was not exorbitant. No profits for outsiders and no fat-cat salaries for top management. Only residents of Anglesey allowed to open accounts. Anyone found to be trying to use the bank as a source of low-interest loan, not using that money within the island, simply found the account refused and since 'our' bank required that any borrowers assets lodged as security for any loan should be assets that were already on the island, then anyone found to be taking advantage by not using that loan within the island simply found their account closed, the loan recalled and, if necessary, their assets seized. It really wasn't worth anyone trying to borrow money at our low rate and then to be operating away from the island – far less risk and trouble, for them, to bank with a mainland bank as normal.

It took Mervyn and his team two years to publicise what they were proposing to do and to obtain written commitment from a large portion of the population of the island that they would open an account with 'our' bank and transfer from the other banks.

Once Mervyn was sure of general commitment he officially opened his bank on New Year's Day 2040 with an office in Llangefni – the 'capital' of the island – and all the Anglesey plc firms that we had founded transferred all businesses and assets to Banc Mona.

Sadly Mervyn died of a heart attack six months later.

Many other businesses rapidly did the same, transferred their business and assets, since our rates of interest were to their advantage and private accounts followed suit. Banc Mona reopened any local bank premises that had shut and started negotiations with the mainstream banks to buy the buildings. These negotiations were a bit one sided really; as Mervyn pointed out to me one evening, all their customers were deserting! By about 2045 all mainstream banks had shut down all their branches on the island although anyone who wanted to could maintain an account with them through their branches in Bangor or Caernarfon on the mainland.

The Anglesey Assembly

Once we had free electricity and our own bank for everyone on Anglesey then, as a Council, we had very strong public approval and support and I thought it was time for us to move on to two developments that had long been gestating in my mind.

One very big factor in the release of greenhouse gases and the resultant pollution of our atmosphere is the use of fossil fuels in industry and transport. Nobody in their right mind on Anglesey was now using either petrol or diesel in an industrial way, with free electricity they would have been foolish to do so. But there was still an enormous number of cars and lorries using – burning – a fossil fuel on the island and sending their waste gases up into the atmosphere. Our air, unlike that of cities, did not smell of these fumes, we were not driven to wear filter masks over our noses and mouths when walking the streets, the wind coming in from the Irish Sea or off the mountains of Snowdonia rapidly dispersed our greenhouse gases but we were still contributing our share of pollution onto the world. But we are a county that is completely surrounded by sea, only connected to the mainland by two bridges – the Menai Bridge and the Britannia Bridge – the former carries foot and motorised traffic, the latter trains and a motorway-style road – the A5.

In 1984 the old Britannia Bridge, carrying rail transport only, caught fire and burned out. The opportunity was taken to strengthen the bridge and construct a motorway-style road above the rail lines and in the early years of the 2000s an entirely new motorway road running from the Britannia Bridge across Anglesey to Holyhead was built to take all traffic from the mainland through to the boat for Ireland. Nearly all of this traffic had nothing to do with the internal economy of the island and, until that motorway was constructed, it had thundered at all hours of the day and night along the A5 through the towns and villages along that route, at considerable inconvenience if not to say outright danger, to the inhabitants. And, of course, adding its share of exhaust gases to the general soup.

I wanted to have all vehicles on the island powered by electricity; to *forbid* any petrol or diesel fuel to come, in any shape or form, onto the island.

Revolutionary.

Fairly easy to do, physically, since the only ways on or off the island are the two bridges, or boat into Holyhead.

We should show the world, just as we had shown them that a whole county could go organic, that a whole county could go fossil-fuel free. And, by extrapolation, that a whole country could do the same, and why not the whole world?

But not easy to do in practice. How to persuade *everyone* on the island to use an electric car and not the conventional one. Their cars had cost a lot of money, no one was going to agree to throw them away or sell them off cheap; and what about those transport firms hurtling huge lorries across from one side of the island to the other along that new motorway en route to and from Ireland?

It took many years of negotiation, compromise and determination until we eventually succeeded and, now, an additional tourist/interested-visitor attraction is the fact that we are a totally pollution-free part of the world, more than just economically viable, our economy is thriving and people, experts, government officials and private individuals, come from all over the world to see how we are doing it and to enjoy our very healthy climate, good food, unique scenery, abundant natural wild life, particularly birds who never seem to stop singing and who you can hear wherever you are since electric engines are not the noisy things that petrol or diesel engines are.

We are as near to Utopia here on Anglesey as anyone is likely to get on this earth! Just as we hoped we would be back there at that informal meeting in Bryn's house, in July 2017.

But that has only happened recently, and I am lucky to be still alive and well enough to see and experience it. I'm eighty-two this year, not many more years to go I suppose; interesting to live through though.

And still lots to do…

I could see that it would take a bit more than just talking to stop those lorries thundering through the night across our countryside; more than persuasion to get people to swap their expensive conventional cars for our, admittedly cheaper, electric cars but which also didn't go so fast!

We needed constitutional clout.

In 2040, aged fifty-seven, I retired from the board of Anglesey Education. I was not by then doing much directly in our Research and Development although it was still maintained as a small firm, having blossomed during the development of the Menai Straits Dams project but was now only a few people investigating the possibility of large underwater turbines in the main oceanic currents of the world.

So I was pretty well free to devote my time to fossil-fuel-free Anglesey and, as a preliminary step, to getting more freedom from the central governments of Cardiff and Westminster.

I was seeking devolvement from Cardiff just as Wales and Scotland had devolved from England in the year 2000.

Self-government, in other words.

To some extent, anyway.

A considerable strengthening of our right to impose some 'laws' – restrictive or advantageous – to anyone who lived or came onto the island.

Let me illustrate this by telling you about one of the measures we were able to implement as a direct result of our becoming, selectively, independent.

I have told you about the cheap commercial video cameras we made and installed in schools, shops, streets, roadsides and anywhere that they might be useful, and you know that we have more police than most places; as a result of this we have far less crime than in other counties.

Now, *anyone* convicted of a crime: be it petty theft, breaking in, drug dealing (although cannabis and marijuana are not considered by us to be substances for which people can be convicted – it is their behaviour after taking such substances, as is the case with alcohol, if their behaviour is anti-social, that can land them in trouble).

Any person from the age of eight upwards, if convicted in a local magistrates court, has a tracer implanted under the skin of their forearm.

This has been done painlessly and without difficulty to dogs and cats, if requested by their owners, by vets for years so that if they were lost from home they could be traced, found and returned to their owners.

So with our criminals. The police doctor implanted a small electronic tracer under the forearm and that person's whereabouts could be picked up by police from helicopter or car or policeman on the beat at any time. A great deterrent against anyone even thinking of committing any crime for a second time.

I'll tell you about our system of punishment for convicted crime another time, although 'punishment' is the wrong word, we find out why they 'needed' to act in an anti-social way and do something about that.

When we first proposed this implant, and particularly when we said it would apply to children of eight and up, and even younger if any magistrate thought it necessary, then a great cry went up about abusing individual freedom.

Our irrefutable reply was that these individuals had stepped outside the bounds of acceptable behaviour and, in doing so, had placed themselves in a group that no longer had a total right to total individual freedom.

That, anyway, all of us living in any society were constrained by the needs of that society, one does not have total freedom of behaviour in a society, one must have consideration for the needs of others.

When convicted, the magistrate stipulated for how many years the implant was to remain, subject to no further conviction. The removal, by the individual, of his or her implant carries severe penalties.

As you can see this was a pretty draconian piece of legislation requiring great confidence in our administration on the part of our population and, before it could be put in place I knew, we as a council knew, that we would require considerable legal power to introduce such a measure in our county. We would be the first legal system to implant an electric trace in our criminals that would remain there *after* they had been fined, done some social service work or completed a prison sentence.

To do all this requires considerable constitutional clout, and I/we had other measures in mind as well – that no petrol/diesel business for a start!

We started negotiations with Cardiff and Westminster in 2040 and got our own 'Right of Assembly' in 2053.

I had been elected Chairman of the Anglesey County Council in 2045 and was elected Leader of the Anglesey Assembly when we were granted that Right of Assembly.

We did not get absolute freedom to make our own laws. Every statute or measure we wished to change or implement had to go to Cardiff for ratification and sometimes on to London. But we could innovate and do things differently from the rest of the mainland – as we did with the electronic implants in 2057.

And we banned any petrol or diesel use on the whole island in 2054.

That was the first really revolutionary measure we put through after gaining our independent Right of Assembly although it was a bloodless revolution and I, together with many other member of the council, had been working towards it for many years.

To start with, after we made electricity free to everyone on the island in 2045, we offered a free, new, electric four-seater car to anyone on the island in exchange for their present car provided it was still on the road, that it still had a current, or very recently expired, road licence and MOT certificate – we weren't out to exchange scrap cars for new!

A lot of publicity went into this – that we hoped everyone would consider the environment and change their vehicle to electric power. Simply putting an electric motor, powered by batteries into the petrol/diesel cars, was not on; their transmission was not geared to this and their design and weight meant that you got very little mileage out of the batteries before they needed recharging.

Mileage was a drawback in the electric cars, as was top speed, when compared with conventional cars. The electric car had a top speed of thirty miles an hour and a maximum range of fifty miles before either recharging or changing a flat battery for a full one.

By that time we had a stock of our special batteries fully charged and held in every garage on the island. To change an empty battery for a full one took no more time than filling up with petrol.

All the same, these limitations of performance, meant that not many people wanted to change their conventional car for our limited range one. We were selling the cars like hot cakes to commuters in cities and we had made a special one-seater, two-wheeled luxury enclosed motor bike for city commuters, rechargeable overnight at any ordinary power plug, that was selling even better all over the world. Anglesey Cars plc was bringing in income hand over fist from making these in our own factories for sale in Europe and, with franchises let to manufacturers in other parts of the world, we as a County Council and later as an Assembly, could easily afford the free electricity for our population and the offer of free cars, and it all helped towards paying our extra teachers, police, and so on.

We sold all the cars that we took in exchange for the electric ones to dealers on the mainland and so got their second/third-hand value back anyway which we returned to the original owners. But this offer of exchange didn't make much of a dent on the total number of fossil-fuelled vehicles on our roads. Not to mention to lorries on the way to Ireland or the tourists' cars that were increasingly coming to visit us. We needed more than just an exchange of vehicle offer.

Something draconian and yet acceptable.

It took from 2045 to 2054 – nine years, with our Right of Assembly being granted in 2053 and us then able to implement the final measure that enabled us legally to enforce the ban on fossil fuels, before we got our pollution free (except that which blew in over the sea or over the mountains) Anglesey. Sir Fôn, its Welsh name which we had been using more and more over the years, Anglesey being an English name imposed on us by those Saison invaders.

I retired as Leader of the Assembly the year after we got that ban installed, although I often attended meetings and am still often consulted about matters. And I have had ten years of most enjoyable retirement, living up here above Red Wharf Bay with

Elen in our house and garden, developing that garden, developing that relationship, both needing constant thought and attention to achieve their full potential.

Elen and I both give constant thought and attention to our diet and, as a consequence, are both very well and fit – for our age. And very well and happy in our relationship compared to many in the times in which we live.

Elen!

I had known her, vaguely, ever since she had married Ianto Morgan. I had been a guest at their wedding. Ianto had been at school with me, played in the school rugby team as fly half where I had been wing forward; Tom Pritchard, you will remember, was scrum half, and Ianto was the first of our local group of lads to get married. He took over the family farm from his father some years later and we met from time to time, by chance, not arrangement, greeted each other, exchanged polite pleasantries and news but were not friends particularly. I knew Elen by sight, not as a personality.

Ianto died many years later, a heart attack while trying to save the lives of two children caught by the incoming tide in Red Wharf Bay. I read about it in the paper, didn't attend the funeral.

The tide comes in very fast over the long, sandy beach. The two kids had been playing at the water's edge, way out on one of the slightly higher sandbanks at low tide, the water had swirled in behind them and cut them off.

Ianto and Elen, walking with their young grandchildren along the beach had seen what was happening, he sent Elen and the grandchildren to get help and went to the rescue. He had got one child across to dry sand and gone back for the other, help had arrived in the meantime but, swimming back across the ever-deepening and widening stretch of incoming tidal water, he had suffered a heart attack; the second child was collected and brought to shore by the men Elen had summoned, but Ianto was dead when they got to him.

I met Elen again, some years after Ianto had died and about ten years after Val's death. I had just been elected Chairman of the County Council and had been attending, in a semi-official capacity, a piano recital of Chopin's music played by John

Griffiths. John was a native of Anglesey and is a world-renowned pianist now. I had been to all of a series of recitals of Chopin's music played by him as a young man in the Ucheldre Centre in Holyhead when I was about eighteen and here he was again invited back to repeat the performance. I had made the re-introductory speech.

Elen came up to John and I, as we were chatting afterwards, just to say how much she had enjoyed the concert. John had had to leave almost immediately and I asked Elen to join me in a cup of coffee in the restaurant before we both went our ways home; she to the family farmhouse that she still lived in, sharing it with her son, his wife, and their two kids; me to my, then, only camped-in, house above Red Wharf Bay.

Over coffee we established a mutual enjoyment of classical music and of Welsh choir music among other things.

A nice, friendly, relaxed person, well dressed, not tall, considerably shorter than myself, pleasant to talk to, not intrusive, motherly even, but still with a good figure; attractive. Warm. And alone, not even with a female friend, at this concert. I asked her to accompany me to a concert to be given in the Pritchard-Jones Hall at the university in Bangor in ten days' time.

'Thank you,' she had said. 'Delighted to. I'll meet you at the door.' We exchanged phone numbers in case either of us couldn't make it and duly met at the door.

No coffee afterwards that time but we stood around chatting to various dignitaries and friends at the interval, neither of us, I noticed, drinking the 'coffee' served in plastic cups from a table in the entrance hall.

I rang her up a few days later, commented on the fact that, like me she had not drunk the ersatz instant coffee on offer at the concert, and did she like real coffee?...

'Yes...' Simply a one word reply, no qualification or further comment... A pause... not very forthcoming...

Would she like to join me for an evening meal in a restaurant bistro up in Llanberis where I knew they served real coffee with real cream after the meal?

A long pause... then a tentative 'Thank you. Yes please, that would be very nice.'

I booked a table and collected her from the family farmhouse near Benllech. I was taken in to meet her son and his wife and their two children who, it transpired, had moved into the farmhouse after Ianto's death. Glyn, the son, had been working the farm with his father and had been living with his young family in a cottage on the farm, moving in to keep his mother company after the tragedy.

That was the first of many pleasant evenings, meals in a variety of places, always searching out restaurants that served quality food, good real coffee being an important criterion although Elen often denied herself the cream, 'taking care of her figure' she laughed. But we always drank wine with our meal and I had my invariable Irish coffee to finish up and she didn't *always* refuse the cream with her coffee. A quiet sybarite, Elen.

Always taking her back, not too late, to the family farmhouse, often invited in for a night-cap before I departed.

After a while we extended the scope of our excursions, driving further afield and going for walks along rivers, among mountains. Less strenuous then the walks I had had with Val, taking much more notice of the smaller things – trees, ferns, wild flowers and grasses, birdsong and the shape of things, sunshine and shadow, mist and wind and rain.

A hardy, strong woman, Elen.

She told me, in bits and pieces, over evening meals sitting on dining chairs, or reclining in soft armchairs by an hotel fire drinking a morning coffee, or outside sitting on rocks or grass covered by a rug, about her upbringing in a large family, barefoot in a small cottage near a tiny hamlet in the middle of Anglesey. Her father, a hardworking, sober, strict man, tractor driver for a farmer in whose tied cottage they had grown up.

'Dad was strict but he never hit us,' said Elen. Her mother driven by the necessity imposed by having to bring up a large family on one man's meagre agricultural wage. Very proud, very independent, immaculate inside the cottage, clothes repaired and passed on to the younger ones; children barefoot until of school age, free to roam the countryside across the fields and down to the sea, 'as long as they looked after each other.' Keeping close as a family and still in contact with each other but each now with families of their own and with fortunes that differed considerably.

Elen had not enjoyed school learning although, on leaving could read and write English well enough, Welsh speaking by preference and in the family of course. She had gone 'into service' as a young nanny to two children of a wealthy family who owned a small 'Plas' not for from where she had grown up.

She was married at sixteen to Ianto. Her father and mother had not wanted her to marry at this early age but Elen, the next to youngest in the family and most decidedly determined, had simply said that she would run away if they didn't give their consent. And they knew she meant it so there it was.

She and Ianto had become a pair while still at school and as the friendship, companionship, developed between Elen and myself she confided more and more detail of her life to me, as I did of my life to her, and I heard of their escapades among hay bales in barns, on piles of dry autumn leaves in quiet woods, on the sunny banks of secret streams, hidden corners of farm fields and, after they were married, in all sorts of ways at all times of the day, in their own home.

A hot-blooded young lady, Elen. Lucky Ianto!

I came to rejoice, with her, in the happiness she had found with him, myself remembering, and telling her, of the joy and pleasure I had shared with Val, each glad for the other that we had had such good fortune in the past. Able to empathise over each other's loss without sentiment or overt sadness, slowly building confidence in each other, slowly getting to know and take increasing pleasure in each other's company.

And then, one evening, after a walk along the river near Dolgellau, up beyond Port Madoc, and an enjoyable meal in a pub in the town she put her hand on my knee as I drove back to Anglesey, squeezed gently and asked why I had never taken her to my house, Ty Gwyn.

'If you will come there now you will see why.' So we drove in the early evening back to Anglesey, along the road to Pentreath, down to Red Wharf Bay and up the farm track to Ty Gwyn. I used to keep the garden grass cut and a woman from a cottage down below did a bit of cleaning, washing-up and general tidying up but, looking at it that evening with Elen I was ashamed of my bachelor pad.

She laughed at me, told me off for living in such scruffy conditions and demanded coffee. We lit the fire – a large open fireplace burning logs of which I had a fine store and I made coffee to the standard she required, standing over me as I did so – why wasn't my coffee kept fresh and cool in the fridge? The coffee percolator should be warmed before use, as should the mugs in which it was to be served. A pinch of salt in with the coffee grains to enhance the taste. And real, fresh cream or nothing!

An epicure, Elen.

The fire burned well, flames flickering in the evening light and as the sun went down and the room darkened she refused to let me switch on electric light. 'Find some candles, much nicer,' she commanded.

Given to dictate (the nicest things and in the nicest way possible. Mostly), Elen.

I had not slept with any woman since Val died. Hardly given sex a thought during all those empty ten years, not having found another partner, believing myself to be getting too old anyway, remembering, when any salacious hint of hunger appeared in my mind, that I had been impotent once and was probably old and impotent again.

But there was Elen on the other side of the fire place, sipping her coffee at ease, one foot stretched out towards the fire, her shoe kicked off, elegant in her own way, still beautiful, attractive, sensual I suddenly, blindingly, realised rather than sexual; soft and alluring. Enticing? Dare I believe?

I remember that hand on my knee in the car and the gentle squeeze. There had been no sexual response from that docile member between my thighs then, but there was one now. A stirring.

Dare I venture? I doubted I could come 'up' to expectation…

Impulse and instinct took over from cogitation.

'Elen. Would you come to bed with me?'

Silence.

Quiet, speculative, deeply beautiful and introspective eyes looking at me across the top of hands folded beneath her chin, resting, considering.

'Well, that's a surprise… don't you think we are too old, and possibly too wise, to do that sort of thing?'

Not to be rushed, Elen.

'I don't know,' I said. 'To tell you the truth I don't even know if I can do it any more. Get an erection, I mean. Never mind producing sperm.'

She laughed, a deep contented, confident gurgle. 'Nor do I, know if I can achieve an orgasm, I mean. Not since Ianto died.'

Peace descended as we both gazed at and listened to the flames, no hurry to take the matter further, no rush upstairs, not at our age.

Then, 'I am very flattered,' she said. 'That any man should find me attractive in that sort of way at my age.'

'You,' I countered, 'are beautiful. Your hairstyle suits you and looks good, your clothes are always obviously thought about and fit and show off your figure. You have a lovely figure.' And I could feel that the normally flaccid member was docile no longer. 'You are totally, sensually attractive,' I said, becoming fully aware of *one* of the aspects of my (by now) infatuation with this middle-aged woman; remembering many times when I had been in her company, the swing of her skirt, the shape of her hips, the warming fullness of her breasts beneath a blouse, the hint of cleavage, the strength of still-shapely leg and arm, the strong grip of hand, the warm curve of lip and soft smile from mouth and eyes.

Infatuated, now, me.

'You,' I said, 'are wonderful. You look good and like the things I like. I hope I haven't offended you but please, could we try?'

Again that purposeful, poised, consideration…

'I'll have to think about that,' she smiled gently, not to hurt but not encouraging either. 'But you'll have to tidy things up a bit. And I like soft clean sheets for my bed.'

Nicely and appropriately fastidious, Elen.

'We'll see,' she said, rising. 'A lot of compliments I have just been hearing. Seduction perhaps? Don't forget I'm a grand-mother!'

'You don't look it and you don't act old. And, anyway, it's probably all myth on my part, I don't suppose these elderly bones can carry out what my mind would like us to do.'

'Well,' she said, 'it's a very nice idea. Take me home now and let me think about it.'

I cleaned that house from top to bottom, bought new soft sheets for the double bed, a new feather duvet and cut the grass; then I invited Elen to supper.

She came, in her own car, carrying a bottle of wine, dressed in a printed cotton, summer dress and sandals, a cardigan loose around her shoulders; comfortable, middle-aged and beautiful. Eyes sparkling with humour and challenge.

'Well, is the house clean, are there soft sheets on the bed?'

No equivocation, direct to the point. Implied acquiescence provided her conditions were met.

An equal, Elen.

My supper came up to scratch, but a walk round my 'garden' provoked exasperation and ridicule: 'You'll have to do better than that if you expect me to visit you here now and then.'

I pleaded ignorance of gardening matters and asked that she should advise and help me.

'I'll think about it,' was all she would commit herself to.

Cautious, not to be rushed, Elen.

But not ruling out the possibility.

We went back in, to the fireside and coffee and, eventually, up to bed.

But first she went outside to her car, returning with a soft carry-bag, 'My nightdress and slippers, toothbrush and hairbrush,' she said. 'Come on, let's have a look at those soft sheets.'

She took my hand and we went upstairs.

A natural.

A gentlewoman, Elen.

We gave each other great comfort in a companionable, sensual way that night. Neither achieving orgasm, but I produced an acceptable erection and, slowly, over the following weeks, months, years, we improved our intimate knowledge of each other, growing in confidence and satisfaction with each other, maturing into our old age in a demanding and intensely happy relationship where sexuality and sensuality blended in an amalgam that cemented our two lives together, making us both two very happy individuals, independently minded, obstinate and upset sometimes but always coming together to renew our relationship, reaffirm our commitment, cementing this, often and reassuringly, in bed in a satiating and sexually exciting session that defied the convention that sex was only for the young. We both continued to achieve an orgasm, not perhaps as frequently as in our youth, but very satisfying for all that.

And I learned to be an enthusiastic and knowledgeable gardener.

A relentless and demanding lady, in the fullest sense of the words, Elen.

She came to stay in my house for days at a time and her family accepted this coming and going. We got married in 2054, eight years after we had met, in the same year that Anglesey Assembly prohibited the presence of any fossil fuel on the island.

No Fossil Fuels

It is one thing to declare that a county be fossil fuel free, another thing altogether to get people to conform to it, to give up the use of the faster, more powerful conventional car and travel more slowly, albeit at no cost for the propellant.

Garage owners had to face a complete change of role and a drop to nothing of their income from fuel sales.

All transport going from the mainland to Holyhead, bound for Ireland, or the reverse, had to be moved from the Britannia Bridge to or from Holyhead.

Three problems: one, to get everyone on the island converted to an electric car; two, to get all those vehicles that simply crossed the island, en route, from either Holyhead or mainland Wales, not to use their own fuel; and three, to persuade all incoming visitors to leave their own cars at the 'frontier'.

It seemed easiest to tackle the 'through' traffic first.

After we got devolvement from Cardiff and Westminster, forming our own independent Assembly, the first thing, as I have told you that we did, was to pass legislation enabling us to implant all persons, young or old, convicted of anti-social behaviour.

The second thing we did was the decree that the 'new' motorway, built in the years 2000 to 2002, was to be declared an 'electric road only' on which NO vehicle using fossil fuel was allowed to travel using its own fuel.

This measure required some preparation. We ordered, from a railway engine manufacturing firm in Birmingham, twelve special engines, built to our own design but utilising their expert knowledge, to be powered by electricity run from our own-design large batteries. These batteries hold enough electricity to pull a heavy load of 'cars' from either the Britannia Bridge entry to the island across to Holyhead, or the reverse journey. Refuel – i.e. change depleted batteries for fully charged ones – at each end of the journey.

The carriages were open flatbeds onto which fully laden heavy lorries, or cars, could be driven, secured and transported from one end of the island to the other. Just as through the Channel Tunnel.

We constructed a rail-road junction station just where the Britannia Bridge crosses from the mainland onto Anglesey, just to its left as you cross the Straits, below the present road that runs to LlanfairPG, well landscaped and partly underground, extending this for quite way along the shore and digging deep underground ready for phase two – the creation of a vast, hidden car park where all the conventional visiting cars could be left. We did the same at the Holyhead end and then declared the 'new' A5 motorway closed to *all* fossil fuel traffic, including local traffic. At the same time the Menai Bridge was forbidden to fossil-fuelled vehicles.

This put anyone living on the island or coming onto the island as a visitor or tourist to some inconvenience. We continued to offer a free electric car or van or lorry to anyone who would change from a conventional one and, slowly over the following ten years virtually everyone who owned a vehicle on Anglesey had converted.

Ordinary trains through, to, or from, Holyhead continued to run on the railway line but were pulled by our electrically powered engines which were attached at Bangor railway station.

There still remained the problem of our tourists who were a very important part of our economy and who we did not want to deter in any way.

We had already constructed the very big car parks near the Britannia Bridge and at Holyhead. We then installed a depot of electric cars. All people, even those who lived on the island, if they came in a fossil-fuel-powered car had to leave it in our, very secure, car park and transfer, lock stock and barrel, to an electric car that was theirs for free while they were on the island. All cars the same, except for colour, all restricted to twenty-five miles an hour. Plug in at wherever you were staying to recharge overnight, free full battery replacement at any garage if required. Any luggage you couldn't fit in the electric car delivered free to your door within six hours.

It made an additional tourist attraction, particularly as it added to the organic, pure air, philosophy of the whole island.

All cars and lorries using this electric 'ferry' used it free of charge. Any local fossil-fuelled car or lorry was forbidden to use it and had to proceed along the old A5 and other secondary roads. Any 'through' traffic using the roads was so heavily fined that it was better to put up with the slight inconvenience of loading onto our electric rail ferry.

This was inconvenient in two ways. The need to stop and load the vehicle onto one of our 'flat' carriages and the fact that the whole ferry only travelled across the island along the railway lines at our set twenty-five mile an hour speed limit. Although it was a *steady* twenty-five miles an hour with no hold ups for other traffic or slow downs for passing through villages so they got there just as quickly in the end.

We imposed this twenty-five mile an hour speed limit on *all* vehicles *everywhere* on the island on the day we opened the ferry for business.

Many cities on the mainland had already fixed a twenty or twenty-five mile an hour speed limit within their confines finding that it cut down the number of accidents dramatically and the severity of the accidents that did occur was reduced. So the concept was already accepted by everyone, we just extended it to the whole island with an immediate drop in accident rate and severity.

That alone was a strong discussion-deciding, factor when it came to legislating against the use of any fossil fuels on the island.

All this was in place by 2054 when Elen and I got married and she moved to live permanently in my house on the hill above Red Wharf Bay.

Our kids and their families come to visit now and then. Under Elen's dictatorship I have become a competent gardener and our gardens give us great pleasure and occupation, we enjoy good home cooking but also eat out on occasion in one of the many well-famed restaurants on the island. Anglesey's economy is well established and booming as is the tourism side of it and we tend to stay within our own place much of the time, the more so as we get older. But the speed limit of twenty-five miles an hour makes travelling by car a pleasure and the abundance of wildlife, particularly birds, makes walking doubly enjoyable.

People on the island are much more relaxed than on the mainland and we travel abroad much less than we used to although Umbria, Florence and Rome still call in early spring and late autumn.

The whole of a, now united, Ireland is well on the way to declaring itself totally organic and fossil-fuel free and England and Scotland will not be far behind. I hope the rest of the world will follow suit but the problems in doing so for India, China, Russia and the Americas are immense, although areas within these continents are already converted, as is New Zealand with Australia well on the way.

Elen

But I leave those challenges to younger minds than mine.

I am a very lucky man, I have Elen and have had a very interesting life.

So there you are! My own little contribution to the archives. I don't suppose that anyone will read them but just you make sure that the grammar and phraseology are good English. I could have made a better job in Welsh.

Diolch yn fawr i chi!